a&b

Muddy Boots and Silk Stockings

JULIA STONEHAM

Allison & Busby Limited
13 Charlotte Mews
London W1T 4EJ
www.allisonandbusby.com

Hardcover published in Great Britain in 2008.
This paperback edition published in 2009.

A CIP catalogue record for this book is available from the British Library.

10 9 8 7 6 5 4 3 2 1

13-ISBN 978-0-7490-7909-3

Typeset in Adobe Garamond Pro
by Lara Crisp

The paper used for this Allison & Busby publication has been produced from trees that have been legally sourced from well-managed and credibly certified forests.

Printed and bound in Great Britain by
CPI Bookmarque Ltd, Croydon, Surrey

JULIA STONEHAM began her career as a stage designer but moved into writing for the stage, radio and television. She was a regular writer on *The House of Elliott* and her radio series *The Cinderella Service* (which inspired *Muddy Boots and Silk Stockings*) was nominated for a Sony Award and was commissioned by Granada TV. She has also written a book of short stories called *Fourteen from Four.*

To my mother, who provided me with the blueprint for 'Alice Todd'.

Chapter One

The dressing-table mirror, like everything else in the boarding house, was old, of poor quality and dimly lit.

Alice Todd peered at her reflection and was disturbed. She still half expected to see the self-confident, pleasantly attractive face with which she was familiar and which, framed and in studio-portrait form, stood on one side of her husband's desk at the Air Ministry, depicting the winsome, contented, middle-class young matron Alice was. Had been. But the eyes that now met hers bore traces of anxiety. The lips of the mouth in the mirror were compressed. The skin, possibly due to the poor quality of the looking glass, lacked lustre. Observing herself carefully, she rearranged her features, composing them as she watched and attempting to achieve the look of confidence and calm which today would demand of her.

The hat would not do. Its half-veil, softening the small, feathered pillbox, suited her but was, she decided, too pretty, too frivolous for the business in hand. She replaced it with a less becoming fawn felt with a heavy brim. The effect reminded her of Celia Johnson in a film that she had recently seen and through which her young son had fidgeted. He appeared now at her elbow, neat in his school uniform, gas mask over shoulder, cap – embellished with his prep school's insignia – slipping slightly to one side on his crisp, curly hair.

'I'll be late for prayers,' he said, searching her face in the mirror, watching it soften as she smiled at him. Snatching up handbag and gloves, she propelled him towards the door, turned off the low-wattage, overhead light and left the room. As they descended the stairs a door opened below them.

'Good morning, Mrs Bowden,' the boy said cheerfully, moving forward to the front door.

''Mornun', Edward-John.' Mrs Bowden edged out into the hallway, effectively blocking it. She had an apron over her frock, a scarf over her curlers, a duster in one hand, a half-smoked Woodbine cigarette in the other. She spoke with the rounded accent and sharp tone of a true Devonian. ''Tis Friday, dear,' she announced to Alice, making a pass at the banisters with her duster.

Alice, still unfamiliar with such approaches where money was concerned, looked blank.

'The rent,' said Mrs Bowden, lowering her voice.

'Oh. Yes. Of course...' Alice balanced her handbag on the

hall table, opened it and searched it hurriedly. 'My cheque book's here...somewhere...'

'I'd rather have money...if it's all the same to you.'

'But a cheque is...'

'Mr Todd always paid cash, dear.' Mrs Bowden stood, implacable.

Edward-John was at the front door, holding it open, the cold February morning blowing in.

'Very well. I'll go to the bank.'

'That's it, dear,' said Mrs Bowden, melting like an ogre in a fairytale into the shadows of her room.

'Oh, Mrs Bowden?' Alice called, her voice, she realised, sounding slightly shrill as Mrs Bowden's face loomed back.

'I should be here by the time Edward-John gets home from school, but if I'm delayed...'

'I'll see to 'im. Don't fret yourself.'

'You're very kind...' Alice smiled uncertainly.

As the front door closed behind the mother and son, Mrs Bowden exhaled, smoke wreathing about her curlered head.

'Poor girl,' she wheezed. 'I dunno... These days...'

Alice withdrew money from the bank and somehow managed to arrive in Ledburton village square at the appointed time. Edward-John, delivered to the gates of his prep school, had hurried through them with the last of the latecomers.

The mid-morning bus from Exeter had been full of

village women returning from their regular excursion to the market. Laden with the week's rations and struggling to control squalling babies and noisy toddlers, they had stared at Alice, the only stranger amongst the otherwise familiar faces. When the bus drew up at the Ledburton stop they watched her as she scanned the village square and saw her react to the beeped horn of a small saloon car, parked in front of the post office. She was seen to approach the car and speak to its occupant through the wound-down window.

'Get in, Mrs Todd!' The speaker was a solidly built woman, dressed severely in a grey coat and skirt. 'If you are Mrs Todd!' she added jovially, grasping the gear-stick as Alice settled into the passenger seat. 'Margery Brewster,' the woman announced. 'Land Army rep for this neck of the woods! We'll be seeing a lot of each other if you take this job!…Ye Gods!' she added as the car protested. 'Mind of its own, this beast!' Then, as they moved erratically forward, she thrust a piece of paper at Alice. 'Can you follow these directions? Not easy with all the signposts gone!'

Occupied by the navigation that took them away from the village into a network of lanes, Alice peered at the scribbled instructions.

'Left at the big willow tree…then down the hill and through the ford…' Margery Brewster crouched over her steering wheel, scanning the muddy surface of the lane in an attempt to avoid the worst of the potholes.

'Understand you've been living in Exeter,' she bellowed.

'Yes,' said Alice, wondering whether the thatched roof she could see on her right was the barn that was to be her next landmark.

'To avoid the London blitz no doubt,' Margery Brewster continued. 'Wise of you. In the forces is he? Your chap?' Had she been observing Alice, Margery would have seen a reaction to this assumption. As it was she missed it, her attention focused on negotiating the crossing of the shallow ford. She pursued her enquiries. 'Which?' she asked bluntly. Alice decided that the thatch was not a barn but a haystack.

'He works at the Air Ministry,' she said. 'His department is being evacuated to Cambridge.'

'Aren't you going to join him there?' Margery's shrewd mind had homed in on something. A sideways glance at Alice's face confirmed her suspicions. Here was an irregularity, a complication.

'Things are...' Alice hesitated miserably, '...a little uncertain.'

'Well, I hope they're not too uncertain, Mrs Todd! We like our hostel wardens to commit themselves for at least twelve months. The last thing Mr Bayliss wants is to find himself with ten land girls on his hands and a warden who goes off to Cambridge to join her husband!' She emphasised this with an abrupt and noisy gear change which flung her passenger forward in her seat.

'Oh, I wouldn't!' Alice said, her eyes scanning the wintry landscape for the elusive barn. 'When I said uncertain,

I meant...well...my marriage...' Margery, embarrassed, interrupted her.

'My apologies,' she said, almost gently. 'Didn't mean to pry or sound hard. But one must have ones priorities, you know. Oh, dear! This war! So many casualties, don't you find?'

Alice was, she supposed, a casualty of the war, having, until recently, been happy enough with her life; for, although deprived of her parents at an early age, she had been cushioned from the hard facts of her loss by affectionate relatives. She remembered, or had been told that she remembered, waving goodbye to her mother and father when she had been left in the care of her Aunt Elizabeth while her parents set off to tour the Black Forest in their new motor car. After the accident she had been surrounded by grave-faced people who ensured that it was several years before the word 'orphan' had entered her vocabulary. When it did, time had blunted the fact of her parents' absence and they had become mythical beings, endowed by her vague memories with invented virtues. It was not an unpleasant situation. Alice barely deserved the sympathy and compassion which her relatives lavished on her but she nevertheless enjoyed it and grew into a well-adjusted young woman with whom James Todd, in his final year at university whilst she was in her first at a domestic science college, had fallen in love. With his degree and his foot confidently on the first ladder of a career in the Civil

Service, he married her. A son, Edward-John, was born the year Adolf Hitler took power, a fact that, together with other signs of an approaching war, discouraged James from adding to his family. Alice had wanted more children and was prepared to take the risk but James had been firm and Edward-John remained an only child.

'Left! Left here!' Alice almost shouted as they passed a gateway through which the elusive barn had become briefly visible. Margery hauled the car round, inserted it into what was hardly more than a track between steep banks topped with hazel bushes and negotiated a slithering descent to the valley floor where the lane levelled and ran pleasantly north, beside a water meadow, for half a mile or so. Then, suddenly, they came upon a cluster of farm buildings.

Alice felt her heart lift. From a distance Lower Post Stone Farm looked idyllic. A classic Devon longhouse with a central porch, pale, pink-washed walls, small, square windows beneath an undulating thatched roof, all of it held protectively between two massive chimneys. The scene suggested a serenity which, since the onset of the war and the disruption it had caused in Alice's previously pleasant life, she had thought had vanished from the world.

Margery Brewster glanced at her passenger's rapt expression.

'Don't like the look of that thatch,' she muttered, searching for firm ground on which to park her car. She had been bogged in mud before now, when visiting remote farmhouses.

'What's wrong with it?'

'Looks damp. And there are things growing on it. Always a bad sign.' Margery brought the car to a stand and pulled hard on the handbrake. She was a worthy woman. Daughter of a clergyman, wife of a solicitor and mother of two girls, both grown up and gone from her, she had, at the outset of the war, offered herself for voluntary work. Shortly afterwards and rather to her surprise, she had found herself face to face with Lady Denman, director of the Women's Land Army. An hour later she had accepted the role of local representative, known officially as a Village Registrar, for that organisation. Her husband, previously unaware of her organising skills, had been astonished to witness the transformation of his wife from docile partner into spruce, committed businesswoman and, although he joked to his friends about her newly discovered vocation, was secretly uneasy, feeling sometimes almost neglected. Margery had never in all her life been happier. From dutiful daughter she had, in her twenties, become a devoted wife and mother. Assuming that this should be enough she had put moments of restlessness down to various time-of-life difficulties. Now, to her surprise, she had discovered that she had a talent for organising and for delegation, for assessing skills, judging character and, as she had already demonstrated on more than one occasion, for dealing with a crisis. She was, however, slightly ashamed of how much she was enjoying the war and tried to compensate for these feelings by being sensitive to those, like the young woman seated beside her now, whose experiences of it were less happy than her own. She switched off her engine and opened her door.

A scatter of clucking fowls approached the car, peering inquisitively at its unfamiliar occupants. More distantly, sheep bleated on the hills that rose behind the roofs of outbuildings visible beyond the farmhouse itself and from the inside of which the sound of hammering was audible. To one side of the farm buildings was a neat, stone cottage. Smoke drifted from its single chimney.

The farmhouse was, Alice could now see, in a neglected state. Great swags of honeysuckle, tangled with a leafless Albertine, swamped the porch and had hauled themselves up over the thatch and towards the chimneys. The pink-wash was sullied with a greenish mould and the window frames were dark with rot. The small, walled front garden was overgrown with rank grass, straggling lavender and unpruned roses, now bereft of leaves but still sporting last year's hips, which shone red as blood in the thin February sunshine. The air in the sheltered valley felt almost warm. Margery heaved herself from her car, her rubber boots sinking a good inch into the mud. She reached into the back seat.

'Better borrow these,' she said, waving a spare pair of muddy boots at Alice.

The porch extended into the garden. It was floored with small cobbles, polished smooth by centuries of use. The disused nests of swallows and house martins clustered where the underside of the thatch butted onto crumbling walls. As Alice and Margery ducked their heads under the lintel of the low door the air inside the house struck cold and the sound of hammering intensified.

The wide hallway – known as a cross-passage – was, like the rest of the ground floor, paved with slate. From it, one on either side, narrow and dark staircases wound upwards. At the far end was a window beside a solid wooden door that, Alice correctly guessed, led into the yard. A door on the right stood open to a gloomy kitchen. Alice could make out the shape of a wooden table, stained with mould. On the other side of the cross-passage a third door revealed a large room, low-ceilinged and beamed, its windows set close to the slate floor. The interior of the farmhouse had been recently whitewashed by someone whose work appeared to have been rushed, for although there were splashes of paint on the beams and on the floors, corners remained cobwebby with signs of mould where the paintbrush had not quite reached.

Someone was descending the right-hand staircase. Someone in stout boots, thick lisle stockings, an apron over her dark, woollen dress and thick cardigan. Rose.

Her face, once pretty, was overlaid now with early middle-age and the strains that five years of widowhood had put on her. The eyes were direct and steady. She had a hardness about her, inherited from her antecedents, generations of farmworkers whose lives had been little more than a losing battle against poor wages, rudimentary accommodation and relentless exposure to elements that were mostly less than kind and often cruel. She stood squarely before them, reddened hands smoothing her apron.

'You'll be Mrs Brewster,' she said, eyeing Margery and ignoring Alice. Her accent was rounded, edged with a sharpness common to Devonians.

'And you are?' Margery asked imperiously.

'Rose,' said Rose. 'Crocker. Mrs. Widowed. I lives in the cottage. My Will were cow-man here. Then my son Dave was. Till he were called up. There be girls doin' 'is work now!' she said derisively. 'I'm to 'elp 'ere, Mr Bayliss says. With the domestic work. Assistant to the warden.' She turned to Alice, ran her eyes over the good suit, the fine gloves held loosely in a well-shaped hand, the soft leather handbag and the diffident expression. 'But you ain't never the warden!' she exclaimed. Alice blanched.

'This is Mrs Todd,' Margery announced, firmly. 'We are here to see your employer.'

'Says 'e'll be five minutes. 'E's busy with the carpenter. I'm to show you round down here. This way.' Rose preceded them into the kitchen, turning to catch Alice's reaction to it for, despite the newly painted walls and whitened plasterwork between the overhead beams, it was gloomy.

'Scullery's through there,' Rose said, indicating a door in the far wall. 'Two sinks it's got and beyond it there be a room where us used to make cheese. Reckon that could serve as a laundry.' Rose noted with obvious pleasure that Alice was clearly taken aback by the kitchen and appeared unwilling to inspect either scullery or potential laundry.

'Of course the bed linen, towels and the girls' overalls will be laundered in Ledburton,' Margery announced comfortingly, but Alice hardly heard her.

'This here's the range,' Rose continued sweetly, pointing to a looming lump of black metal, the doors to its ovens sagging from their hinges. 'And Mr Bayliss has ordered a paraffin stove with four burners. Now, if you'll follow me...' She led them back through the cross-passage and into the room opposite the kitchen. 'This here's the parlour,' she said. 'Leastways 'twas the parlour. Mr Bayliss says it's to be a recreation room for the girls now. He's getting in a piano and a gramophone and there'll be easy chairs and a sofa I daresay...' The room was large and square. Two low windows faced south and through the swags of creeper, sunlight speckled the stone floor. Two other windows, facing north, looked out onto the yard. It had the same low beams as the rest of the ground floor and a wide fireplace in the chimney wall. 'And this through here will be the warden's room,' said Rose, opening a door through which a second, smaller room was visible. It too had a double aspect. The bulk of the chimney breast intruded into it, producing an interesting effect of two areas, each with its own window, one south, one north, and with a small fireplace where the room narrowed. Alice was immediately taken with this room. A divan bed at either end. One for her, the other for Edward-John. Her mother's desk opposite the fireplace. An armchair on either side of it. It was possible. Someone entered the room behind her.

Roger Bayliss was a gentleman farmer. An educated man whose family had owned its acres for several centuries, living a mile away from this building in the modest but comfortable farmhouse known as Higher Post Stone, to which each generation had added various extensions. Elizabethan solidity had been succeeded by Georgian elegance and Victorian affectation, the result being more interesting than architecturally significant. The man was tall. Alice's first impression of him was of strong shoulders and a face that, although lacking any particularly distinctive feature, was acceptable, even handsome. His greying hair had once been dark and his eyebrows were showing the first signs of eccentricity. He wore riding breeches, a lightweight waterproof jacket and well-polished leather boots. He held a riding crop in his right hand and stood tapping it irritably against his left palm. It occurred to Alice that he might have been using it on the carpenter. She was dismissing the thought as unworthy while Margery greeted him.

'Roger!' she said, extending her hand. 'Haven't seen you since the Blatchfords' Christmas bash! How the hell are you?' Alice suspected that for a split second Roger Bayliss was unable to place Margery but he recovered quickly, said that he was well and enquired, not however by name, after the health of her husband. Now it was her turn to look blank. 'Gordon? He's fine as far as I know,' she said, laughing. 'I'm so damned busy these days I hardly see the man!' This reminded her of the purpose of her visit. She turned to Alice. 'May I introduce Mrs Todd?'

In Alice's hand Roger's felt large, rough and warm. Hers in his struck him, although her grasp was firm, as cold. Her smooth, narrow fingers slipped through his as she withdrew them. Margery was talking.

'As I told you on the telephone, Mrs Todd hasn't quite as much experience as we would like, but she does have a Certificate in Domestic Science and before her marriage took a cordon bleu cookery course in Paris.' Alice saw one of Roger Bayliss's eyebrows lift. 'She has, until the outbreak of war, run her own home, of course, and raised her son…' It sounded weak. Behind them, Rose cleared her throat, eloquently suggesting her own lack of confidence in Alice. Without looking at her, Roger asked Rose to show their visitor over the upper floor. He did not say please. There was a silence as Alice and Rose left the room. Roger waited until their footsteps had faded. Margery smiled.

'Your Mrs Crocker seems a bit hostile!' she said. Roger shrugged.

'You know these Devonians, Margery. Distrustful of

strangers to a man.' He peered out of the north window, checking on the horse he had tethered to the yard gate. 'This Mrs...'

'Todd,' Margery finished for him and waited.

'Isn't she a bit...'

'Genteel?' Margery ventured, hoping he would not bring up the matter of Alice's lack of experience, confidence or natural authority.

'Some of these girls are going to be pretty rough characters. Will she be able to handle them?' Margery avoided giving him a direct answer by flicking through the notes she had attached to Alice's application form.

'She's not quite what we're looking for, I know. But there's absolutely no one else I can offer you! Beggars can't be choosers, Roger!'

Upstairs, Rose's tour was almost complete. Alice was paying little attention as she had already decided that the prospect of running a hostel in this building was not only beyond her but that her prospective employer shared this opinion.

At one end of the upper floor partitions were already in place, transforming the available space into one large bedroom containing three beds, two slightly smaller rooms, each housing two beds, and a fourth rather cramped room which would also accommodate two girls. Each bedroom had its own low, square window and, as well as its beds, just enough space for the dressing table and wardrobe that would shortly be moved into it. At the other end of the building, studs were in position for another room, which would make provision for a further two land girls who might be required either to join Roger Bayliss's workforce, or whose labour could be hired out to one or other of his neighbours. There was also, above the porch, a small space with a tiny, high window, which Rose described as a boxroom, and next to this a bathroom equipped with a stained, white enamelled bath with claw feet, its brass taps bright with verdigris. In one corner was a hand basin, in the other a lavatory.

'Only one bathroom!' Alice breathed.

'One more'n I've got!' Rose snapped. 'The range heats the water but there'll not be enough in the tank for separate baths. Reckon they'll have to share. Still, 'tis better than a tub in front of the kitchen range, which is what I 'as to make do with!' she finished virtuously.

At the foot of the stairs they encountered Roger and Margery. Roger dispatched Rose to unpack a box of crockery that had arrived that morning.

He stood, regarding Alice, making her feel as though she might be an item of livestock he was considering bidding for at a cattle auction and she wished, more fervently than she had ever wished before, that James was here. That he would put a protective arm round her and explain that it was all a misunderstanding. That she was, of course, to accompany him to Cambridge. But she knew that this was not going to happen and she had recently guessed why.

When Penelope Fisher had first been assigned to James as his secretary and personal assistant, he had mentioned her quite freely and frequently to Alice. My secretary thinks this, says that, has been reading this or that novel, liked this or that film. One evening, before the move to Exeter, he had brought her home for dinner. She was a nice-looking, soberly dressed girl. Rather thin. Rather quiet. Slightly humourless. Harmless enough, Alice had thought. But as the months passed, James had spoken less and less of her to Alice. In fact he had spoken less and less to Alice about anything. Apart from brief discussions of the day's news of the war and any domestic matter that needed his attention, they communicated very little. When she had asked, over supper one night, whether Miss Fisher would be going with him when his department moved to Cambridge, James had hesitated a touch too long before answering, yes, of course she was going, adding that she was a valued member of his department. Roger Bayliss had begun to speak.

'Not too daunted, I hope, Mrs Todd?'

Alice hesitated. She wanted to say, yes, she was daunted. She wanted to look helpless. To apologise for wasting his time. To be aboard the bus, travelling back to Exeter. To re-enter the depressing safety of the rented room. She cleared her throat and forced herself to meet his eyes.

'I hadn't realised quite how…' she hesitated.

'Primitive the place is?' he finished for her.

'You'll think me foolish. But I didn't know. Wasn't told... that this building was not already in use as a hostel.'

'I need more labour,' he said. 'Lower Post Stone has been lying idle. Seemed sensible to use it as a billet.'

'I understand that. But I'd expected to be taking on an establishment that was—'

'Up and running?' Margery cut in brightly, attempting to ease the tension between the woman who needed work but not this work and the man who needed a warden but not this warden.

'It's a valid point, Margery,' he conceded, glancing at his wristwatch. Margery launched into a spiel.

'Most of our smaller hostels are very much like this one, Mrs Todd. We'll see you get all the standard equipment – a bread-slicer for the sandwiches and so on. There's a telephone in the barn across the yard – for emergencies – and a generator for the lights so you won't be dependent on oil lamps – at least not downstairs.'

'If you feel it's going to be too much for you, Mrs Todd...' Roger Bayliss sounded dismissive. He had looked at her, listened to her and found her wanting. She felt insulted.

She asked for the weekend to consider, but he shook his head and said it was out of the question. Then he said he had to leave them. That running his farm almost single-handed meant that his time was short. He asked Margery to give Alice his telephone number. 'Ring me by noon tomorrow if your decision is positive, Mrs Todd. Otherwise I'll assume it's not. All right with you, Margery?' Margery glanced at Alice and nodded. He excused himself and left them. Rose came into the room with an armful of the old newspapers in which the crockery had been packed. She dumped them in the fireplace, straightened and wiped her hands on her apron. She saw Alice flinch as the yard door slammed noisily behind her employer.

'That's Mr Bayliss for you!' she said, enjoying the effect of her words on Alice. 'On a bad day you can hear his door-slams two fields off.'

Buses from Ledburton into Exeter were infrequent and it was dusk by the time Alice arrived back at the boarding house. She hurried up the stairs, anxious to confirm that Edward-John was safely home.

He was in the rented room, sitting at the table playing Happy Families with his father. He smiled at his mother as she entered but the looks that passed between his parents reaffirmed what he already knew and he sat looking gravely from face to face.

James seemed thinner than Alice remembered. His face was almost gaunt. Guilt perhaps. Or maybe simply the strain of wartime London. His suit was a new one. His appearance was altogether sharper, more suave than when she had last seen him. The bones of his face were as familiar to her as her own and yet he seemed almost a stranger now that she did not share or even know his plans. She wished she could tell him about the awful farmhouse and the impossible job but she could not. She felt her son's eyes on her.

'Have you had your tea, Edward-John?' When he shook his head Alice took two pounds and fifteen shillings from her purse and told him to give the rent money to Mrs Bowden and to ask her if she would very kindly make him some beans on toast for his tea. He protested, appealing to his father to be allowed to stay.

'Off you go, there's a good chap,' James said. Edward-John sighed and left them.

'This is so awful for him!' Alice began. 'I don't know how you—' She stopped. Reproach was useless and James did, to his credit, look as wretched as she felt. 'Why are you here?' she asked. 'I wasn't expecting you until Edward-John's half-term.' James got to his feet and walked about the room, making the loosened floorboards creak. His shoes were new and well polished.

'This situation…' he began.

'So your wife and your child are "a situation", are we?' James sighed and sat down. After a moment he began again.

'Penny thinks…' So it was 'Penny' now. He paused. 'No…I think…' He wasn't going to blame his lover or hide behind her feelings. Alice hated him for being so considerate, so noble. 'I think it's best if I remove the rest of the stuff I have here and…'

'And leave us?' Alice completed the sentence for him and stood, searching his face. 'Just…leave us, James? Here?'

The scene which followed, conducted in lowered voices so that neither the other tenants, Mrs Bowden or Edward-John should get wind of it, was bitter. As they argued James packed a suitcase with the clothes he had previously left in Exeter. He took several of his books from a pile that was stacked against a wall. Since bomb damage had forced the family from the house they owned in Twickenham, their furniture had been stored. Exeter had been thought of as a temporary refuge until a more permanent home, safe from the bombings, could be arranged. As a result of this, James's personal belongings had been scattered between a warehouse, rented rooms in Exeter and the small flat in Finchley that he was currently sharing with a young colleague. He was closing the suitcase as his son came back into the room. Edward-John looked at the case and then from one parent to the other.

'Say goodbye to your father, Edward-John,' said Alice and she went to the door and stood, holding it open. Edward-John and his father shook hands. Then James took the weight of the suitcase and went out through the door.

In a corner of the public bar of the Ledburton Arms two young women were sitting over half-pints of shandy. Their skirts were short, their jumpers tight and their hair, which had spent the day in curlers under headscarves, was marvellously dressed in sausage curls in the front and long, unravelling tresses at the back. Their eyebrows were plucked into carefully shaped crescents, their lashes were stiff with mascara, their lipstick was beetroot red and they sat smoking moodily. Marion, the taller of the two and who had dyed her mousey hair a rich plum colour, screwed her fag-end into the ashtray and sighed.

'Sod Bayliss,' she breathed.

'Bugger hostels,' echoed Winnie, blowing smoke. During the two years they had been deployed to work on the Bayliss farms, and while Roger had been able to retain the three labourers who had only recently been conscripted, Winnie and Marion had been billeted at the village pub. This had ideally suited them, for here, after work, when they could emerge from the chrysalis of dirty dungarees, rain-soaked coats and muddy boots and become the sort of creatures blokes buy drinks for, take to the flicks and to the dance halls in Exeter, they could meet whomever was on offer or had strayed in their direction from any of the several military and naval establishments in the area. Now it seemed that their boss was about to take on another eight girls and billet them in the disused farmhouse that he had acquired some years previously when he had bought out a neighbour. Once installed in the new 'hostel', which was over a mile from the village, Marion and Winnie knew how rarely they would encounter anyone but aged, groping farmhands or boys unfit or too young for the armed services and therefore too broke or immature for their purposes. Furthermore, the hostel would have rules. And a warden to enforce them. And Mr Bayliss for her to report to if she was disobeyed. The news of this change in their circumstances had been broken to them earlier that evening on their arrival back from work when, in the kitchen of the pub and still clad in their working clothes, their landlady had set before them their plates of dinner which, as on most Thursdays, consisted of fried sausages, a pile of mashed potato and another of swede, all of it doused in thick Bisto gravy and followed by suet pudding under a spoonful of golden syrup. Then, just as they had drained their shandy, smoked the last of their fags and the future seemed bleak, the door of the bar burst open and a bunch of likely lads came stumbling in. They sported various uniforms: Fleet Air Arm, Navy and Army. On setting their eyes on Marion and Winnie they responded at once to the girls' body language. Their bearing altering perceptibly, they slowed, regrouped and then, swaggering and grinning, approached their quarry.

'Oh, aye!' said Marion under her breath to her friend, baring her teeth in a wide smile, her Geordie accent warm in the thick air. ''Ere come the lads!'

Alice was at her dressing table smoothing cold cream into her skin when she became aware of Edward-John at her elbow. He was wearing his pyjamas and his hair was on end where he had lain on it.

'You should be asleep,' she said.

'I woke up,' he said. 'I was worried.'

'Try not to be.'

'You are,' he said. His eyes were huge, missing nothing. 'Anyway, where were you when I got home from school?' Alice had almost forgotten about the other disaster of the day.

'I had to go out into the countryside,' she told him. 'And then wait ages for a bus back again.'

'I didn't know where you were and I don't like not knowing where you are.' His voice was thick and she knew he was close to tears, which she guessed had as much to do with his father's visit as her own, earlier, absence.

'I'm sorry, darling. Won't do it again. Promise.' Then she lightened her tone and asked him whether he had remembered to brush his teeth. He smiled sheepishly and she watched him go to the hand basin and squeeze paste onto his toothbrush.

'But where did you go?' he persisted, shoving the brush around his mouth.

'To see about a job,' she said. Impressed, Edward-John stopped brushing.

'Gosh!' he said. 'Like a workman, you mean? What would you have to do?' The memory of the unsatisfactory interview swept over Alice but she controlled her voice and almost cheerfully told her son that this particular job entailed looking after land girls. Cooking their meals and supervising their hostel. 'What's a hostel?' was his next question, between spitting and turning off the tap.

'This particular hostel is a farmhouse,' Alice answered, a vision of the crumbling, damp building solidifying as she spoke. But her son's eyes were widening.

'A farmhouse? A real farm? With animals?' Alice had not noticed any animals.

'I don't remember seeing any,' she said, discounting the chickens in the yard and the distant sheep. 'But I suppose there must be animals there...' Her son was transformed by this news.

'Animals! And haystacks! And carts and tractors and things! Can we go there? Can we go tomorrow?' His delight was infectious. She found herself smiling with him as he pleaded, climbing beguilingly onto her lap, hugging her, pressing his cheek against hers, engaging her eyes via the dressing-table mirror.

'I don't think so,' she said.

'Why not?'

'It would be too far to get you to school each day... You'd have to board...except for the weekends...' He was interrupting her, his keen eyes inches from hers.

'I don't care! I don't! Let's go there, Mother!'

In the pub, as the landlord called time, Marion and Winnie, closely pressed by several uniformed male bodies, were at the centre of a group clustered, singing, round the piano. The chorus of 'You'll Never Know' filled the smoky air and in Marion's handbag were two lipsticks, a bottle of crimson nail varnish and several pairs of silk stockings.

Margery Brewster's 'office' was a desk in the corner of a small ante-room in Exeter Town Hall. There was a sign that read 'Women's Land Army', a telephone, an in-tray and an out-tray, stacks of papers, tidily clipped together, and an immaculate blotter. She invited Alice to sit in the chair opposite to her own and sent a girl for two cups of tea. She knew, from Roger Bayliss, that Alice had accepted the job and had been asked to report to the Land Army office to complete the formalities.

'So your son's needs made up your mind for you, did they?' Margery Brewster asked when Alice had explained the reasons for her decision. 'I was almost sure you would turn us down!' Alice took the cup and saucer in her hands and declined sugar.

'I'm hoping he will be happy on the farm,' she said. Margery looked at her sharply.

'And will you be?' she asked, sliding Alice's contract across the desk and indicating the places that required her signature. Alice felt that she was unlikely to be happy anywhere but she told Mrs Brewster that she thought she would be. The interview was obviously over. The tea was too hot so she left half of it in the cup, got to her feet and shook the proffered hand.

'Monday week,' Margery said. 'At the farmhouse. As early as possible.'

A thin girl, dressed in a long dark coat, thick stockings, lace-up shoes and with her felt hat in her hand, approached Margery's desk and stood uncertainly, her eyes on Margery's face, as though awaiting a command. Her face looked scrubbed, the skin stretched and almost transparent. She wore no make-up. Her pale auburn hair was drawn back into a bun on the nape of her neck. Alice, as she moved away, heard Margery say 'Next!' and saw the girl creep forward.

'Name?' demanded Margery.

'Tucker, Miss,' whispered the girl. 'Hester Tucker.'

Roger Bayliss sent a man in a truck to fetch Alice and her belongings. The man, Ferdinand Vallance, was a labourer who, in his late teens, had been injured in an accident on the farm. One leg, so badly crushed that it was barely saved, remained twisted. This gave Ferdie a weird, gyrating gait and prevented him from working as fast or as efficiently as he had done before the injury. It also made him unfit for active service. All this information was imparted to Alice when, after delivering Edward-John and his luggage to the preparatory school where he was to spend weekday nights, Ferdie drove the truck out through the suburbs of Exeter and onto a minor road which wound over the hills to Ledburton.

'Baint that I doan wanna do me bit in the forces like

any other fella,' he had told Alice, almost unintelligibly. 'Mean, no one ud choose to 'obble 'bout the place like I 'as to do!'

Her leave-taking from Edward-John had been easier than Alice had expected, due in part to its rushed and peculiar circumstances. They had hugged. On Friday night he was to be put on a bus to Ledburton where he would be met. She promised him two whole days on the farm and left him smiling at the prospect.

Her few pieces of furniture were unloaded from the truck and installed in her room. Two threadbare Persian carpets had been spread, one in each of the floor areas and, as well as her mother's desk and the two armchairs, there was a low rosewood table and a bookcase, presumably contributed by her employer. A fire was burning in the grate and another roared up the wide chimney of the recreation room.

'Mr Bayliss says as we're to keep 'em in day and night till the place dries out,' Rose informed her. 'These walls has got a dozen years of cold stored in 'em! Once they'm warm 'twill feel better, he says but 'twill take weeks, I reckon!'

In the kitchen the range had smoked sulkily, refusing to draw until Roger himself climbed to the chimney and removed the generations of jackdaw nests that were blocking it. After that the kitchen too began to heat up, steaming as the damp was drawn out of the walls, condensation misting the slate floor.

Rose was working at speed. Unlike Alice, she knew where everything was, which of the deliveries of furniture had already been made and when others were expected. She had decided where the pots and pans would be stored and which drawers would contain the cutlery and which the ladles, kitchen knives, potato peelers and sieves. This, she was well aware, gave her advantages over Alice. She could show off her efficiency and her energy to Mr Bayliss and did so, literally running rings round Alice as the cold of the house seeped through the thin soles of Alice's shoes from stone floors still barely above freezing point.

They had less than three days before the first intake of girls was due and, as Rose eagerly pointed out, still had no chairs, no saucepans, no mattresses and only half the required linen.

'And this is a list of their next of kin,' Margery had begun, sitting beside Alice on one of two packing cases and spreading her paperwork on the kitchen table. 'Put it in your file and don't lose it whatever you do. There'll be eight to start with; another couple later in the season.' She produced a second sheaf of papers. 'Ah...here are the travelling arrangements. One copy for me and one for you... Winnie Spriggs and Marion what's-her-name will be fetched from their billet after work. One girl...Tucker, Hester Tucker, is coming over by bus from Bideford. She'll need meeting at Ledburton at three-thirty. There'll be a couple – a Mabel Hodges and an HM something or other – on the London train and two more coming via Bristol. This one…Georgina Webster…is being driven over by her parents. So we can cross her off our lists of worries.'

In her warm and sunny bedroom, Georgina was, at that moment, trying on her Land Army uniform. The corduroy breeches fitted well and did not displease her. The fawn aertex shirt was very like the white ones she wore for tennis and although the green jumper was thick enough to flatten her breasts, her figure was too lithe, athletic and, where appropriate, rounded for any garment to significantly diminish its charm. She looked, in fact, very much like the girl on the posters advertising the Land Army, which were, that year, widely displayed up and down the country. Georgina's hair was straight, thick, dark and silky. She wore it in an almost 1920s bob, which not only accentuated her good bones and compelling, grey eyes but was easy to dry after swimming in the summers and after riding in the rain during the winters. She laced up the heavy shoes. The khaki socks felt rough against her skin but were thick and would keep her warm. She reeled under the weight of the greatcoat with its ugly, wide lapels and buttoned it, barely able to breathe, across her chest. But the hat! The hat she could not, would not, tolerate. She went noisily down the polished wooden stairs and into the dining room where her parents and her brother were finishing breakfast. They stared, laughed as she clowned with the hat, then fell silent, their smiles fixed. Her mother rose from the table and began gathering the dishes.

'It rather suits you, darling!' she said gamely. 'I feel as though I'm packing you off to boarding school again! Uniform and all!' She was not happy about her daughter's virtual conscription into the Land Army but there was a war on and people were having to make sacrifices. Hers, she knew, were less irksome than most. Her husband got to his feet, tucked his folded newspaper under one arm, held his daughter at arm's length and told her, not for the first time, that she was a good girl and that he was proud of her. Both mother and father left the room while the brother and sister remained, looking at one another, she, smiling, he, increasingly downcast.

'What's the matter, little brother?' Georgina asked. 'Come on. Tell.'

'I'm embarrassed, Georgie,' he said. 'I don't like what's happening.'

She laughed, removing the hat and sending it skimming through the air to land on the window-seat.

'Well, neither do I but who cares!' she said breezily. But Lionel was not to be cheered.

'I don't mean the bloody hat,' he said. 'You shouldn't be going.'

As a condition of war, exemption from military service was permitted to one son in each farming family. Second and successive siblings, male or female, were required to do war work of some description. Georgina, at twenty and able to avoid combat by enlisting in the Women's Land Army, had done so willingly, not only to protect her nineteen-year-old brother but because she herself, influenced by the convictions of her parents, was a pacifist. While not enthusiastic about the prospect of the Land Army, she found it tolerable and was pleased that she would be allowed to continue with a correspondence course, run by the Ministry of Agriculture, which would, if she was successful, give her recognised qualifications and develop the skills she might one day need in order to farm either her own land, or someone else's. Lionel, whose interests lay elsewhere, would replace one of his father's men until the war ended and then go to university. Although logical, the plan left Lionel with a nagging conscience, which neither his sister nor his parents could ease.

'It'll be ghastly, George,' he announced flatly. 'You'll be homesick and as lonely as all get-out! If your lot are anything like the land girls on the Marshalls' farm they'll be moronic!'

'Shut up, Li!' She was gentle. Persuasive. 'It has to be done. We both know it. I've spent enough time helping out here for the work to be familiar. I shan't be far away! I'll get home! And I daresay I'll be so exhausted that all I'll want to do with my spare time is sleep!' Her brother still looked unconvinced. 'It'll soon be over and we'll forget about it in no time. Think how much worse it would be if we were both boys and one of us was going to have to fight!' He smiled, slightly soothed.

'I could come over on the bike and take you for a spin?' he offered.

The breeches that had been allocated to Georgina had been manufactured in a small factory off the East India Dock Road. Its proprietor, Frederic Sorokova, together with large numbers of his close relatives, had emigrated from their native Poland soon after the end of the First World War. One of his current employees was his niece, Hannah-Maria who, at eighteen, like several of her cousins before her, was learning the business from the bottom up. Unlike them, she detested it. She hated the smell of fabric and of the oily machines. She hated their rattling clamour and the power they appeared to exert over the operators who spent their days bent over them as though attached by their flying fingers and strained eyes to the plunging needles.

Hannah-Maria had been in the dispatch room, folding corduroy breeches commissioned by the War Agricultural Committee for use by its land girls, and packing them, a dozen to a box, in cardboard cartons, when the idea first occurred to her. She was uncertain what land girls were or what they did. Her curiosity revealed that they were being employed on farms so that male workers could be released from vital agricultural labour and sent to fight the real war. According to the posters on the advertising hoardings these young women spent their time in idyllic countryside, riding on hay-wagons, driving tractors, bottle-feeding lambs and sprawling in the sun with their backs to honeysuckle-covered hedges. Hannah-Maria did not know honeysuckle from ragwort but, once planted in her mind, the notion of wearing one of these stiff pairs of breeches, rather than packing them, had taken hold and things had developed quickly from possibility to reality. She had called at a local recruitment centre where an elderly female officer looked her up and down, pulled a fresh application form from a file and began to fill it in.

'Name?'

'Hannah-Maria Sorokova.' The woman recoiled. 'Everyone calls me Annie,' Hannah-Maria explained. 'Except our gran. She calls us all by our proper Polish names.'

'Polish?' the woman repeated foolishly. 'I had assumed, from your accent, that you were...'

'Local? Yeah, well, I am. Born in Duckett Street, just off the Mile End Road. Same as me mum and dad. But their folks come from Cracow.' The woman looked at the thick dark hair, the soft eyes and the small oval face.

'I see,' she said.

'I'm not a German spy or nothing!' said Hannah-Maria defensively, her vision of the countryside fading under the woman's stare.

'Of course not,' said the woman. 'My concern is that you have a very urban background, Miss Soro...Sorok—'

'What's urban?' Hannah-Maria interrupted.

'It means...of a town or a city. You'd have to go wherever you are sent, you know. That might be a very long way indeed from your family and friends.'

'Look,' said Hannah-Maria urgently, 'the day I left school I was stuck in front of a sewing machine with twenty other girls, all of us doing the same thing, thinking the same thoughts. Since the war started we've been making breeches. For land girls, right? Thousands of 'em! Great towering stacks of 'em! I don't want to sew 'em, Miss! I want to wear 'em! Oh, please, Miss!' Hannah-Maria had a fleeting impression that the woman was suppressing a smile.

'Don't you think the countryside would seem very strange to you?' she asked.

'No, Miss!' Hannah-Maria was emphatic. 'I've been to the countryside! Honest! Hop-picking! Every year since I can remember! Till the war started, that is.'

She was given the address of a local doctor, a chit from the Ministry to cover the cost of a medical examination and told to report back with her certificate. A week later she was interviewed again and informed that she had been accepted into the Women's Land Army. She would receive one pound one shilling a week out of which ten shillings would be deducted for board and lodging. She would be trained on the job as there were no available places at the instruction centres. If she proved suitable her wage would rise to twenty-five shillings and the cost of her keep to twelve shillings and sixpence. She was given a rail ticket from Paddington to Ledburton Halt, near Exeter, told to make the journey on the following Wednesday and to inform her next of kin that her address would be care of Bayliss, Higher Stone Post Farm near Ledburton. There was a telephone number, strictly for emergencies only. Hannah-Maria ran all the way back to her uncle's workshop. She had exceeded her lunch break by fifteen minutes.

Chapter Two

Alice was floundering. Aware that neither Roger Bayliss nor Rose Crocker had any confidence in her ability to run the hostel and that even Margery Brewster's support was more in the interests of her own reputation than of Alice's, she felt increasingly exhausted.

Until the girls had arrived and their ration books were in her possession, Alice was able to buy only an emergency supply of basic food to tide them all over until the shopping could be put on a regular footing. Fred, an elderly labourer, normally attached to Bayliss's farm, was detailed to drive her into Exeter. She sat in the passenger seat of the truck that would soon be carrying the girls to and from their various sites of work. Its worn leather still reeked of a sick sheep that had recently been transported in it. Alice stocked up with scrubbing brushes, mops and as much food as was possible without the essential ration books.

Since her arrival at the farm she had been shaking. Whether this was caused by depression or anxiety or by the intense cold of the interior of the building she was unsure, but while she was in Exeter she spent some of her precious clothing coupons, and almost the last of her cash, on two pairs of woollen slacks, some warm socks, a thick sweater and a pair of leather boots whose inch-thick soles would distance her, that much at least, from the cold floors.

When she returned to the farm she found Rose watching Roger Bayliss, who was trying to assemble the paraffin cooker. Earlier, he had discovered Rose, absorbed in fitting its components together with the aid of the manufacturer's instructions. Assuming that she was incapable of the task, Roger relieved her of it and now she stood, ignoring Alice and observing him. After some time, convinced that he was holding some vital part or other upside down, Rose could no longer contain herself.

'I think you'll find, sir,' she ventured, her contempt thinly disguised as respect, 'if I may say so…that this bit goes there.' She took the piece of metal from him and inverted it, flushing with pleasure as it slid, without resistance, into place.

Rose had also contrived to tame the kitchen range, bullying it into submission and then persuading it to draw so vigorously that it now glowed almost red hot, its heat filling the room, spilling out into the cross-passage and rising through the ceiling into the rooms overhead. The tank above the bathroom was now filled with scalding hot water, which meant that the airing cupboard was warm and the linen could be unpacked and loaded into it. Alice's respect for Rose was huge but the woman refused to accept her praise and seemed determined to avoid eye contact with her.

Sacks of potatoes and swedes, together with nets of sprouts and carrots, were delivered from the Bayliss farm, which was, Alice learnt, situated on rising ground a mile further up the valley. Three hens, past laying, were killed, plucked and prepared for the table. Too tough for roasting, they were to be stewed for the first evening meal on the following day and served with mashed potatoes and cabbage followed by prunes and custard.

By Tuesday afternoon the beds in two of the double rooms, together with the three in the largest room, were assembled. Each was equipped with a pillow, two sheets, three blankets and a coverlet. Alice, now wearing her new trousers, thick sweater and boots, at last felt warm. She was at her mother's desk, working on menus which would utilise the limited supplies at her disposal when Roger called to check on progress and was greeted by Rose, shrilly cataloguing a host of problems.

'There's two beds not yet come, sir, and the man as is fetching over the kitchen chairs has broke down. We're still short of cutlery and there's a funny noise in the bathroom pipes… And if you could tell Fred us'll need another load of logs if we're to keep the fires up 'cos these walls is going to take a lot of heating through.' Roger Bayliss ignored Rose's concerns and asked where he could find Mrs Todd.

'She'll be working on her lists, sir,' Rose replied, her tone suggesting that her own contribution to the situation was vastly more to the point than Alice's.

When, moments later, Margery Brewster arrived with a bunch of snowdrops for Alice's room, Rose curtly acknowledged her arrival before trotting away on some pressing business.

'You'll have to watch her,' Margery warned Alice later, arranging the flowers in an old cup. 'Keep her in her place or she'll undermine your authority with the girls!' The looming prospect of the girls' arrival made Alice start to tremble again. It was an interior shaking which, fortunately, did not seem to be apparent to others.

'She's extremely capable,' Alice murmured. 'I think she could run this hostel without me!' If Margery gave her a quick, sharp look, Alice did not see it.

'There's a lot more to it than Rose Crocker is even aware of, Mrs Todd, and don't forget, any discourtesy on your charges' part, or failure to obey the rules may – in fact, should – be reported to me so that I can give you my unstinting support.' Margery's words, intended to reassure Alice, only added to her dread of possible confrontations with the eight unknown girls who were soon to invade the farmhouse.

That night, after the last of the workmen had withdrawn and Rose had retreated to her cottage across the yard, Alice was alone in the empty farmhouse and already becoming familiar with its creaking and with the wuthering of the night wind round its chimneys. She sat beside the fire in her room. Images gathered, surrounding her: Rose Crocker, who was hostile; Ferdie Vallance, who was lame; Roger Bayliss, who was disdainful; Margery Brewster, who was anxious; Edward-John in his boarding school dormitory; James, somewhere, probably in bed with Penelope Fisher.

In Alice's purse were five pound notes and half a crown. For months James's salary had been thinly spread between his needs in London and those of Edward-John and herself in their rented room in Exeter. The school fees, James's flat, her expenses in Exeter and the cost of the storage of their furniture had put a strain on their finances, as a result of which Alice found herself with less income than she had received as pin money in happier times. And tomorrow eight strangers, who Margery anticipated would be both discourteous and disobedient, would arrive at the farmhouse. Not only had Alice's life collapsed, not only had she lost home, husband and the presence of her son but she had contrived to deliver herself into a sort of hell. She had tried hard to do the sensible thing. To find work that would give her an income and put a safe roof over her head and the head of her child but this had proved difficult with a young boy's needs to consider. Because of him many occupations were barred to her. His safety was paramount so she could not consider working in a major city because of air raids, or volunteer for any of the military services that offered employment more suited to her education and the lifestyle with which she was familiar. There was no one to whom she could turn now that her Aunt Elizabeth was dead, leaving, quite understandably, all her money to her own daughter and not to the ward for whom she had so generously cared and who was, as far as Elizabeth had been aware, well provided for by the worthy husband that James had seemed to be. Faced with such a limited choice and although the prospect of running the hostel was clearly challenging, it had not, when Alice decided to accept the work, appeared to be the nightmare in which she now felt trapped. She stayed by the fire, in her dressing gown, past tears, too tired to get into her bed, while the grandfather clock in the hall chimed away each quarter, each half, each hour. Finally, in the interests of self-preservation, she made herself cross the room to the divan and try to sleep.

The arrivals began soon after noon. Two girls, Christine Wilkins and Gwennan Pringle, were met from the Bristol train, given a spam sandwich for their lunch and driven over to the Bayliss farm to be shown the ropes of the poultry sheds which was where they were to work in the mornings and late afternoons, spending the rest of their time helping out wherever they were required.

Christine was small, blonde and pretty; Gwennan, Alice thought, looked difficult. She was lean and dark with a Welsh accent so strong that Alice, Rose and Margery had difficulty understanding her. At thirty-two, she would be the oldest of the intake. Both she and Christine had previous experience in the Land Army and had brought dungarees, boots, sweaters and waterproof jackets with them. Christine was polite about the tiny room which she was to share with Mabel. Gwennan, because of her seniority, was allocated the smallest of the double rooms which she would have to herself, at least until the workforce was increased at harvest time. She accepted this arrangement as her due and complained about the draught whining through the ill-fitting window frame.

As Rose and Alice snatched a late lunch consisting of a cup of tea and a sandwich made from what was left of the spam, they listened to the wireless, which was powered by the same small, temperamental generator that provided lights for the ground floor. Reception was poor in the deep valley but through the whistling and crackling, John Snagg's voice informed them that the Eighth Army had taken Tripoli. To Alice this news and the familiar voice was a thin, precious thread, connecting her with the world from which she felt separated. Tears formed and before she could control them, ran down her face. Rose's chair scraped back across the floor, she picked up Alice's plate and her own and carried them out into the scullery. When she returned Alice had collected herself and was sipping her tea.

'Bit of a madam, that Welsh one!' Rose said nastily. 'Just as well no one has to share with her! Wonder how they'll all get on with each other! The woman at the big hostel over to Aunton had a couple there as scratched each other's eyes out!' Knowing very little about the in-coming girls, Alice had allocated the rooms on the basis of age and qualifications. Hannah-Maria with Hester because they were both only eighteen years old, Georgina with Winnie and Marion because they were all in their early twenties, Christine with Mabel because they both had previous Land Army experience and Gwennan alone, in deference to her age. It seemed inevitable that clashes of temperament, personal taste or hygiene habits were going to make some of these pairings unsatisfactory.

'We'll just have to see,' Alice said. 'If they want to change partners, they may.'

'I'd make 'em do as they're told!' Rose snapped caustically. 'Show 'em who's boss!'

By four o'clock Mabel Hodges and Hannah-Maria Sorokova had been collected from the London train and delivered to the farm. The list read simply HM Sorokova and M Hodges. As they ticked the name of each arrival on Mrs Brewster's list, neither Alice nor Rose, who were both preoccupied with the preparation of the evening meal, had time to go into detail regarding Christian names. Alice proposed leaving the introductions until all the newcomers were assembled round the kitchen table and had, she prayed, been fed. Rose had raised her eyebrows at this plan but seemed prepared to comply with what was, in fact, Alice's first tentative attempt at taking charge of the situation.

It was dusk when Fred's truck arrived with Hester Tucker, who had stepped down from the bus in Ledburton and stood, transfixed, until he identified himself and persuaded her into the passenger seat beside him. Marion and Winnie had kept him waiting while, at the pub, they lingered over what they feared would be their last hot baths until the bells of victory sounded.

Hester, dressed as she had been when interviewed by Margery Brewster at the Exeter recruitment office, clutched a carpet-bag and stared about her as though she had been delivered into temptation which, of course, she had. Marion and Winnie, casting their eyes over Hester's dark clothes, thick black stockings and lace-up shoes, decided she was a freak with whom they would have nothing whatsoever to do. Hester, for her part, blushed at the sight of their lipsticked mouths and mascaraed eyes. On arrival at the farmhouse she lowered her lids and stared at her feet.

'Come on, dear,' Rose ordered, almost pushing the bewildered girl into the porch.

It was at that moment, while Marion and Winnie were unloading several bulging suitcases from the truck, that the Websters' car, driven by Lionel and containing Georgina, lurched over the cart ruts and stopped outside the garden gate. The suitcases that Lionel lifted from its boot had been a birthday present from Georgina's godmother. They were made of soft leather and initialled GW in gold leaf. Georgina emerged from the passenger seat, hat in hand, immaculate in her uniform. She smiled at Alice and Rose, extended a hand to Alice and introduced herself.

'I'm Alice Todd,' Alice responded. 'Your warden. And this is Mrs Crocker, my assistant.' Georgina smiled at Rose, said hello to her but did not shake her hand. This, Rose's expression told Alice, was something Georgina would live to regret. Fred, his eyes fixed approvingly on Georgina, took her suitcases from her brother and was about to carry them into the house when Marion's voice cut the air.

''Ere! You!' she said, indicating the unglamorous clutter of luggage at her feet. Fred knew at once it was him she meant. 'What about a hand with these ones then!' Marion stood, implacable, Winnie simpering beside her, as Fred relinquished Georgina's cases to Lionel and took the weight of the heaviest of Marion's. Georgina smiled but Marion's expression was that of a gloating victor. Teetering on stiletto heels, she followed Fred into the farmhouse.

The meal, planned for six o'clock and despite the stew-pan going off the boil several times and the potatoes boiling dry on the paraffin stove, was less than half an hour late.

Pieces of chicken were doled out onto the plates by Rose, who made a good job of the distribution, managing to save two portions, one for Alice and one for herself, to consume in peace after the girls had been fed. Alice had just invited her charges to help themselves to the vegetables when Hester, flushed with embarrassment, spoke. To begin with no one could quite hear the mumbled words and Alice had to ask her to repeat them.

'No one's said Grace, Miss,' Hester mumbled, still almost inaudibly, her face pink with misery. The girls were aghast and several giggled but Rose tapped a plate with her serving spoon and looked at Alice.

'Perhaps you would like to, Hester?' Alice suggested.

Hester gathered herself, lowered her head and muttered, 'For what we are about to receive,' and then stopped, her lower lip trembling, Winnie and Marion smothering their amusement as the freak made a fool of herself. Then Rose's voice cut in, sharp and authoritative.

'May the Good Lord make us truly thankful. Amen,' she concluded, glaring round the table and repeating the 'amen' so fiercely that Hannah-Maria, Christine, Georgina and Gwennan all joined her.

Rose had knowingly shaken her head when Alice had decided to present the mashed potatoes and cabbage in large dishes from which each girl could take what she required. Unfortunately Mabel, Winnie, Marion and Gwennan required rather more than their share, so that by the time the dishes reached Hester and Georgina they were almost empty. At subsequent meals Alice would distribute the meat and Rose the vegetables.

Mabel, Winnie, Marion and Gwennan ate quickly, using pieces of a thickly sliced loaf to soak up the gravy on their plates.

'What's for afters,' Mabel enquired with her mouth full. Her bovine frame would always be eager for food.

'Prunes and custard,' Rose announced.

'Nursery food,' said Georgina sociably.

'You what?' Winnie and Marion looked genuinely curious.

'Prunes and custard,' Georgina repeated politely. 'What my brother and I always called nursery food because...' She looked around at the eyes which were observing her, some hostile, some amused. 'Because we used to eat that kind of thing in our nursery,' she finished lamely.

'Eew!' said Marion, inaccurately imitating Georgina's accent, 'Eeen the narsery, what? La-di-da-di-dah!' Winnie, reacting to Alice's obvious disapproval, nudged her mate and told her to hush up.

'Tinker, tailor, soldier, sailor,' chanted Christine, happily counting her prune stones. 'I'll need four, 'cos my Ron's a sailor! Minesweepers, he's in. We're gonna save up all our pay so when the war's over we'll have enough for a place of our own!'

'Isn't that lovely!' said Marion sarcastically. Winnie giggled.

'Love's young dream!' she added, with her mouth full. For a while no one spoke and cutlery clattered.

'Perhaps we should introduce ourselves,' Alice suggested tentatively. 'We could go clockwise round the table. Would you begin, Christine?'

'OK then,' Christine smiled round the chewing faces. 'I'm Christine Wilkins. Everyone calls me Chrissie... Me and Ron got married two months ago...'

'Up the spout, are you?' Winnie asked, nailing Chrissie with her shrewd eyes.

'No, as it happens,' Chrissie said cheerfully. 'We're not having kids till the war's over... He looks like Leslie Howard, my Ron. I'll show you his photo after. He got a forty-eight-hour pass for our wedding and I haven't seen him since!' There was a murmur of sympathy as she turned to Gwennan. 'Your go now,' she said.

'Gwennan Pringle. From Builth Wells. My folks are both dead and I live with my aunt and my uncle, who is an undertaker.' The girls stared at the narrow face with its prim mouth and at the hard, dark eyes that seemed to be daring anyone to make some joke or other at an undertaker's expense.

'A "taffy", eh!' said Hannah-Maria. 'How do, Taff!' Everyone laughed and suddenly the room felt warmer.

'Next!' demanded Chrissie.

'Georgina Webster. My people farm in Taunton Deane.' Winnie and Marion nudged and giggled. Georgina paused and then continued in a clear voice. 'I volunteered for the Land Army so that my brother could stay on the farm.' There was a slight intake of breath. Rose, about to dispense the last of the prunes, paused, spoon in mid-air.

'And not get called up, you mean?' asked Gwennan in her clipped, sing-song Welsh voice.

'He's a pacifist,' Georgina said and then, her words dropping into a heavy silence, continued, 'and so am I.'

'What's a pacifist?' asked Hannah-Maria while Hester's eyes went anxiously from speaker to speaker because she didn't understand a word anyone was saying.

'Someone who…' Alice began, searching for a definition that would not provoke further dissension.

'Who's a friggin' coward!' Marion interrupted sharply. 'And what's more, Mrs Todd, me and Win's not sharing a bedroom with no bloomin' conchie!'

'We didn't want to come here in the first place!' Winnie chimed in, self-righteous and injured. 'We liked our digs in the village!'

'Yes!' said Rose. 'And there's some as knows why!' Marion and Winnie gasped. Hester was now thoroughly alarmed by all this shouting. Hannah-Maria and Gwennan exchanged speculative glances, Georgina dropped her eyes and smiled at her plate as Rose continued, 'But whilst you'm 'ere you'll sleep where you'm told! And be in be ten o'clock, like it says in the rule book!' Alice was slightly taken aback by the ferocity of Rose's tone and placed a restraining hand on her arm.

'I noticed that there's a small single room,' said Georgina coolly. She was in the habit of getting what she wanted. 'If you would allow it, Mrs Todd, I'd prefer to sleep there.'

'Fine by us!' spluttered Marion.

'Yeah!' echoed her shadow.

'Quiet, you two!' Rose commanded and the girls subsided into a stunned silence. Alice said she thought it could be arranged, although the room Georgina proposed using was very small. Georgina said she didn't mind a bit and the matter was closed. Rose offered the last of the prunes and Mabel accepted them with an alacrity that amused Chrissie and Hannah-Maria.

Later, in the double room they were to share, Hannah-Maria, who at supper had invited everyone to call her Annie, was unpacking her suitcase. Hester, whose one change of clothes was already stowed in the wardrobe and in the lower drawer of the shared dressing table, watched, fascinated as Annie shook out frilled blouses, floral frocks, sleeveless Ceylonese nightdresses with lacy inserts and two pairs of cami-knickers, which, she told Hester, had been a farewell gift from her boyfriend, Pete, who had run a barrow in Petticoat Lane until being recently conscripted, but only into the catering corps on account of his flat feet. Hester stared at the curlers and the face powder and the little jars of Pond's Vanishing Cream and Cold Cream and the bottle of Amami shampoo, which now stood on Annie's side of the dressing table.

'What with all that fuss with Georgina, we never got round to you, did we!' Annie said, adding, when Hester shyly hung her head, 'Come on! Your name's Hester. And…?!'

'And me dad's a dairyman,' Hester said. She had difficulty in understanding her room-mate's cockney accent but, despite worries about Annie's appearance and shocked by the colours and the cut of her clothes, found that she was reluctantly, almost guiltily, responding to her friendliness.

'Yeah?… Go on, then!' Annie persisted, smoothing out the creases in a blue crêpe de Chine frock before hooking it onto the rail in the wardrobe.

'And he preaches, Sundays.'

'Oh!' said Annie.

'We belong to the Brethren. It's a religion.'

'Yeah,' said Annie. 'Well, it would be, wouldn't it! Is that why you wear dark colours and that?' she enquired, running out of coat hangers.

'Bright colours is sinful.' Hester's accent, Annie noticed, was like Mrs Crocker's only softer. 'It says so in the book.'

'What book?' Annie asked innocently, her face already betraying her response to Hester's convictions.

'The Bible!' said Hester as though there was only one

book. Annie, her unpacking finished, had pulled a packet of Woodbines from her handbag and was searching unsuccessfully for matches. She caught Hester's look.

'Oh 'eck…I suppose smokin's a sin an' all?'

'Yeah, 'tis,' Hester muttered almost inaudibly.

Annie got to her feet, showed her teeth in a wide smile and crossed the small space to the door.

'Reckon I'll have my fag next door then,' she said.

Hester sat on her bed beside her carpet-bag from which she lifted a framed photograph of her father, her mother and her young brother. She stared for a moment at the hard eyes of her father and then positioned the photograph carefully on the small table which separated the twin beds.

In the neighbouring room Marion and Winnie had rapidly appropriated the extra space left by Georgina's decampment. The unoccupied third bed was now strewn with brightly coloured garments and half a dozen pairs of new silk stockings. Winnie lay sprawled on her bed reading a film magazine while Marion, one foot braced against the dressing table, daubed blood-red varnish onto her toenails. When Annie put her head round the door and asked Marion and Winnie if they had a match they responded in unison.

'Yeah!' they chorused, 'your face and my bum!' Then Marion, tossing a box of Swan Vestas in Annie's direction, asked sharply whether their visitor had ever heard of knocking.

Although not invited into the room, Annie smiled and lingered in the doorway, smoking.

'Nice colour,' she said, nodding at Marion's nail varnish. 'Many blokes round here?'

'If you know where to find 'em,' Marion said.

'Or if you like your men under sixteen or over sixty,' Winnie giggled, adding to Marion, 'Hey! She could come with us, Sat'day night, down the pub.' She hesitated, silenced by a sharp look from her friend and then asked tentatively, 'Couldn't she?'

Marion's glance as she screwed the top tightly onto the nail polish was designed to shut Winnie up and close the subject but Winnie persisted. She would have been happy enough for Annie to join them. There were always more than enough men to go round on a Saturday night. But Marion remained adamant, exercising her well-developed facility to lie.

'No, Win,' she said, 'she can't 'cos we're going on, aren't we!' She began running a razor over a smooth shin.

'On?' Winnie echoed. She was, Marion considered, very stupid at times.

'To Exeter, Win! To that dance! Gary and Sergeant Whatsit's got a staff car for the night and there's only room for them two and us. Sorry,' she added, glancing coolly at Annie.

Marion was not beautiful. She was not even pretty. It required a lot of hard work to make her sharp face, mousey hair and angular body attractive to men. She employed most of the devices available to her and spent a large portion of her small income on smoothing out the sharp corners of the raw material against which she had been fighting a running battle ever since she had first admitted to herself that she was plain, bordering on ugly. In her raw state Marion would have been passed unrecognised by the same men with whom, foundation-creamed, plucked, rouged and powdered, her contact could hardly have been more intimate. She was very aware of competition. Winnie, small, soft and silly, was the perfect companion. She laughed at Marion's jokes and was impressed by her shrewdness. She was happy to sit smiling in the pub until Marion attracted the men and Winnie willingly linked arms with the soldier, sailor or airman who, for one reason or another, did not link arms with Marion. Annie, on the other hand, struck Marion as competition. She was not only attractive but pretty, if not downright beautiful. Added to which she had exactly the sort of personality blokes like best. As a consequence she would have to make her own way into the unreliable, fluctuating social scene of the Ledburton area for neither Marion nor Winnie would initiate her, a fact which, although Marion would not have considered it so, was no disadvantage. As Annie stubbed out her cigarette she caught sight of the silk stockings.

'Blimey!' she exclaimed, 'where d'you get all them?'

'Where d'you think!' Marion snapped, enjoying Annie's envy.

'From an admirer!' Winnie said smugly. 'Three pair each, we got!'

'Jeez!' said Annie, deeply impressed. 'He must've been feeling generous!'

'Well, he was feeling *something*!' Marion shrieked and the ensuing laughter echoed along the corridor and was even faintly audible to Rose as she knocked on the door of Alice's room.

After supper and the washing-up and the setting of the table for tomorrow's breakfast and the putting of porridge oats into a pan to soak, Rose had retired to her cottage where she had eaten the plate of chicken which, despite being reheated, was not quite hot enough to be pleasant. Try as she might – and for her own, complicated reasons – to harden her heart, she could not forget the look of exhaustion on Alice's face when her day's work was at last completed. Unable to stomach the chicken, Alice had given her portion to a cat that, discovering the farmhouse to be once again inhabited, was clearly planning to take up residence in it. Rose fretted for a while and then left her fireside, returned to the farmhouse, heated a pan of creamy milk, filled two cups and made her way through the house to Alice's door.

'Only hot milk,' Rose said breezily. 'Six tins of cocoa we ordered but d'you think I can put my hands on 'em?' Alice was at her mother's desk. She looked, Rose thought, like an exhausted child.

'We must reorganise that store cupboard tomorrow,' Alice said, reaching for notepad and pencil.

'Never you mind that now,' said Rose, putting one of the cups of milk into Alice's hand. Alice thanked her.

'Bit of a baptism of fire, that supper!' Rose stood, her own cup in her hand.

'It certainly was!' said Alice. 'And the awful thing is that we have to do it again tomorrow... And the day after... And the day after that!' She was trying to laugh but Rose felt, uncomfortably, that she was very close to tears. 'Sit down,' she invited Rose. 'Join me, won't you?' She indicated one of the two armchairs but remained where she was, at her desk. Rose sat. She looked round the room and complimented Alice on how nicely she had arranged it.

'The other bed's for your boy, I suppose?' Rose said. The thought of Edward-John, alone in his boarding school dormitory brought Alice close to tears. She nodded at Rose and there was a small silence while both women sipped at the hot milk. 'They're a rough old lot, these girls!' said Rose. Alice looked at her in surprise.

'D'you think so?' she asked.

'I *know* so!' Rose replied. 'And that Georgina! Make my blood boil, conchies do! When I think of my Dave...out there...riskin' 'is life! While her sort—'

'It's called freedom, Rose. It's what the war is for.' Alice's quiet statement failed to convince Rose.

'So they say,' she scoffed. Alice allowed her the last word and again they slipped into silence. 'Christine seems a charming girl, don't you think?' Alice said, trying to find something positive to say.

'Bit lippy, if you ask me,' Rose snapped. 'Wilful, I reckon!'

Alice smiled. 'You're awfully hard on them,' she said gently.

'Maybe,' said Rose. 'And maybe you're not used to that class of girl, Mrs Todd! Hardly the sort of person you've mixed with, are they!' Aware that Alice was looking at her, Rose turned her head and stared at the heavy curtains, which, too long for that window, lay with their hems dragging. 'No more'n what I am, come to that,' she concluded in a low voice, at once regretting having introduced a sour note into what she had intended to be a soothing gesture towards Alice.

'Rose… Please…' Alice began, after a short silence and then, catching Rose completely off guard said, 'Won't you use my Christian name? I'd really like you to!' Rose, flushing with pleasure, was about to respond when the two of them were interrupted by a tap on the open door. Christine, a dressing gown wrapped tightly round her, stood in her slippers.

'I need to ask you something please, Miss,' she said to

Alice, ignoring Rose who got to her feet and took Alice's empty cup from her.

'I'll say goodnight then...Alice,' Rose said, glancing at Christine to see whether or not she had noticed her use of the warden's Christian name.

Alice invited Christine to sit opposite her by the fire and asked what she could do for her.

'Well... It's my 'usband, see... He's got a twenty-four-hour pass!' She spoke with a soft West Country accent which Alice couldn't quite place 'We haven't seen each other since the night we was wed, Mrs Todd! He's in Plymouth... And he sails Friday! Can I go and see him when I finish work tomorrow? Fred...the driver fellow...he says he'll drop me off at the railway after work and meet the milk train next morning. Lord knows when Ron and me'll see each other again! *Please* can I go? I won't miss no work!' Alice considered and could see no reason why, in these particular circumstances, permission would not be given. She told Christine she would ask Mr Bayliss and basked in the girl's gratitude, enquiring, as she rose to leave, whether her bedroom was comfortable.

'Yeah,' Christine answered. 'I'm sharing with Mabel. She seems like a good sort, except...' She hesitated delicately.

'Except for what?' Alice asked.

'I don't like to say, Miss,' Christine said, colouring. 'Prob'ly she just got too hot on the train... Mr Bayliss will let me go to Plymouth, won't he?'

'I'll do my best for you, I promise.'

'Ta. Night, then.'

'Goodnight, Christine.'

In the small, dark bedroom above, Hester and Annie lay in their narrow beds under the roof-beams and tried to sleep. From the next room Marion and Winnie, unused to early nights, were amusing themselves, giggling together and keeping up an endless, bantering conversation. Eventually Annie struck the partition with her closed fist.

'Leave it out, you two! We're trying to sleep in here!'

'Go to buggery!' Winnie shouted but, more because they were becoming drowsy than in response to Annie's request, silence fell.

It was the absolute silence of a still country night. It dropped over them like a blanket. The world beyond the valley might have ceased to exist as the farmhouse, with its complement of assorted women, sailed on into the night.

But the act of thumping on the partition had roused Annie.

'Listen…' she whispered.

'What to?' said Hester, half asleep.

'It's like when we was hop-picking,' Annie said. 'The quiet always kept us awake the first coupla nights…' They lay in the silence; their feet, cold when they first got into their beds, were warm now. Then the vixen barked, its shriek close and hideous.

'Jesus!' said Annie, lurching upright.

'S'only a fox!' Hester murmured and Annie dropped back shuddering, burrowing into her hard pillow and pulling the skimpy blankets up around her shoulders.

'Whew! I near enough shit meself!' she said. There was a pause before Hester spoke, almost reluctantly, as though her conscience was driving the words from her.

'Annie.'

'What?'

'You shouldn't say "Jesus" like that.'

'No?'

'No.'

'OK then,' Annie sighed, yawning. 'No fags... No Jesus... OK? Night, Hester.'

'Night.'

It felt like the middle of the night when they were roused and came, still smelling of sleep, down to the kitchen, where the porridge had caught slightly and the toaster, a wire contraption that had to be balanced on the paraffin stove, proved intractable and was abandoned in favour of the toasting-fork method. In front of the open door to the range, the girls noisily competed for space until Rose organised an orderly queue.

Outside, in the freezing darkness, Fred sat in the idling truck, his headlights picking up the figures of the girls as they emerged through the porch and came groping and stumbling towards him through the darkness. One by one they climbed, or were hauled, up into the back of the lorry where they seated themselves on benches that ran along each side of it.

'This is it, then!' said Annie. 'Life in the Land Army! Shivering in the back of a truck as stinks of cow shit!'

'In the middle of the night!' added Christine, happy and uncaring because of the prospect of seeing her husband that evening.

'Baint the middle of the night!' said Hester, who was used to rising early.

'Feels like it!' whined Winnie, who never would get used to it.

'My feet are freezing,' said Gwennan, her Welsh voice half singing the words.

'Should wear two pairs of socks inside your boots this weather, Taff,' Marion muttered through chattering teeth. Gwennan told her to go teach her grandmother to suck eggs. Fred tried to hurry the stragglers by sounding his horn.

'Doan wanna be late the first mornin', do ee?'

'Where are you takin' us?' Annie, in the passenger seat beside him, shouted over the revving engine.

'To the Bayliss farm first off,' he replied. ''Igher Post Stone, it be called.' In the back Christine was counting heads.

'Six, seven, eight… All aboard!' she yelled. As Fred shoved the gear lever into position Rose appeared in his headlights, several bulging brown paper bags in each hand.

'Wait, Fred!' she commanded. 'They 'asn't got their samwidges!' Alice, in Rose's wake, carried an armful of the same small packages which the two women rapidly distributed amongst the girls.

''Ere!' Rose called. 'Georgina! Taffy! Hester… Catch!' And while Fred swore at the delay, the girls chorused back, 'Thanks, Mrs Todd! Ta, Mrs Crocker!'

As Alice and Rose picked their way back to the porch they could hear the truck labouring up the incline towards the Bayliss farm.

'That's them gone!' said Rose, sitting on the porch bench to heel-off her boots and slip her feet into the plimsolls that, over a pair of her late husband's socks, she had taken to wearing about the farmhouse. 'And good riddance, I say!' She followed Alice through the cross-passage and into the kitchen and, glancing at the scatter of dirty porridge bowls, plates, cups and saucers, lifted the teapot.

'Reckon there's enough in 'ere for a cuppa each,' she said and began to pour. Glancing at the dishes she added, 'Deserve one too, afore us tackles that lot!' Alice sat heavily down at the table.

'We're going to have to cut their sandwiches—' she began and Rose interrupted, finishing her sentence.

'The night before! I was just thinking the same thing myself.'

* * *

As the morning lightened, Taffy, Marion and Winnie were shovelling dung from the Bayliss cowshed into the back of a cart. Ferdie, lurching past them, snarled, 'C'mon, c'mon! Put some muscle into it!' and continued on his way, unaware that Marion's middle finger was jabbing at the air behind his back.

Inside the byre Georgina was showing Mabel how to coax milk down through an udder and into a galvanised bucket.

'It was pigs, mostly, where I bin!' Mabel gasped, fingers slipping, cow fidgeting.

'Keep the rhythm going!' Georgina urged, encouraging her. 'That's it! Nice and easy!' She steadied the bucket as the animal lurched, rolling its eyes at Ferdie as he approached.

'Hold still, you varmint of a cow!' he growled. 'Can't you see as the young lady's on'y learnin'? And very well she'm doing, too!'

'Thank you, Mr Vallance!' said Mabel, her plump cheek pressed against the cow's flank. Ferdie eyed her. He liked a big woman. Not that it mattered what he liked. Since he had been crippled he had learnt to accept the fact that no girl would go with him. He understood that there was nothing personal in their decision to exclude him from the ranks of possible mates. It was simply impractical. A girl needed a man who could provide for her and her babies. Ferdie, with his rolling gait and his weakened back, could not. But the girl squatting before him, her huge, khaki-clad thighs spilling over the edges of the milking stool, her hair thin and lank, her face pocked with on-going pimples…she might not be too choosy. As he approached her he became aware of the pungent, animal smell that emanated from her, penetrating intoxicatingly into his susceptible nostrils.

'You can call me Ferdie,' he said and, turning to Georgina, asked if her name was Webster. When she nodded he went on, 'Boss wants to see you. Nine sharp in his office, he said. 'Tis the door round the side. You can't miss it… If I was you,' he continued more gently, returning his attention to Mabel, 'I'd move that there milking stool in a bit closer, see?' Mabel did as he said, her smile revealing uneven, unbrushed teeth as she thanked him for his advice and, with something close to coyness, used his first name.

Georgina tapped on the door of the farm office. A voice said 'Come' and she went in. The man sitting behind the desk, his feet clad in riding boots resting on its surface, was much younger than Georgina had expected. He in turn seemed surprised by her appearance.

'I say!' he said appreciatively.

'Excuse me?'

'You should be in the WRNS with your figure!'

Georgina was not unused to compliments, sought or, as in this case, unsought.

'Driving some admiral about in a shiny motor car? No thanks. I'd rather be doing something useful.'

'The WRAF, then,' the young man persisted, undaunted

and misreading her reaction. 'The girls in Fighter Command see lots of action, I can tell you!' He moved his eyebrows suggestively.

'I don't want to "see action",' Georgina stated soberly. 'I happen to believe that war is—'

'Oh, Lord!' he cut in, 'so what do you suggest then? "Dear Herr Hitler, please would you stop bombing London and give Poland back?" That approach didn't work, duckie! Ask Mr Chamberlain!'

'I don't know what you're so smug about!' Georgina retaliated, feeling herself flush stupidly. 'You're not in uniform!' He threw back his head and was laughing at her when Roger Bayliss came through the door and stood, tapping his riding stock against his palm.

'Morning, Miss Webster,' he said, as the young man quickly swung his legs off the desk and got to his feet. 'Introduced yourselves, have you?'

'Sort of,' the young man said, smiling at Georgina's reaction. Then he excused himself and left them.

Roger Bayliss sat behind his desk and motioned Georgina into the chair opposite him.

'My son, Christopher,' he said, searching for something amongst the scatter of papers on his blotter. 'He's in fighters.'

'Fighters?' Georgina echoed, aghast and then seriously embarrassed.

'Yes. Spitfires mostly. And Hurricanes. Ah… Here it is…'

Roger Bayliss consulted a list and Georgina was grateful for the few moments in which she was able to collect herself. Then he told her that he had been looking through her application form. 'In view of your education and…how shall I put it…your obvious…' he hesitated, 'superiority… I'd like you to act as forewoman. Nothing complicated, you understand,' he added, misunderstanding her reaction. 'Simply need someone who can keep the worksheets in order and distribute the pay packets on Fridays. Manage that, could, you?'

'I should think so, sir,' she said coldly and had begun to tell him about the Forewoman's course she had almost completed, and of her work experience on her father's farm, when she was interrupted by the ringing of the telephone on his desk. He lifted the receiver, said 'Bayliss,' and listened for some moments with, it seemed to Georgina, increasing impatience. 'Absolutely not, Mrs Todd,' he said. 'She'll get Saturday afternoons and Sundays off, the same as the rest of them!' Georgina could hear Alice Todd's voice coming down the phone line until Mr Bayliss interrupted her. 'I can't start making exceptions whenever their spouses get leave! Good day, Mrs Todd!' He hung up sharply and returned his attention to Georgina.

'I shall need a permanent dairy-hand,' he said.

'Mabel Hodges, perhaps?' Georgina suggested. She watched him find the name on his list and try to connect it to a particular girl.

'Hodges... Is she the overweight, plain one with the bad smell?' Georgina felt a surge of defensive anger rise in her.

'Unfortunately we don't have the privilege of choosing our looks,' she said primly. They were words her grandmother had once used to her when, as a small child, she had poked fun at the long-nosed verger at their local church and she had never forgotten them. 'Mabel has a natural aptitude for dairy work and gets on well with Mr Vallance,' Georgina concluded firmly. Her employer laughed.

'With Ferdie! Does she! Does she indeed!'

'And you'll need someone to deputise for her, of course,' Georgina continued, ignoring his amusement. 'When she's on leave, or sick or on her day off. I would suggest Marion Grice. She tells me she's been milking on and off for the past two years.'

'Yes,' Bayliss said, impressed by the speed with which Georgina had not only familiarised herself with her fellow workers but was instinctively dovetailing their various skills and temperaments into the running of his farm. He thought better of confiding to her his well-established dislike of Marion Grice, shuffled his paperwork into a tidy pile, told Georgina he would consider her suggestions and dismissed her.

In a corner of a field a mile from the Bayliss farm, Christine, Hester and Annie were loading a cart with swedes, heaving them from the straw beneath which they had been stored through the winter until now, when they were needed as fodder for the livestock. A cold, fine rain beaded the girls' hair and was being absorbed by their clothes. Their hands were blistered by the pitchforks and the muscles in their backs and thighs were already tightening. Christine, a smudge of mud across her nose, leant on her pitchfork, arched her back to ease its stiffness and then laughed as Annie groaned under a load of swedes.

'Wish you were back at your sewing machine?' she asked and then ducked as Annie lobbed a clod of mud at her.

As dusk fell the girls had tumbled out of the truck and come roaring through the rain into the porch where they were confronted by Rose, her voice cutting the air like a whetted knife.

'Don't think you'm comin in 'ere in that state,' she bawled. Gwennan, ahead of the others, was brought up sharply against Rose's aproned chest.

'We're freezing cold and soaked to our skins, Mrs Crocker!' she whined.

'That's as maybe! Get those boots clean under the pump! Then into the linhay with you! Take off your wet things in there!' Leaving their cleaned boots in the porch they did as they were told. Soon the linhay was hung with damp dungarees and soaked sweaters. As Marion, Winnie and Gwennan, now clad only in shirts, socks and knickers, went shivering through into the house and up the stairs to fight over the first bath, Annie, Mabel and Georgina stumbled into the linhay and began to peel off their own muddy, rain-soaked garments.

The meal that evening, ready on time and consisting of shepherd's pie and trifle, was received appreciatively. Rose, taking each loaded plate from Alice and adding carrots, found herself with an extra portion and counted the heads round the table.

'Six...seven...' she said. 'Who's missing?'

'Chrissie,' said Mabel with her mouth full and her attention on the food which was disappearing swiftly from her plate. 'She's gone to bed. Didn't want no supper. She's upset she wasn't allowed to go to Plymouth.' Several of the girls looked at Alice who, catching Rose's eye, resisted the temptation to assure them that she had tried, on Christine's behalf, to get permission and had not been in agreement with their boss's decision to refuse it.

'Reckon it's a shame!' Annie said.

'Yeah. Me too,' said Mabel, polishing her plate with a wedge of bread. Annie eased herself uncomfortably in her chair and complained about her aching back.

'Wait till tomorrow!' said Marion.

'You'll be that stiff!' Winnie added, cheerfully unsympathetic.

'Know all about it, don't you!' Annie muttered.

'Should do!' said Marion. 'Been at it long enough!' Rose made a small but significant sound that caused both Marion and Winnie to turn and stare accusingly at her.

'Did you say something, Mrs Crocker?' Marion demanded.

'Just clearing my throat, dear,' Rose answered innocently. Another silence followed, this time broken by Georgina who said that some of the girls had not yet been able to have their baths.

'The hot tap ran cold, Mrs Todd,' she said, trying not to sound censorious. Mabel, still eating, announced that she would have her bath on Friday.

'Don't bath that often, me,' she said. Winnie and Marion became convulsed with laughter. Even Hester was forced to smile. 'What's funny?' Mabel asked, looking from face to face. She had amused them but couldn't for the life of her see the joke herself. She laughed anyway, which set them off again.

'You'm gonna have to share the bath water,' Rose informed them and relishing the look of horror on Georgina's face, continued, 'Don't look so shocked, my lover! I shared a tub with my three sisters till the day I wed and after that with me 'usband! There'll be enough for two good bathsful when you first gets back each night. That'll take care of four of you. The others'll have to wait till after supper for it to heat up again!' They ate in a subdued silence.

'Down the pub we had as many baths as we liked, didn't we, Marion!' Winnie grumbled, remembering the handfuls of hyacinth-scented bath salts and the slippery, sodary, pink-tinted water.

'Yeah. Steamin' hot they was. Lovely!'

Rose snatched Marion's plate from under her nose, reached for Winnie's, then Gwennan's and began, noisily, to stack them.

'The least said about "down the pub" the better, if you ask me!' she said harshly, everyone following her progress as she moved towards the scullery.

Although the huge task of feeding the girls on time with food that was as plentiful and as nourishing as possible had been successfully performed there was still work to do. After the washing-up of the dishes and the setting of the table for breakfast there were eight cut lunches to prepare which, with very limited ingredients to put between the slabs of bread, was a formidable task. Alice positioned first one and then another of the long, square loaves into the slicer and worked it to and fro.

'You mind out for your fingers,' warned Rose, darkly, spreading margarine. 'A warden over to Yelverton cut the top clean off of one of 'ers las' week!' They mashed a tin of corned beef, sliced up some beetroot and filled the sandwiches. Rose divided up a ginger cake that she'd baked that afternoon. The individual sandwiches and portions of cake were then wrapped in greaseproof paper and stacked ready for the morning. Then the airing racks were lowered from above the range and the day's damp clothes were brought through from the linhay, spread out on the racks and hoisted up to dry.

'Reckon we should get 'em to do this for theirselves,' Rose gasped, almost speechless with fatigue.

'I'll work out a roster,' Alice said and later, sitting up in her bed, her pillows at her back, a notebook on her knees, had begun to do so when she fell asleep.

Chapter Three

Christine waited on the windswept platform of Ledburton Halt for the Plymouth train which, delayed by bomb damage to the track near Slough, was almost an hour late. She had changed out of the thick, muddy layers of her work clothes and was wearing a silk dress that, under her winter coat, left her shivering. Every minute the train was late shortened her precious time with her husband but, an hour and a half later, when she stepped down onto the platform in Plymouth and he put his arms round her and ran with her across a deserted street and into the small bed and breakfast hotel where he had booked a double room for their single night, the waiting and the cold and the loss of time together evaporated.

The bedroom walls were papered with a design of leaves in crude autumnal colours. Sagging floorboards caused the furniture to lean dangerously and the stale reek of fried food which had greeted them in the hallway below had permeated the bedrooms and the lavatory on the landing which, together with the luxury of a hand basin in their room, was as far as ablutions went in this establishment.

Christine bounced happily on the edge of the bed while Ron put her coat on a hanger and hooked it over a peg on the back of the door. He then made a flying tackle in the direction of his wife, spreading her under him. She squealed with pleasure, pretending to fight him off before surrendering provocatively, enjoying his mouth and the feel of his hands sliding up under her skirt. But when she felt him hard against her she wriggled free, giggling as he kissed and kissed her, preventing her from speaking.

'You have got some what's-its, haven't you?' she managed, finally and breathlessly.

'Ah, shit, Chrissie!' he said, the mood broken. She put her lips against his moist, sulky mouth.

'You'd better get some, lovey,' she whispered, meeting his eyes. 'I know…' she coaxed. 'But remember what we said.' The decision not to have children during the war had been mutual. It would be just their luck, she told him, for them to take a chance and get caught out. He capitulated, climbed off her, took her hands in his, turned them and kissed the palms, watching her eyes widen as he forced his tongue between her fingers.

'Hey, what's this?' he said, examining the row of rosy blisters across her right palm.

'Swedes,' she said proudly and mimed the loading of the farm cart. 'Up and over! A whole ton we shifted, me and my two mates!' Ron kissed the blisters and looked tenderly into her happy face.

'Wish you didn't have to!' he sighed.

'What?' she laughed. 'You reckon I should sit at home while you go off and have your war! I want *my* war!' She pushed him playfully away from her. 'Go on!' she said. 'Sooner you go the sooner you'll be back.' From the door he told her that he loved her. As it closed she called after him.

'Fetch us some fish and chips while you're at it! I'm famished!' He mock-saluted and she laughed at him. After the door had closed behind him she took the new nightdress out of her attaché case and spread it on the bed. It was deep pink with a lacy bodice decorated with tiny bows of white satin and she loved it. Then she sat down at the dressing table and slid the grips from her hair so that it fell down round her shoulders.

Ron found the chemist, asked directions to the nearest fish and chip shop, queued for five minutes and was making his way through the deserted streets, the warm, clammy, newspaper-wrapped parcel under his arm, when he heard the plane.

Christine heard it too. She was standing in front of the looking glass, wearing the nightdress, turning this way and that, watching the way the imitation silk skimmed her nipples and her hips before falling away over her thighs. She felt like a film star.

Sigurd Wender, the twenty-two-year-old pilot of the Junkers Eighty-Eight, had been on a raid targeting the RAF repair and storage unit at Aston Down, east of Bristol. With half his bombs gone he had dropped his port wing and was bringing the aircraft round in a slow sweep, sighting up his target for a second run, when he was struck by shrapnel from an ack-ack shell. It smashed through the body of the plane and ruptured a fuel tank. With a brief plume of ignited aviation fuel in his wake Sigurd fought to control the aircraft. The tail rudder was responding erratically and he was choking on acrid fumes. There had been the sensation of an impact against his left side and as soon as he felt the plane stabilise he examined the damage. A piece of shrapnel which had penetrated the floor of the cockpit was lodged in his seat. It had pierced the canvas valise that contained his 'chute, slicing through the folded silk before lacerating his thigh. At first he felt nothing but a physical and mental numbness which affected both his flesh and his intellect. Under this sensation was the absolute, yet unacceptable certainty that he was not going to survive this. In a reflex response to his training he asked his crew for their assessment of the state of the aircraft. His bombardier reported that the shell had knocked out the release mechanism in the bomb bay and that there was too much structural damage for him to manually discharge their remaining two-hundred-pounder. In view of his own injuries, the loss of fuel and the uncertain performance of the tail rudder, Sigurd told his crew to bale out, assuring them that, after setting the plane on a course that would take it as close as possible to their target, he would follow them. Unaware of his injury or that his parachute had been destroyed, they obeyed him, their 'chutes opening behind him as he carefully eased the stick over and began a slow, banking turn. The fire was out now but the pain from his leg was beginning to reach him. He was overwhelmed by a sense of outrage at what was happening to him. He muttered his mother's name, conscious of how much he wanted the life of which he was about to be deprived. His eyes burnt with tears in the lingering fumes as he clenched his teeth and made his decision. He was hardly more than a child but he would fly his plane at the target, taking his remaining bomb and his life directly into it at maximum speed. Pushing through the nausea of shock and blanking the prospect of certain death, he lined up the airfield and the scatter of hangars and workshops which were intermittently visible through strips of mist below him. He eased the stick forward and began his run. As he approached, tracer floated up and drifted past him. The beam of a searchlight licked through wisps of cloud. The aircraft bucked and juddered in the concussion of exploding shells and metal fragments whacked into its fuselage. Pain was sapping his energy now and the effort to stay focused and functioning made him sweat. Briefly he blacked out. Seconds later, as he lurched back to consciousness, he found himself flying through dense cloud. The probing searchlight and the tracer attack had been swallowed by a swirling darkness. Easing the throttle forward he pulled back the stick, emerging suddenly from the clag into the pale light of a waning moon. Below him the cloud mass was solid. With difficulty he circled, searching for a landmark which would establish the position of his target. Finding none he checked his compass bearing and headed south. He felt weak. The inside of his left flying boot was warm and wet, filling, he guessed, with his blood.

As he approached Southampton the cloud thinned and he could see activity over the Portsmouth area. A raid was in progress. The sky was alive with searchlights, tracer and ack-ack fire. As he watched, explosions blossomed silently amongst the warehouses and marshalling yards which were under attack. He still had his bomb but he was weakening now and the intense cold combined with the shock of his injury was deadening his senses. To his left he could make out the line of the Channel coast and was drawn to it, seduced by its delicacy. He dropped his starboard wing and let the machine drift westwards, out over the Solent, leaving the Isle of Wight to port. The land, white with hoar frost, lay peacefully against the silver sea. Darkened villages and small towns were virtually invisible. He lost concentration and the plane began to yaw, lurching from side to side. Instinctively he fought the damaged rudder and levelled out. Poole Bay slipped behind him, then Portland and the sweep of Chesil. With one tank gone and the other possibly leaking, he was low on fuel. He could have turned then and slipped across the Channel, perhaps making it back to the airfield at Caen where he was based. With his undercarriage damaged it would be a crash landing. Provided the impact failed to detonate his bomb he might, just possibly, survive but a thought, clouded by pain and blood loss, had drifted into his mind, lodged there and now obsessed him. He would not simply slide into oblivion. Something must be achieved before his life ended. Fifty miles further west was Plymouth where, two years previously and on his debut operational flight, he had taken part in the raid which had blown the heart out of that small, naval city. He was losing height as Torbay passed under his starboard wing.

Ron listened to the sound of the solitary plane. He was familiar with the tones of aircraft engines. One of ours, surely. No. One of theirs. But no anti-aircraft fire. No siren to warn people of a raid. Must be coming in low. Under the radar. He stood on the pavement opposite the boarding house, the parcel of fish and chips warming the inside of his arm. He could see a narrow streak of light escaping through the blackout curtains of the room in which Chrissie was waiting for him.

Over Start Point and as the cloud thickened below him, Sigurd had slipped into unconsciousness, regaining his senses only when the change in the tone of his engines penetrated his dulled mind. He must, he was certain, be close to Plymouth now. He nosed down through the cloud and there was the breakwater, a thin, dark line across the Sound. And the Tamar, snaking inland, narrowing sharply, creeks and mudflats shining in the faint moonlight. He identified the dockyards and let the plane drift round, throttling back, pushing the pain in his leg away from him. Then he was in cloud again. Either cloud or the other mist which kept forming in the cockpit before his eyes or in his brain. He flew blind, easing the stick forward now, losing altitude, his head emptying.

It was obvious to Alice that the best if not the only time for her to use the bathroom and be sure of hot water was immediately after the girls had left the farmhouse each morning. First she and Rose cleared the kitchen table of breakfast dishes and while Rose washed them and stacked them in the wooden racks over the sinks, Alice toasted slices of bread and spooned out the remains of the porridge into two bowls, one for herself and one for Rose. Over breakfast she planned the evening meal and then, leaving Rose to start work on the vegetables, went to her room to collect towel, soap, talcum powder and clean underwear. There was plenty of hot water at this time of day and she lay in the bath while shafts of sunlight lit the steamy room which was permanently rich with the warm, suggestive smell of girls.

While Alice was still suffering from the stress of her undertaking it was now Friday and she was conscious of having somehow survived four days of it. As long as she was able to keep her mind off what her life had been and still should be, or let herself dwell on what it had so suddenly become, or worry about the uncertainties of the future, it seemed she could at least remain calm. The waves of panic and the feelings of desolation had subsided.

She dried herself, dressed, brushed her thick, dark blonde hair and coiled it at the nape of her neck. She powdered her face and put on lipstick. Apart from the trousers, shirt and thick sweater, her appearance, reflected in the steamy mirror, was recognisably her own.

They had decided on toad-in-the-hole for supper. It would be served with mashed potato and tinned peas. Rose raised her eyebrows when Alice said that as wartime sausages consisted mostly of bread they would put extra eggs into the batter to make up for the lack of protein. Rose longed to know what protein was but, unwilling to disclose her ignorance, did not enquire.

'There'll be eggs in the barn be now,' she said, being

familiar with the habits of the farmyard fowls. 'Shall I collect 'em or will you?' Alice said she would.

The morning was warm for February. Alice pushed her feet into the rubber boots with which Margery Brewster had issued her. She walked, without her coat, through the sunshine, around the building, skirted the yard and entered the barn. The hens, Rose had informed her, tended to lay in a disused manger at the far end of it. Here Alice collected five warm, brown eggs which, with the half-dozen which were already in the kitchen, would be enough for tonight's meal. On her way back to the house Alice stood for a moment with her shoulders against the barn wall. The air was soft. She closed her eyes, feeling the warmth of the sun on her lids. In the scullery, as she peeled potatoes, Rose was singing about the white cliffs of Dover. Alice heard the sound of a vehicle arriving on the far side of the farmhouse. The butcher's van, probably, bringing tonight's sausages and some stewing steak for tomorrow. She would be calm. She would take each day as it came and not think of the past or the future.

She opened her eyes as a young man appeared round the corner of the building. He was dressed in an Able Seaman's uniform, which was dusty and soiled. Blood was seeping through a grubby bandage on his right hand, his hair was dishevelled and on his face there was a look of total despair.

* * *

Mabel had known there was something wrong as soon as she reached the lorry. Breakfast had been chaotic, the girls tumbling, still half asleep, into the busy kitchen, swallowing their porridge, smearing margarine and a scrape of jam onto their toast, gulping tea, snatching up their packed lunches and, pulling on boots and waterproofs, hurrying out into the darkness where Fred sat, engine running, sounding his horn to hurry them. Mabel had picked up Chrissie's lunch as well as her own and was the first to reach the truck.

'Where is she?' she hissed, through the driver's window, over the rattle of the idling engine.

'She weren't on the train,' Fred told her and saw her eyes widen and her face blanch in the glare reflected from his headlights.

'What am I gonna do?' she wailed and behind them Georgina, who had been the last to leave the kitchen, shouted, 'All aboard, Fred.'

'I'd keep my mouth shut if I was you,' Fred murmured and when Mabel remained, white-faced, breathing noisily, he released the clutch and added, 'C'mon, girl! Get in!'

The young man and Alice stared at one another. 'You the lady in charge?' he asked finally and, when she said she was, began to tell her what had happened. In the kitchen, Rose had continued to sing, her voice drifting out over the clatter of saucepans and of tap water running into the deep sinks. After 'The White Cliffs of Dover' she had begun another song; now she was making a big finish on 'I'll Be Seeing You' after which there was a short silence before she threw open a window and called out to Alice that it was time for their elevenses.

Alice led the young man into the recreation room, persuaded him to sit and hurried through to the kitchen. Rose was standing at the table pouring their tea. She looked at Alice and froze.

'What's happened?' she demanded, thinking at once of her son.

'It's Chrissie,' Alice said. 'She went to Plymouth.' Rose experienced a wave of relief and was immediately angry with Christine for giving her such a scare.

'Didn't I say she was wilful,' she blustered, spilling a little of the tea before steadying herself.

'You don't understand,' Alice said. 'There was an air raid. The boarding house was hit while her husband was out buying their supper. They dug her out at five o'clock this morning. She's dead, Rose!'

Rose stared. 'Oh my Lord!' she breathed, her hard face collapsing into the softer folds of shock. 'I thought it was Dave! I thought you was going to tell me that my Dave…! Oh, that poor girl!'

They brought Ron into the kitchen where it was warmer and made him sit and drink some strong, sweet tea. He sat with the cup between his battered hands and stared for some time at the floor. Then he looked slowly round the kitchen.

‘I wanted to come ’ere,’ he said. Alice noticed that his accent was similar to Chrissie’s. ‘To see where she was. She told me she liked it ’ere… And there’s ’er things. I’d better take ’er things.’

After Ron had been driven away in the naval car that had brought him, a suitcase containing his wife’s clothes on his knees, Rose went to the room Chrissie had shared with Mabel and stripped the sheets and pillowcase from the bed in which she should have spent the previous night.

Using the bicycle which Margery Brewster had provided, Alice pedalled up the valley to the Bayliss farm where she encountered Mabel and asked where she could find their master.

‘He’s in his office,’ Mabel told her, adding anxiously, ‘What’s up, Mrs Todd?’

Roger Bayliss listened while Alice told him all she knew of what had happened. When she finished there was a silence. Then Roger sighed.

‘What am I supposed to tell Margery Brewster?’ he asked Alice. ‘That my warden fails to make certain that the girls in her charge are accounted for each night? That they are roaming about all over the county without permission?’

‘One girl,’ said Alice lamely. ‘And she did ask permission to visit her husband and you refused it. So she—’

‘Disobeyed!’ he cut in. ‘And you failed to notice her absence!’

‘I was told she had gone to bed early.’

'By whom?' he persisted. 'Whoever told you that must have been covering for her!'

'I'd rather not say who it was. It was my responsibility. I should have checked. I'm sorry. It won't happen again.' Roger Bayliss didn't respond. Then he asked her if she would inform Margery Brewster or whether she would prefer him to do so. Alice got to her feet.

'I'll tell her myself. Of course,' she said. He opened the door for her and stood aside as she moved through it.

Georgina had been sent to fetch King, one of the farm's three carthorses, from the farrier's and was enjoying leading the great, clumsy, gentle creature back to its paddock when she saw Christopher Bayliss leaning against the gate, his father's hunter tethered nearby. She had not spoken to Christopher since their initial encounter and it occurred to her that she should take this opportunity to apologise to him. He was lighting a cigarette as she approached, managing to conceal from her the shake of his fingers. He flicked the spent match away from him, blew smoke and smiled.

Georgina slowed the horse and when Christopher did not move, said, 'Excuse me. I need to open the gate.' He made a great play of moving away from the latch and then reached across to unfasten it for her.

'Allow me,' he said but she was there before him, had the gate open and was leading her charge through it. Slipping the halter from King's huge head, Georgina turned to find

Christopher blocking her way back through the gate. She stood, glaring at him. He laughed.

'For a pacifist you do seem remarkably aggressive, if I may say so!'

'You may not,' she said.

'OK,' he smiled. 'The subject of the war shall be taboo. And I promise not to comment on your appearance, however divine you look!' He blew smoke.

'You simply can't resist being offensive, can you!' He was still smiling, still blocking her way.

'Offensive?' he repeated incredulously. 'I'll have you know there are girls who would be delighted with a compliment from me!' It was an idiotic conversation and at the back of Georgina's mind was the fact that not only had she previously misjudged him but that she was talking, as though he was some pushy flirt she had encountered at a tennis club hop, to a man who had repeatedly, albeit misguidedly, risked his life for his convictions. Nevertheless, she found herself suggesting that if such girls existed, he should go and compliment them, rather than wasting his time on her.

'Have dinner with me,' he said suddenly. If only he hadn't still been smiling his self-satisfied smile, or if she had understood that the smile was masking a sort of desperation, she might have been kinder. But she declined his invitation and was watching his smile fade when to her surprise he reached out and made a grab for the halter she was carrying, twisting it tightly round her hands and pulling her towards him. She wrenched free and in doing so slammed the gate towards him so that its bottom rung caught his shin. He grimaced and his face reddened with suppressed anger. Georgina, deeply embarrassed, apologised at once.

'No, no,' Christopher said, recovering quickly. 'My fault. My fault entirely!' She stood and watched as he unhitched his horse, hauled himself into its saddle, turned it, kicked it into a trot and moved off while she disentangled the halter from her wrist, fastened the gate and stood cursing her stupidity and her short temper. Fred's voice reached her from the yard. Mr Bayliss was looking for her, he said. She found him in his office. He told her to sit.

'Bad news, I'm afraid,' he said.

None of Georgina's immediate family was in the armed services. Nor were they where enemy bombs fell. When she had left them they had all been in good health. An accident perhaps? Lionel's motorbike? Her father's hunter? Her mother's car? 'One of your colleagues,' Roger Bayliss began and, as Rose had done, earlier, Georgina felt a sense of guilty relief that no one close to her was involved. She was shocked by the news of Chrissie's death, and did not relish the idea of calling the other girls together and breaking the news of it to them as Roger Bayliss was requesting her to do.

In the kitchen of Lower Post Stone Farm Rose was breaking eggs into a deep bowl and whipping them into a batter.

Alice paced about the room and Margery Brewster, a cup of tea cooling in front to her was, as usual, calm in the face of what she would later define as a crisis, her heavy features and slightly hooded eyes suggesting concern and concentration on the matter in hand.

'Most unfortunate,' she sighed and the clock ticked on. 'But the point is that even if you had checked at what… six o'clock, was it?' Alice said yes, it had been about then that it had been noticed that Chrissie was not at supper. 'Then it was impossible for you to have prevented her from going,' Margery concluded. 'She would have already been in Plymouth by then!'

'That's what I keep tellin' her!' Rose muttered, tight-lipped in the background. Margery was becoming irritated by Alice's pacing and told her to sit down. 'Do the girls know what happened?'

'They will by now,' said Alice miserably. 'Mr Bayliss was going to ask Georgina to tell them.'

The girls sat in silence on each side of the swaying lorry as Fred drove them through the dusk, back to the hostel. Heavy cloud had lifted, leaving the western sky a cold, hard, greenish colour which suggested to those who knew about such things that the coming night would be a frosty one. Having discovered that it was slightly warmer in the cab, Winnie and Marion were already in the habit of squeezing in together on the passenger seat next to Fred, their faces and his solemn tonight, in reflected light from the dimmed headlamps. After a mile or so Marion said, 'Sod Jerry!' and Winnie echoed, 'Sod buggering Jerry!'

'She were a lovely girl,' Fred said, remembering how light and soft Christine had felt when he had lifted her down from the truck three short days ago. Where the descent towards Lower Post Stone steepened he changed gear. ''Tweren't a regular raid,' he told them. 'Said on the news that a stray Jerry bomber crash landed. Still loaded, 'twas. Hit a row of boarding houses opposite the station. Flattened the lot! Stupid bugger!' Behind him, in the back of the lorry, Mabel burst into noisy tears.

After a silent supper, the girls drifted away, some to their bedrooms, others to huddle round the fire in the recreation room, one or two to the bathroom for, despite their shock at Chrissie's death, tomorrow was Saturday and from midday on, those not on dairy duty would have the afternoon and all of Sunday to themselves. Fred collected Edward-John from the bus stop in Ledburton, Alice gave him his supper in her room, escorted him to the bathroom and then, promising him a tour of the farm immediately after breakfast next day, left him in bed, reading his latest Biggles book and went in search of Mabel, who, more distressed than the other girls, had gone to her room and even refused her supper.

At first, when Alice tapped on the door to the room Mabel had shared with Chrissie, there had been no response. Then, her voice muffled, Mabel said, 'Go away. I don't want to see no one.'

'I've brought you a cup of tea,' Alice coaxed. 'And a slice of Rose's cake...' Mabel opened the door. Her face was puffed and her eyes were almost lost under swollen, reddened lids. Instead of drinking the tea and eating the cake she sat on the edge of her own bed and looked at Chrissie's while fresh tears spread down her wet cheeks.

'It was my fault, Mrs Todd,' she wailed and when Alice said she must not blame herself she interrupted her. 'But I put her up to it! I said if it was me I'd go to Plymouth whatever Mr Bloody Bayliss said! And she went! And now she ain't never coming back! It's no good, Mrs Todd! There's nothing you nor no one can say as'll ever change what I done!' Alice took the girl's sweaty hands in hers.

'Listen, Mabel!' she began. Mabel sat gulping. 'Just suppose that Chrissie hadn't gone to Plymouth.'

'Then she'd still be alive, wouldn't she!' Mabel howled angrily.

'Listen to me!' Alice persisted. 'Supposing she hadn't gone and her husband had gone off, back to sea, in his minesweeper...' Mabel was beginning to pay attention now, her wet, reddened eyes widening. 'And supposing,' Alice went on, 'that tonight, in the Western Approaches, his ship had been torpedoed...'

'Yeah...?' Mabel said, imagining it.

'And he'd been lost,' said Alice. 'How would Chrissie have felt then?'

'If she hadn't gone to Plymouth to be with him, you mean?'

'Yes. On the last night they could have had together? D'you see? D'you see how…' Suddenly Alice was enveloped in Mabel's soft, malodorous bulk and held in a tremulous embrace.

'She wouldn't never of forgiven herself, would she!' Mabel said, her moist face pressed against Alice's.

'No!' said the warden, gently disengaging herself. 'Never. It's anyone's guess where it's safe to be and where it's dangerous, Mabel.' Mabel's heavy frame still juddered as her sobs subsided. Then she began to hiccup. 'Eat your cake and drink your tea,' Alice said. 'Then try to get some sleep.'

'It's still bloody awful though. in'it,' Mabel said shakily.

'Yes,' Alice said. 'Bloody awful.'

When Alice returned to the kitchen Rose was still at work, finishing the last of the clearing up after the evening meal. The next day being Saturday there were no sandwiches to cut. The girls' damp clothes were airing on the rack.

'I'll be off now,' Rose said, folding her apron and hanging it over a chair-back.

'You're very late,' Alice said. 'I'm sorry to have left you to it. What with Edward-John arriving and…' She stopped, her throat closing as the events of the day overwhelmed her. Rose shrugged off the apology and when Alice asked whether everyone was in, replied heavily that no one had gone out.

'No...I suppose not,' said Alice, sitting down wearily at the table and putting her face in her hands. The promised gramophone had not yet been delivered but in the common room someone, with one finger, was picking out a Glenn Miller tune, sight-reading it from a music sheet. Annie, one syllable at a time, was tentatively singing the lyrics.

'I'm simply not up to this,' Alice said suddenly and as much to herself as to Rose. Then she raised her head. 'I shall telephone Mrs Brewster in the morning and tell her I can't manage here.'

'You'll do no such thing!' said Rose. 'You'm just tired! And upset!'

'It's not only that.' Alice spoke quietly, her hands clasped in front of her on the scrubbed table. 'I realised today just how inadequate I am. I'm used to running a home, Rose. Caring for a husband and one small boy. All this is too much for me...!' She glanced round at the hateful kitchen, realising suddenly that everything was in the wrong place. There were no working surfaces beside the range where they were needed. Nowhere for food to be served, no place where clean dishes could be piled before use or dirty ones stacked, ready for washing-up afterwards. No wonder the preparation and serving of the meals was so chaotic... 'I should have observed Chrissie more closely!' she went on. 'I should have realised how upset she was about not being allowed to go to Plymouth. Her husband could have come here!'

'He could not!' said Rose, familiar with hostel rules.

'I mean to the village!' Alice said, sharply enough to make Rose's eyes widen in surprise or possibly with the beginning of respect. 'They could have spent the night together at the inn in the square...' She paused. In the recreation room a couple of the girls had joined Annie and the three voices repeated the chorus of the song as Alice continued to speak, almost to herself. 'If all I had to do was to feed them and keep the place clean...even that would be enough, but there's so much more to it! Eight young women...!'

'Ten! When the rest of 'em come!'

'Full of themselves, their lives, their problems!' Alice had forgotten Rose and was sliding towards desperation. 'I don't know who they are or what they think!'

Rose's manner was changing. She looked concerned. Guilty even. 'Nothing you can't handle!' she said defensively. Alice laughed.

'You'm doing all right, I reckon!' Rose said staunchly.

'You don't mean that, Rose! You don't think I can cope here. Nor does Mr Bayliss and nor does Mrs Brewster! I'm only here because there was no one else and I shan't be here much longer so you'll all be able to say how right you were!'

'No!' said Rose.

'Yes!' Alice felt a sense of release as she turned to look at the hard-faced, self-righteous woman with her sharp eyes and spiteful tongue. 'Every time you look at me your face tells me exactly what you think of me, Rose. And you are right! I shouldn't be here and very soon I won't be! So... goodnight,' she finished dismissively and waited for Rose to go. But Rose sat down at the table and stared at its scrubbed surface. Alice's gaze moved to the badly situated cupboard where the saucepans were kept. She found herself considering where, in the interests of streamlining the cooking processes, it should be sited.

'Lot of how you feel is my fault,' Rose began in a low voice. To begin with Alice did not appear to be listening to her. 'See, when I heard Mr Bayliss was gonna open up this place and board his land girls here, I thought...' She paused, took a deep breath and plunged on. 'I thought as he was gonna put me in charge!' Alice, her attention caught at last, turned and looked at Rose.

'Stupid, wasn't I,' she said, 'to go thinkin' that!'

The cause of Rose's unpleasantness suddenly plain to her, Alice hesitated, sensing that her reaction to this disclosure must be a cautious one. Concealing her surprise she said carefully that it was far from stupid, adding, 'I wonder why on earth he didn't?' Rose's eyes widened. 'You'd have been the perfect person for the job!' Alice continued. 'You know the building inside out, you're a wonderful cook, you understand the kitchen range and the plumbing and you're awfully good at keeping the girls in order!' Rose was confused. Was she being praised? Did

Mrs Todd…Alice…mean what she was saying?

'But there's other things, i'nt there,' Rose said. Alice shrugged and said she couldn't think of any.

'Well,' said Rose and it was now her turn to carefully consider her words. 'Between the two of us I reckon we make a good team, you and me, and I won't hear another word about you quittin' and givin' the boss and that busybody Bewster woman the satisfaction of saying "told you so"! It's been a rough old day, this has, what with poor little Chrissie and all…but it don't do to make decisions on bad days!' She got to her feet. 'I'm going to my bed now, Alice, before I falls over with tiredness and I suggest you does the same.' She wanted to get away by herself and think over the astonishing scene that had just taken place. 'Now, where's my boots?' she said, busily making her way out into the cross-passage. 'That yard be a quagmire this weather…'

'Goodnight, Rose.'

'Night Mrs Todd.'

'Alice!' Alice called after her.

'Yes,' Rose said and smiled. 'Alice.'

Alice followed Rose down the cross-passage and as the outer door closed she slid the bolt, feeling through her near exhaustion a small, surprising sense of satisfaction as the ancient, blackened rod of metal slipped into place. All her charges, except for the one who had chosen to defect, were safely under her roof. She stoked the range, closed it down for the night and made her way through the old parlour to her own room where Edward-John lay asleep, his book on the floor.

The Bayliss farmhouse was, by that time, in darkness. Father and son had eaten the meal that the housekeeper had cooked and cleared. As it was the last night of Christopher's leave there had been stuffed capon served with roasted potatoes, buttered parsnips, carrots and Brussels sprouts. This was followed by crème brulée which had the reputation of being Christopher's favourite pudding. Roger had opened a bottle of Chateau Neuf du Pape which, having been preceded by a couple of large glasses of sherry, had left the two men relaxed enough to be unconcerned about the several long silences that fell during the course of the evening. After a glass or two of port Christopher excused himself on the grounds of his early departure next morning. His father got to his feet while they exchanged farewells, smiling at each other, wishing each other good luck. Although acutely conscious of the fact that this might well be the last time he saw his son alive or, come to that, dead, Roger's manner revealed nothing of his anxiety for the young man who stood before him, smiling gamely.

Roger's life, for as long as he was able to remember, consisted of an accumulating collection of compartmentalised feelings, many of them quite painful and which he had long ago decided were best dealt with by keeping them very much under wraps. As people had suggested at the time, he had probably been wrong to marry Frances. She was the only daughter of a neighbouring landowner, one of whose farms Roger had subsequently added to his own. He had met her when, at eighteen, she had been recovering from a bout of tuberculosis. She had told him, on their first meeting, that she thought it unlikely that she would ever marry as she wanted to be a farmer's wife and since her illness no one would consider her healthy and strong enough for that role. Haunted, for reasons he did not analyse, by this confession, Roger found himself drawn to her and had, soon afterwards, proposed marriage and been accepted. Christopher, their only child, was in his first term at boarding school when she suddenly died of an illness quite unconnected to the tuberculosis. The boy had stood in Ledburton churchyard beside his father as the flower-laden coffin was lowered into the mud. Afterwards Roger had suggested that it might be better if, for a while at least, they did not speak of the dead woman who had been his wife and his son's mother, as to do so was too painful for both of them. Christopher was sent back to school, returning, at the end of the term, to a house that was always to remain different from the one he had lived in when his mother was alive. To make up for this, his father indulged him, unstintingly bestowing on him the best toys, ponies, push-bikes, motorbikes and eventually sports cars, that he could afford. At the age of seventeen Christopher had expressed the wish to learn to fly so that when war was declared it seemed both logical and attractive to him to join the RAF rather than take the place at Seale-Hayne Agricultural College which his father had arranged for him.

Alone on the upper floor of the farmhouse, Christopher had run a hot bath which, instead of relaxing him, had the opposite effect. He sat smoking in his bedroom, trying to suppress a familiar, rising anxiety, until the chill of the unheated room drove him to bed. Here, again, he ran through the events of his unfortunate encounter with Georgina and cursed himself for his stupidity.

Shortly after he started flying fighters he had shut down his feelings. Initially the knowledge that he had on several occasions escaped death by inches or by seconds had made him nervous in a healthy and predictable way, raising the hackles on his neck and providing him with a cracking yarn to tell over a pint. But, like many of his peers, the continuous pressure of his situation had begun to damage him. To begin with he and the small group from within a larger group with whom he had done his training regarded themselves as a band of brothers. They would survive because they willed it so. They were indestructible. But as the months passed and their numbers were reduced, in many cases by death, in others by horrific injury, the comradery faltered and changed. Mess banter became increasingly brittle. Relationships with wives and lovers suffered and new conquests tended to be considered only on the briefest and most shallow terms. The girls too, the FANYs, Wrens and WAAFS, found the going tough and hardened themselves in self-defence against the daily news of lost men. Men downed over enemy territory. Men ditching in the freezing Channel. Men with their skin burnt off them and their limbs shredded by shrapnel. Excesses increasingly became Christopher's only escape from the cruel events that confronted him on a daily basis. Drinking, risk-taking and love-making became frenetic fixes, short-time diversions, while the fact of his own mortality, something with which the young should not have to deal, faced him each day.

Christopher had no way of knowing how close to the edge he was and so he continued, taking his orders, carrying them out, coming home for spells of leave and returning to base when the leaves were over. Although he knew that he was misreading people and had lost the art of communication, mostly he behaved well, responding much as he would when returning a lob in a game of tennis or driving a cricket ball into the outfield. It was when he was faced with a situation which involved feelings beyond the superficial that he floundered into the sort of stupidity that had ruined his chances with Georgina. Yet when he asked himself 'chances of what?' he had no answer. Perhaps, on his next leave, he would try again, approaching her differently. But how? He concentrated on assembling her face in his mind and finally fell briefly asleep in an appreciative contemplation of her steady grey eyes, only to wake with a start. Downstairs the clock began to strike. If it was five he would get up. If it was four he would try to sleep again. If it was seven he was already late. It was three. He lay for some time unable to control his imagination which, as soon as he relaxed his grip on it, had him plummeting out of the sky in a burning Hurricane. He swung out of his bed. On the upstairs landing he opened the heavy curtains. There was a glimmer of light from the last quarter of the moon. Enough for him to see his way down the stairs. His father, before retiring, had opened the curtains in the first-floor drawing room. Christopher made his way to the drinks table, poured himself a finger or two of whiskey and stood drinking.

Roger Bayliss may have been woken by a creaking stair board. The slightly larger than usual amount of alcohol he had taken that evening had made him thirsty and his bedside carafe was empty. He would go downstairs and refill it from the kitchen tap where the water was best. At the same time he would check up on the sound he thought he had heard. Probably a window left unfastened. Or one of the farm cats raiding the pantry. The wind was rising and a scud of cloud brought the first rattle of rain against a west-facing window. It also drowned the faint sound of Roger's slippers on the stairs so that when he saw the outline of his son, standing beside the drinks table, and spoke to him, Christopher spun round defensively.

'Couldn't you sleep?' his father asked, adding uncharacteristically, 'Bit uptight about tomorrow, perhaps?'

Christopher laughed. He had been trying to refill his glass and now, for some reason, could not seem to do so without the lip of the decanter repeatedly striking the rim of the glass so violently that it seemed likely to shatter it. Roger removed the two objects from his son's hands, replenished Christopher's drink and poured one for himself.

'You are all right, aren't you?' Roger said casually, after a few moments. No point in making the boy think you were nervous about him. 'I mean, we might be able to organise a spot more leave, if you feel you need it. They've been driving you pretty hard these last few months.' Christopher swallowed a gulp of the whiskey, shook his head and assured his father that he was perfectly fine.

'Too much grog, Dad! Makes the old heart go pitter-pat!' They both chose to ignore the fact that Christopher was, at that moment, adding considerably to the amount of alcohol in his blood. They drained their glasses in silence.

'Think I'll pop down and check the kitchen,' Roger said. 'Reckon we've got a marauding tomcat!' Christopher mimed picking off the cat with a shotgun. They smiled at each other and, relieved that an awkward moment had been painlessly passed, parted for the second time that night.

Chapter Four

Over the next four weeks the occupants of Lower Stone Post Farm settled into something approaching a routine. A spell of icy easterly winds was followed by a heavy fall of snow that caused the lorry to slither into a ditch, where it remained for three days, forcing the girls to make the ascent to the Bayliss farm on foot, trudging in single file through fields parallel to the lane, which was filled to hedge level with soft snow.

A land girl called Iris Butler took Chrissie's place as roommate for Mabel, whose odour was diminishing daily due to pressure put upon her by the other girls who encouraged her to bathe each night, insisting bluntly that she took the last turn in the second filling of the tub, thus ensuring that no one had to use the bathroom after she had – at least not until it had been well ventilated.

Alice and Rose, despite the farmhouse being briefly snow-bound, managed to keep the girls fed, the hostel clean, reasonably warm and mostly dry. Edward-John arrived happily each Friday night and stoically returned to his school early on Monday mornings. To begin with, the attention he received from the girls overwhelmed him but he soon began to respond, developing an almost flirtatious relationship with them, which made Rose frown and left Alice slightly uneasy. Almost certainly the girls' risqué jokes and bawdy laughter went over his head but on more than one occasion his mother had cautioned them to watch their language in his presence. He made friends with the ploughman, Jack, who allowed him to ride the carthorses when they were driven along the short lane to the paddock into which they were turned out at midday each Saturday. Once, after a morning spent at the pig-pens and over Sunday lunch, Edward-John delivered a graphic account of the birth of a litter of piglets.

'The mother pig has this special place,' he announced, his eyes moving from face to face as he addressed his captive audience around the table. 'It sort of opens up and out comes the piglet and blood and things!' The girls howled in disgust and Alice was dismayed.

'It won't do him no harm, Mrs Todd!' Mabel assured his mother, mopping gravy from her plate with a second wedge of bread. 'He's gonna learn sooner or later, i'nt 'e!' Alice confined herself to suggesting to her son that in future he must chose his topic of mealtime conversation more carefully.

One night, as Alice tucked him into his bed, he asked her what a 'monthly' was and remained only partly satisfied when she explained that it was anything which happens every month.

On the coldest nights, before the snow fell, it had proved impossible to adequately heat the recreation room and the girls had spent their evenings in the kitchen, sprawling round the table, taking it in turns to press their feet against the hot metal of the range while Alice sliced up loaves for the next day's sandwiches and Rose mashed up canned sardines before levelling the result thinly over the margarine-spread slices. Some of the girls helped her, taking knives from the cutlery drawer and spreading the filling.

'Not too thick, now!' Rose cautioned them, mainly in order to reinforce her own, superior status within the hierarchy of the kitchen.

'Yessuh, Sarge!' said Annie and the girls, comfortable together and easily amused, giggled at her because, in response to Rose's brusque manner, Annie had already nicknamed her Sergeant Crocker.

'Mrs Crocker, to you!' Rose snapped, peering at the family snapshots which Gwennan was showing round. 'Which is you then, Taffy?' she asked. 'The one in the hat, is it?'

'Noo!' Taffy wailed. 'Tha's my gran!' A chorus of laughter. 'This one's me, yer!'

Mabel was knitting a scarf on a pair of thick wooden needles. It had reached two feet in length and was striped in assorted, garish colours.

'It's for me bruvver,' she told them. 'Gran give me her leftover wool 'fore I come here. But I'm runnin' out, see? This is me last ball.'

'I'll ask Mrs Brewster if she could get you some more,' Alice said, measuring out porridge oats in preparation for the morning. 'She's been organising the villagers to knit blanket squares for refugees and there might be some spare wool.'

'Organising!' muttered Rose. 'Pestering, more like!'

'Ta, Mrs Todd!' said Mabel and she pulled a dog-eared photo from the envelope of a letter she had recently received from home and laid it before them on the kitchen table. 'This is Arthur,' she said, pronouncing the name Arfer, her face ruddy with pleasure and pride.

He was a lumpen child, about eighteen months old, his straggling hair and slightly gross features resembling Mabel's.

'He don't half look like you, Mabel!' said Iris and everyone laughed when Marion added, 'Never mind! As long as he's healthy, eh!' Mabel's face had reddened. Her stubby fingers closed clumsily round the picture. She fumbled it back into the envelope, stuffed it into her cardigan pocket and resumed her knitting.

Mrs Brewster did provide some leftover wool. It came from her own knitting box and Mabel's scarf, which had begun with stripes of harsh reds, greens and sharp blues from the Hodges family, became progressively quieter as she incorporated into it the softer beiges, lavenders and crushed raspberry shades favoured by Margery Brewster.

The early mornings remained the least pleasant part of these winter days. In pitch darkness Alice's alarm clock dragged her from sleep. She would pull on her clothes before the cold struck her and then, as she made her way through to the kitchen, where her first act would be to open up the fire in the range, she shouted to the sleeping girls in the partitioned rooms above her head.

'Wake up everyone! Breakfast in ten minutes!' Rose would arrive from across the yard, shuddering with cold and bearing reports of icicles, frozen puddles and a piercing wind. The porridge, which had simmered through the night, would be brought to the boil, the tea brewed, the milk fetched, ice-cold, from the pantry as the first of the girls, bleary with sleep and depressed by the prospect of another day of exposure to sub-zero temperatures, came stumbling into the kitchen.

'Is something the matter, Winnie?'

'She's got a pain, Mrs Todd! It's her monthlies! She should be allowed to stay in bed!'

'It's not an illness, Marion,' Alice told her, adding,

'There's aspirin on the dresser if you need it, Winnie.'

'And if you're still poorly when you get home lunchtime,' Rose interjected sweetly, 'it being Saturday, you can put your feet up all afternoon, can't you!'

'What?' Winnie whined. 'Spend me half-day in bed?'

''Twouldn't be the first time, I daresay…' Rose muttered. Alice glanced at her but Rose had assumed a convincing air of innocence.

Edward-John, dressing gown over pyjamas, joined them and pleaded to be allowed to go with the girls to the Bayliss farm that morning. Initially Alice refused to give him permission but, as it was half-day and Annie promised to keep an eye on him, she allowed herself to be persuaded, encouraged him to finish his porridge and sent him off to dress quickly and warmly, cautioning him not to get mud over the tops of his boots and to stay within earshot of Annie until the lorry arrived at midday to bring them all back to Lower Post Stone.

'There was someone I haven't seen before in the yard last evening, Rose,' Alice said, as they sat over their breakfast, after the girls and Edward-John had left. 'A youngish man, slightly stooped and wearing black.'

'That'd be Andreis,' Rose said. 'He come at the start of the war. From Amsterdam or some such place.'

'He's Dutch?'

'Yes…Jewish. A relative of Mr Bayliss. Or perhaps 'twas his wife's. I don't know as I would 'ave allowed it meself –

foreigners around the place with a war on. But he's a law unto himself is Mr Bayliss!'

'The authorities know about it, presumably?' Alice asked.

'Oh yes. 'Tis all above board. He's got some sort of permit or other and Mr Bayliss is responsible for him. Feedin' 'im and that. The idea was that he should work on the farm but it seems he's an artist, see, and Mr Bayliss says as he can do as he pleases, in the way of labourin' – which isn't that much, according to Ferdie Vallance!' Rose refilled their cups with tea that was by now tepid and too strong for Alice. 'He lives in the loft at the end of the long barn.'

'In the barn? This weather?'

''Tis where the shepherds lived in the old days,' Rose said defensively, 'during the lambing season that is. There be a stove in it. Quite snug it is. Andreis is doing paintings, Ferdie says. I 'aven't seen 'em meself but that 'Anna-Maria Sorokova 'as!'

'Annie?'

'Oh yes!' said Rose. 'Saw her and him talking in the yard. Last Saturday afternoon it were. And then she went with him, into the barn!' Rose smiled at Alice's expression, enjoying the fact that she appeared both surprised and uneasy. 'Girls will be girls, dear,' Rose murmured, stirring Alice's concern. 'And a pair of trousies is a pair of trousies these days! Dutch refugee or whatever else he be!' She paused, adding casually that she thought bread pudding might be a good idea for 'afters' that night.

Later, when Alice had collected the eggs, she wandered on, across the yard and into the long barn. Since the dairy herd was now housed at the Bayliss farm the milking stalls at Lower Post Stone were unoccupied and the space was now used to store hay and straw bales. Alice could hear the creak of the boards above her head as someone moved about the loft. As her eyes grew accustomed to the semi-darkness she saw that a ladder ran up the wall ahead of her. She cleared her throat, raised her voice and asked if anyone was about. There was a short pause and then Andreis's head appeared at the top of the ladder.

He looked pale in the half-light and his lank hair fell forward. A look of concern left his face as he recognised her.

'You are the Mrs Todd?' he asked. 'The warden of the girls?' The accent was thick and although his command of English was fluent the phraseology was, Alice noticed at once, charmingly odd. 'Pleased to come up into my loft if you wish it,' he said.

The loft was lighter than Alice had supposed. Three glazed windows had been let into the northern slope of its roof, presumably when the space had been used to accommodate the shepherds. This, with Andreis's canvases and easel, immediately suggested the studio into which he had turned it. He wiped paint from his right hand and extended it to Alice.

'I am Andreis Van Der Loos,' he said, smiling shyly. His hand felt cold. Alice had transferred three hen's eggs from her basket into her pocket. She took them carefully out and put them into his hand. He smiled.

'They lay in the old stalls at the far end of the barn,' Alice said. 'I'm sure Mr Bayliss would like you to help yourself to them whenever…' She paused, wondering whether he had already discovered this source of food.

'I have heard the hens,' he said. 'But I wait for Mr Bayliss to send supplies, which he does often and with much generosity to me.'

Alice looked round. There was a table, a chair and a narrow bed piled with blankets and an eiderdown, which presumably had also been provided by her employer. On a pot-bellied stove an iron saucepan was simmering. Andreis was following the course of Alice's eyes as she examined his quarters. A shotgun stood against an angle of the walls and from a nail a rabbit hung, beads of blood congealing in its nostrils.

'I shoot it,' the man said. 'Two of them this morning I get. Perhaps you hear the shots?' Alice said she had not. 'One in the pot with potatoes and swede for my meal tonight. And one for tomorrow.' He smiled briefly and then his narrow face fell back into the blank pallor which had been Alice's first impression of him.

'You must be…' She stopped. Something in his face warned her to choose her words carefully. 'Lonely?' she finished and his expression held a suggestion of relief. He shook his head and paused before answering her.

'If it was simply loneliness that I feel I should be fortunate. I thought this was what I should do, you see. Come here, I mean to say. My family and my friends said I must come. Some of them, too, came in time away from Amsterdam before the Germans invaded us. Others, for various reasons or refusing to believe the worst, waited until it was too late.' His eyes held Alice's and searched her face anxiously. 'Now I paint them, you see.' He indicated the canvases on which there appeared to be a succession of portraits. Men, women and children. 'Friends,' he said. 'And family. Painted from my recollection of them. As a memorial. For some of them are no longer alive. And for others I have a great fear.'

'I'm so sorry,' Alice said inadequately.

'But I have no longer any canvases left,' he went on, as though he had not heard her. 'So I have begun to work onto the panels, you see?'

At one end of the space was a partition of wide boards which appeared to divide it from the larger part of the loft beyond it. This Andreis had already prepared with a coat of white paint on which he was beginning to lay-in a vast composition. 'It is to be the story of this war as I experience it,' he said. 'It will show what happened to my people,' he paused, searching her face. 'It is all I can do, you see.' Alice stared at the charcoal marks on the white panelling and then at Andreis, feeling his desolation and his sense of helplessness.

'Oh, Andreis,' she said. 'This is so sad!'

He shook his head. 'No,' he said. 'It will make me happy I think.'

She smiled back as encouragingly as she could and then said she must go. She had, she told him, eight girls to look after and to cook for. As she turned towards the hole in the floor and was about to reach for the top rung of the ladder she caught sight of a sketch which was lying on Andreis's table. It was a charcoal drawing on a piece of brown paper. The lines were flowing and free and the face which was its subject was unmistakably Annie's. The artist had captured and perhaps exaggerated the girl's Jewishness. Now he followed the direction of Alice's eyes and saw her attention focus and sharpen as she recognised her charge. 'It is Hannah-Maria, of course,' he said. 'You see the likeness?'

'Yes I do,' said Alice. 'She…she was up here? Posing for you?' She sounded, in her own ears, both suspicious and prudish.

'Should she not be?' he asked. He looked confused. Almost hurt. 'I ask her for permission to draw her. Just her head, you see, not…' he met Alice's eyes carefully. 'Not from the life,' he said. 'Not nude.'

'No!' said Alice and found herself flushing slightly at the suggestion that she had misjudged his intentions towards Annie. 'Of course not! And of course she may. Pose for you, I mean. If she chooses to.'

'Chooses?' he asked.

'If she wants to. But…'

'But?' he echoed. Alice paused and tried to simplify her words to him. To avoid hurting or confusing him.

'You see, Andreis, it is difficult for me. I am responsible for these girls. Some of them are very young. Annie – Hannah-Maria – is barely eighteen. They are beyond the supervision of their parents so I must be…' She was going to say careful but Andreis interrupted.

'Their *Mutta*… Their mother, I mean to say. Yes, I understand. So, if I were to ask your permission to make a painting of your "daughter", of Hannah-Maria, would you permit this? If she chooses? She has, you see, the perfect face of the Jewess. The shape of her eyes and of her head, the line of her jaw, the flare of her nostrils. The long neck. I wish to use this Jewishness. When my painting is complete you will understand why. Will you allow me?'

Alice gave her permission and afterwards defended her decision to Margery Brewster and Roger Bayliss, both of whom accepted her judgement without much enthusiasm.

'It's not our business to chaperone them during their free time,' Roger Bayliss said, looking at Alice's dark blonde hair and fine, grey eyes and feeling that she would have been his choice were he to wish to commit to canvas any of the women at Lower Post Stone Farm.

'As long as she's in by ten,' had been Margery's only comment, delivered with an indifferent shrug as she gave Alice several more balls of leftover wool for Mabel's scarf.

So Annie spent her Saturday afternoons sitting on a bale of straw in the small loft. On the first occasion the intensity of Andreis's scrutiny embarrassed her and she attempted to keep up a flow of light conversation with him, feeling that silence was somehow impolite. But soon she came to understand that he liked the silences that formed between them, stretching sometimes into whole hours in which she became aware of herself not as herself but as an object, the lines and contours of which were necessary to Andreis's work, to the small, meticulous drawings which were later to become part of a larger, intricate composition. It was an entire race, he explained, that was to be depicted in his new work and shown to be threatened, scattered, shackled and herded into railway wagons. For this much Andreis knew, though not the horror of the destination of these involuntary travellers. Bad enough that they were forced from their homes and separated from their families and from the lives they had, until the Nazi invasion, been blamelessly living.

After an hour he would suddenly apologise for keeping Annie so long without a break. If she was cold he would invite her to come close to the stove on which his kettle simmered. He made tea for her and they sat, smiling, while Annie eased her stiff shoulders and Andreis wrapped cold fingers round his enamel mug. Not until the light failed did he let her go and then he thanked her, taking her hand, bowing formally over it and kissing it lightly.

On the second occasion Annie had run quickly through the dusk, across the yard and into the noisy, warm farmhouse. Tonight there was a hop in a neighbouring village. Fred was going to drive the girls over and collect them at eleven o'clock which, on this occasion, was to be curfew hour. Before his arrival there would be the usual fight for hot water for baths and hair-washing. All the girls except Hester were going to the dance. She sat on her bed watching Annie slide a printed rayon frock over her head, carefully leaving undisturbed the curlers in her hair.

'You should come, Hes!' But Hester shook her head as though refusing the apple from the serpent. 'Ain't no harm in it!' Annie persisted. 'Just a bunch of local lads barely out of short pants most likely!'

'Marion said there'd be soldiers,' said Hester nervously. 'American GIs and that.'

'So what? They won't eat you! You can borrow one of my frocks if you want. The blue one'd suit you. C'mon! Dare you! You don't have to dance. You'd make a lovely wallflower!' But Hester had resisted temptation and, after the girls had clattered through the cross-passage and out into the cold night in response to Fred's blast on the truck horn, she had wandered into the kitchen where Edward-John seized upon her as a suitable opponent in a game of Snap.

'But it's cards!' Hester said in alarm and it took Alice half an hour to convince her of the innocence of the game. Edward-John taught her the rules and soon she was shouting

'Snap!' and triumphantly seizing her matchstick winnings, her pale face flushed with excitement while Alice, using the flat-iron, smoothed her son's school shirt, ready for Monday.

Hester's parents and most of her immediate relations were, the girls had discovered, members of a small, religious sect which was an offshoot of the better known Plymouth Brethren. Hester and her brother Ezekial had been reared to unquestioningly obey their father whose role as head of the East Cornish Church of the Pentecostal Brothers, as they called themselves, had encouraged a tendency in him to bully and dictate. Their mother, too, unquestioningly obeyed him. According to his lights, women and daughters were no more than chattels whose inclination to sin must at all times be curbed, while sons, until they had proved themselves worthy, required discipline and protection from corruption in a wicked world. His daughter's compulsory contribution to the war effort had been limited, not only by her short and hardly heeded education but by her timid personality, to a choice between ammunition factory and Land Army. Her father had considered that the second occupation would put his daughter in less jeopardy than the first. Soon after he had made this decision on her behalf he learnt that land girls had a mixed reputation and that, despite the discipline imposed by hostel wardens, many were straying from the path of righteousness. He cautioned his daughter and stressed the power of temptation and how, for the sake of her immortal soul, she must keep herself separate from these women who, if not quite fallen, were heading in the general direction of damnation and would almost certainly try to drag Hester with them. Consequently, when she first arrived at Lower Post Stone Farm, Hester had regarded everyone with deep suspicion, avoiding eye contact and restricting communication, whenever possible, to a simple yes or no. Of Mrs Brewster she was plainly terrified. She kept so effectively out of Roger Bayliss's way that he was barely conscious of her existence. She avoided Ferdie Vallance's randy eye and treated Alice with the deference with which she had faced her school teachers, saying 'Yes, miss,' or 'No, miss,' whenever she was directly addressed.

Although some of the girls ignored Hester and others were not above throwing the odd spiteful remark at her, several, including Annie, her room-mate, were kind, drawing her into their conversation, encouraging her to experiment with her appearance and inviting her to join them on various outings. This she stoutly resisted but on the evening of the hop, after Edward-John had been sent to bed and she had filled her hot-water bottle and climbed the stairs to the upper floor where the doors stood open to empty bedrooms chaotic with perfumed preparation for the girls' night out, she felt isolated and abandoned. She lit the lamp in the room she shared with Annie and sat down on her bed. The wardrobe was open and the frock Annie had offered to lend her was on its hanger, lamp-light illuminating its soft, blue folds. Hester had never, in all her short life, worn any colour but grey, black or dull brown. She looked at the photograph of her father, his hard face flanked by her brother Zeke on one side and their timorous mother on the other. Perhaps because she had spent the evening in the easy company of Edward-John and Alice, because she had laughed and shouted with excitement over the game of Snap, or because the obvious influence of the girls was, for once, not pressuring her, she felt calm and faintly inquisitive. What, she wondered, would she look like in blue? With her hair loose around her shoulders instead of hauled back into a bun? With lipstick on her mouth and mascara on her lashes? It didn't mean that she would ever dress in blue, or paint her face, or loosen her hair but should she not be allowed at least to experience and identify the sins she was resisting? She undressed, pulling her grey jumper up over her head and stepping out of the long black skirt which her mother had sewn by hand. Then, instead of putting on her nightdress, she slid her arms into the sleeves of Annie's blue frock. She felt the silky texture of it slide down, settling round her waist and ending at her knees. She pulled the net from her bun and shook out her hair, reached for Annie's lipstick and, spreading it on her mouth, worked her lips together as she had watched Annie do it. Then she turned to the long mirror which was set into the door of the shared wardrobe. A stranger faced her. Transfixed by the image in the looking glass, she failed to hear either the arrival of the truck or the sound of the girls who, later than they should have been, stealthily re-entered the farmhouse, slipping off their high-heeled shoes and coming silently up the stairs.

'Hey!' said Annie, taking in at a glance Hester's willowy figure, her narrow waist nipped in by the wide belt, her small breasts rounding out the silky bodice, her mass of auburn hair, rouged mouth and gently accentuated eyes. 'Hey, Hester!' But the eyes, Annie saw at once, were brimming. Tears were washing the mascara down Hester's white cheeks. She was looking at the photograph of her father as though half hypnotised.

'I shouldn't have!' she gulped reaching for cotton wool and scrubbing the colour from her mouth, her eyes still on her father's. 'I'll go to hell, I will!'

Annie soothed and calmed, pleaded and cajoled but Hester's distress continued until she had stripped off her borrowed finery, pulled her flannelette nightdress over her head, plunged under the covers of her bed and buried her head in her pillow. 'He's looking!' she moaned. 'He can see!'

'If you wasn't so bloomin' pathetic, Hester Tucker, it'd be funny!' Annie said. 'But as it is, you make me sick!' Hester, tear-streaked, sat up and stared at Annie. 'You tried on me frock, that's all! You put on lipstick and brushed out your hair! What if he did see? It's not a crime!' But Hester's eyes kept straying back to the photograph. 'If it's him that's bothering you he's easily dealt with!' Annie said and she picked up the photograph and shut it firmly into a drawer in the dressing table. Then, because she'd had several shandies at the hop and because Hester's face, now that her father's image had vanished from sight, was such a picture of confused relief, Annie started to laugh and, once started, couldn't stop. The thud of Marion's fist on the partition added to her amusement and Hester, her delicate nerves stretched and sensitised by various emotions, found her weeping dissolving into a slightly hysterical giggling. The more Marion beat upon the wall the funnier it all seemed and both Annie and Hester were soon speechless and choking with laughter. It was Alice, coming to check that all the girls were accounted for and that the outer doors were locked for the night, who finally quietened them.

That night began an accelerating change in Hester. Instead of the lowered head and evasive eyes, the girls encountered shy smiles and open curiosity on womanly matters. If Hester had been previously equipped with the facts of life by her mother and the elders of her church, they were different facts and a different life from those with which the rest of the girls at Lower Post Stone Farm were familiar.

'I don't reckon she knows which hole is which or what for!' Winnie had sniggered after one frank and open discussion. Little by little Hester's horizons widened. One Saturday afternoon she went with Annie into Exeter and returned without her bun. The soft, reddish hair, released from restriction, floated round her face like a pale gold cloud.

'It weren't meant to go like this!' she beamed helplessly at Alice. 'It did it by its own self, soon as it were cut! D'you like it, miss?' Alice said she did and it was true. Hester, despite the changes to her appearance, for a while at least, retained the sweet timidity that set her slightly apart from the coarseness of Marion and Winnie, the hardness of Gwennan and even the assured self-satisfaction of Georgina's well-groomed attractiveness and the dark intensity of Annie's Jewish beauty. But she still would not go out with the girls, blushed when they teased her and trailed round the kitchen while Alice, alone while Rose had her day off, cleared Saturdays's high tea from the kitchen table.

'I'll wash the dishes, Missus Todd… I'll help peel the tatties for Sunday dinner…' In return for this assistance Alice found herself endlessly plied with questions.

'Do you go to church, miss?'

'Sometimes.'

'There's some as say 'tis a sin not to go regular.'

'You must learn to live and let live. It says so in the Bible.'

'Do it? I never heard Father say that.'

Early each Sunday morning a group of Pentecostal Brothers collected Hester in a horse-drawn wagon and bore her off with them for several hours of prayer and hymn-singing in the barn of a local dairyman who embraced their particular faith. On the Sunday after her visit to the barber's Hester had managed to confine her hair under her church hat but, back at the farm at dinnertime, told Alice and the girls that the wind had caught the hat and carried it off, bowling it down the lane and how the brethren had stared at her as she retrieved it and stuffed her hair back out of sight.

'Bugger them!' Marion suggested.

'But they could see as it's cut!' Hester wailed, passing a hand ineffectively over her drifting halo.

'So?' said Annie, her mouth full.

'So I might be damned!'

'Damned?'

'Cutting hair is a sin!' Hester whimpered. The girls groaned unsympathetically and the conversation moved on.

On the following Saturday afternoon most of the Post Stone girls went, as usual, into Exeter to visit the cinema and then, depending on what was on offer, either to a pub or a dance hall for the evening. Mabel, who had plans of her own, spent the afternoon in the warm kitchen, knitting Arthur's scarf and writing home, printing the words laboriously. 'Dear Gran, hope you are well...love to Arthur, kiss, kiss, kiss...' Annie, who would meet up with the girls later in the day, presented herself as usual on Saturdays at Andreis's studio.

'Do you get letters from your folks?' she asked him when they broke for a cup of tea. His mind was on his composition and she watched his expression change as he addressed her question.

'To begin with, ya. But then not so often and from some of them none at all any more.' He sipped, wincing as the hot tea burnt his mouth. 'I try not to think, Hannah-Maria, not to imagine, for to do so is painful. While I work on my painting – which is my account of things – my mind is easier, you see.' They sat in silence. Annie could not share the intensity of his feelings. Her own Jewishness was something of which she was not often aware although she knew that it grieved her grandparents that their children and grandchildren paid only lip service to their faith.

The farmhouse was quiet. Alice, having prepared a cold supper for those few of her charges that were not out for the evening, had gone for a walk with Edward-John.

In the room Hester shared with Annie the light was already fading. The dress which Annie was to wear that evening lay across her bed. Hester, having darned a hole in her khaki-green Land Army-issue socks, sat looking at the dress. Its colour, a rich garnet red, attracted her. The fabric was soft to her touch. The photograph of her father had been restored to its prominent place and his eyes regarded her balefully until she reached suddenly forward and placed the picture face down on the bedside table. She breathed deeply for a moment and then was on her feet, stepping out of her long shirt, dropping her thick sweater on the floor and easing Annie's red frock over her head. Its colour, as she surveyed her reflection, did not flatter her as obviously as the blue dress had done. Nevertheless, against her pale skin and the floating red-gold of her hair, it worked a sort of alchemy, lending to the overall impression a glowing pre-Raphaelite richness which astonished her.

In the kitchen Mabel had heard a timid tap on the front door. She put down her knitting and lumbered along the cross-passage, lifted the latch and pulled open the door.

The young man in the porch was silhouetted against the fading sky so that all Mabel could see of him was the narrow-trousered dark suit and skimpy jacket, from the sleeves of which large wrists and hands protruded as he bent to remove bicycle clips from his bony shins. She did not notice that the boy's hair was the same pale gold colour as Hester's.

'Yes?' Mabel said cautiously, for visitors were rare at the farmhouse and male ones were taboo. She was unsure of herself and wished Alice would return from her walk.

'I'm here to see Miss Hester Tucker,' the boy announced, just as he had rehearsed it and sensing that Mabel, although bulky, presented no threat to his mastery of the situation. She was undoubtedly evil. Her jumper was too tight across her breasts and there was a faint suggestion of nipples under the pilling wool. Flushing, he lowered his glance to the safety of the stone floor aware, nevertheless, of the fleshy shins below Mabel's skirt. Without turning her head or removing her eyes from the young man's face Mabel raised her voice and bellowed Hester's name. Hester heard her, responded instinctively and got as far as the top of the stairs before hesitating. She was still dressed in Annie's frock. But the voice that had summoned her was only Mabel's, so she came quickly to the head of the staircase and stood, peering down, instantly recognising the young man who was standing, flat-footed, in the cross-passage. She stared, her hands flying guiltily to the bodice of the dress as though attempting to conceal its cut and its colour from him.

'Zeke!' Her voice was thin with surprise 'It's me brother!' she added, for Mabel's benefit. Mabel relaxed slightly and decided that a visiting kid brother was acceptable, at teatime at any rate.

'Best take 'im into the recreation room,' Mabel said, moving back towards the kitchen. 'I'll fetch youse a cuppa.'

Left alone, brother and sister gaped at one another. He stood, peering up at her as though doubting what he saw. After a moment of silence she came down the staircase, opened the door to the recreation room and went through it. Zeke followed her. The air smelt faintly of cigarette smoke. The fire was laid but unlit and the room struck cold. But it was lighter than the cross-passage and for the first time Zeke could clearly see his sister's red frock and the loosened, brilliant hair. He froze.

'I didn't know you was coming, Zeke!' she said, desperately. His eyes, the same light grey-blue as hers moved incredulously over her.

'Go see your sister, Father said.' His voice was young and barely broken. 'Go see how she is.' He paused, wretched. 'Look at you, Hester! Your frock! Your hair!'

She clasped her hands together, avoiding contact with

the fabric of the dress. Her voice was a plaintive whisper. 'There's…there's no harm in it, Zeke! Inside the dress I be the same as always!' It was the truth. She was innocent. Unsure. Scared. They faced each other, the brother and the sister, the established relationship yawing between past influences and present pressures.

'But Father!' Zeke's voice was querulous. 'What would he say?'

'You won't go tellin' 'im, will you, Zeke?' Pleading, she took a step towards him but he drew back, raising an arm as though to ward off the evil she represented. He stood, tense and miserable.

'He's gonna ask. What shall I say to 'im?'

There was a pause, both of them wilting at the prospect of their father's anger.

'You mustn't lie, Zeke. That's for sure,' she said with a low hopelessness, resigned to what would inevitably follow.

'So what shall I say to him?'

'That it baint my dress… That I only borrowed it…!'

'But you shouldn't of!' He was shouting at her now. Sounding like their father. Suddenly she remembered Annie's words and felt a sharp surge of self-defence rise in her.

'But why not, Zeke? I like pretty colours! Why's pretty colours sinful?' She could hardly believe she had said it. The words hung in the air and Zeke shook his head as though trying to keep the sound of them out of his ears. He knew, because he had been told, they both had, that colours and laughter and loosened hair were signs of debauchery and wickedness. She stared at him in hopeless defiance. 'Them that comes for me, Sundays,' she said, 'to take me for prayers. They told Father that I'd cut my hair! That's how he knew! And now you'll go off home and you'll tell him the rest, I suppose! About me having on a red dress! Well then, you do it, Zeke! You go tell him! But I baint a sinner, Zeke! Leastways I 'aven't done nothin' as I'm ashamed of, so there!' She stood, breathing hard in the silence, holding her brother's eyes until he faltered and looked away.

'That woman,' Zeke said flatly. 'She looks like a whore!'

'Mabel?' Hester breathed, incredulous. 'No, Zeke! She's kind! When I first come here and I was homesick for you and our mother, Mabel was good to me! Nearly all of them was! Mabel and Annie and Missus Todd! You'd say they all was evil sinners but they baint!' She was interrupted by Mabel who came carefully into the room bearing two brimming cups, her tongue protruding as she concentrated on delivering them without slopping tea into the saucers. Then she watched, astonished, as Hester's brother went, without a word, past her to the door and through it.

In the lane Alice and Edward-John stood to one side as the cyclist pedalled past them. By the time they reached the kitchen, Hester, who had changed back into her black skirt, had joined Mabel at the kitchen table where the two of them sat sipping tea.

At five o'clock Mabel announced that there was a calf she wanted to check on at the Bayliss farm. She asked if she could borrow Alice's bicycle. Alice was surprised at this request but agreed to it and Mabel, her face rosy with quiet determination, departed leaving Alice, Edward-John and Hester to eat supper alone that night. Afterwards Hester declined Edward-John's invitation to play Monopoly and went to her room where she read her Bible for an hour and then sat with it open on her knees, wondering, despite herself, where Annie and the other girls were and what they were doing. She was in her bed before the lorry which had met the last bus from Exeter to Ledburton deposited them in the muddy lane outside Lower Post Stone Farm. When Annie entered the shared room, Hester pretended to be asleep.

'Calf, my eye!' said Rose, when Alice told her about Mabel's excursion on the previous evening. 'Tis Ferdie Vallance she'm after! Or maybe 'tis he who be after 'er! He's been that lonesome since his mother was took! Well, perhaps not so much lonesome as incapable!'

'Incapable?'

'Of washin' 'is clothes! Cleanin' 'is cottage! Cookin' 'is meals! I hear all about it from Mrs Fred, see.' As usual other matters intruded on this conversation. More often than not Alice was unable to come to grips with any situation before it was overtaken by another and a scenario which, one day, would seem complicated and possibly threatening to one or other of her charges had, the next, been replaced by another, involving a different girl.

At the Bayliss farm there were two adjacent labourers' cottages. In one, Fred and his wife, who was known as Mrs Fred, had raised their daughters, both of whom were now married and gone. In the other cottage, Ruby Vallance, widowed early, had mothered her Ferdinand and when, at nineteen, he had been maimed by a rolling tractor, had refused to permit the doctors to saw off the mangled leg. She had gritted her teeth and nursed him back onto his feet. The farm's insurers had paid for a labourer to take Ferdie's place while he mended and the rent for the cottage was part of the injured boy's wages so he and his mother had, at least, a roof over their heads. But throughout his recovery they lived on charity and the vegetables and hens that Ruby raised in the tiny patch of garden behind the cottage. So focused was she on keeping herself and her son fed that she had little time or energy for housework and as she aged, and after Ferdie became mobile enough to resume at least some of his work in the dairy, she grew exhausted, then weak, then sick, until one morning, Ferdie came down to a cold kitchen, no porridge in the pot and his mother stone dead in her chair. After that he had used the cottage more or less as an animal uses its cave. He made no attempt to clean it. When all his clothes became so stiff with sweat and dirt that he could barely get his limbs into them, he dumped them into the copper and boiled them up as he thought he remembered his mother doing. Woollen jerseys became slimy, colour bled from his shirts into his pyjamas and his combinations. His entire wardrobe took on a khaki-ish, greyish tone. Mrs Fred gaped at the line of strangely pegged, monochrome washing. She considered offering her help but Ruby had always been a slut and what had Ferdie ever done for her?

'I've got meself a lovely piece of stewing steak for me tea,' Ferdie had announced to Mabel during the course of the Saturday morning milking, 'and a couple of kidneys...' Mabel thought of the high tea which, after a hot meal at lunchtime, would be all she'd get at the hostel. 'You much of a hand at cookin'?' Ferdie had enquired casually and in the course of only a few minutes Mabel had agreed, in return for a share in the resulting meal, to make her culinary skills available to him later that day.

When she entered the cottage at five o'clock Mabel quickly became too engrossed in the preparations of the meat and vegetables and the mixing and rolling out of the pastry for the pie to pay much attention to the small, dark, cluttered room which served Ferdie, as it had served his mother before him, as kitchen and living room. A galvanised tin bath hung from a nail on one wall and it was in this, in front of his fire, that Ferdie occasionally – and only occasionally – submerged himself in soapy water. The walls were coated with a film of accumulated grease, the result of many years of smoky cooking and through which the outline of the pattern of a floral wallpaper was only faintly discernible. A few framed pictures, each subject a dark blur, hung haphazardly and askew and the mirror over the tilting sideboard revealed nothing more than a speckled, silver haze.

Soon an aroma of the baking pie filled the kitchen and Ferdie and Mabel, while they waited for their meal to be ready, passed the time sipping home-brewed cider, the effect of which, together with the warmth of the kitchen and the welcome respite from the unremitting cold in which they had laboured all week, loosened them. They chatted about this and that, Mabel reacting with appropriate enthusiasm as Ferdie expounded several of his theories on farming. She sympathised volubly while he described in detail the accident that had maimed him. How for three hours he had been trapped under the overturned tractor before another could be found to pull it off him and how Christopher Bayliss, then only a boy in short trousers, had crawled under the wreckage and fed him brandy from the master's hip-flask to deaden the pain in his crushed leg. For two months Ferdie had lain with the limb supported in a wooden frame, until the flesh had healed sufficiently for the splintered bones to be set in plaster. After that, for a whole summer, he'd hauled himself about on crutches and, when the plaster was removed, been left with a leg that bore very little resemblance, either in appearance or performance, to its mate. The ligaments and sinews had been so damaged that the mechanism of both knee and hip refused to articulate and it had taken years for Ferdie to maximise the wrecked limb's performance and to evolve the curious, gyrating limp which now bore him about the farm.

'So there's been no courtin' for me, Mabel!' he concluded. 'No fiancée, no bride, no young 'uns.'

'No,' she said and then, trying to look on the bright side, 'But no war, neither!'

'I'd 'ave gone though, Mabel! If I could of! Like a shot, I would.'

''Course you would!' she soothed, adding, 'Reckon we should mash them spuds now…'

They ate speedily and with mutual relish, wolfing the food and mopping up the gravy from their plates with doorsteps of bread. Their faces shone. There was potato in Ferdie's beard and grease on Mabel's chin.

'Next time you come us'll have pudden!' Ferdie announced, for Mabel's cooking had passed muster. This had been the best meal he'd eaten since his mother's death and he wanted more. Just how much more he had not at that moment decided for, although he knew that no good-looking girl would give him a second glance except in response to his twisted shape and rolling gait, he resisted any ambition to regard Mabel as a possible wife. Although she was gross and clumsy he guessed that she too had her own ideas about the man she'd wed and would, should Ferdie make advances to her, repel him just as all the others had done before her.

Resigned to his isolation, Ferdie had given up his attempts to end it. But Mabel also had an agenda and her own hungers. The feelings of lust which warmed her prettier sisters also heated her. Like Ferdie and for much the same reasons, she knew she had little chance of satisfying her cravings. His cottage was unlike any other human habitation she had seen. She sensed the filth and the neglect. But it had walls, windows and a roof. These, for reasons of her own, Mabel needed. So she smiled at this strange, benign, whiskery little man and spoke to him promisingly of spotted dick, apple pie with dollops of Devonshire cream and of suet pudden with golden syrup spooned over it, until the clock struck ten.

Her mittened hands tight on the handlebars, Mabel negotiated the steep lane, letting gravity bear her home. The pale gold circle of light from Alice's headlamp bounced over the ruts while moonlight flickered blindingly through the leafless hedge, disorienting Mabel so that she pitched dangerously from side to side, her legs spread and her rubber-booted feet fending off first one and then the other of the mossy banks that walled the narrow track, expecting at any moment to be thrown into the mud and unable to do more than try to keep the bucking machine on an even keel. Feeling herself to be delivered body and soul to the whim of God she surrendered to the careering descent and laughed aloud, shrieking 'Whee!' into the darkness. Across the dark valley sheep turned enquiring faces in her direction.

* * *

It was Margery Brewster's policy to keep meticulous records of the hostels in her care. Every six weeks she had meetings with the wardens in order to review the running of each establishment. The consumption of food and fuel was monitored. Visits by the land girls to doctor or dentist were noted, together with any time off a girl might have taken, due to illness or family obligation. Requests for leave were discussed before referral to Roger Bayliss. Each warden would, at the end of the meeting, be given the opportunity to air any problems.

So, one blustery day towards the end of March, Mrs Brewster's car nosed up to the front gate of Lower Post Stone Farm. Rose was predictably and visibly insulted when Mrs Brewster, after accepting the offer of a cup of tea, made it clear that when she and Alice withdrew for their meeting, Rose's presence would not be required.

Alice led her visitor through to her own quarters where Margery spread her notes across the table, settled her spectacles and, as was her habit on these occasions, opened the proceedings by scrutinising the warden's appearance. In Alice's case she seemed pleased with what she saw.

'You're looking better, my dear,' she announced.

During the six weeks since her arrival at the farmhouse Alice had given very little thought to how she was looking and even less to how she was feeling. It was all she could do each day to get through her workload, keep herself and her clothes clean and spare some time on Saturdays and

Sundays for her son. The initial bewilderment had settled into an almost unrelieved grind of labour and responsibility. Sometimes she had despaired of ever getting the routine organised enough to pause for breath and consider her situation. But perhaps such consideration would have depressed her and possibly it had been easier to submerge herself in her duties than to lift her head and contemplate her future.

Margery's voice droned on.

'...And apart from the unfortunate incident involving Christine what's-her-name there have been no serious problems and no complaints from either your employer or your charges. So. Well done. During the cold snap you did rather overdo the consumption of logs and paraffin but I'm sure Mr Bayliss sympathises with your intention to keep the girls as comfortable as possible – however he did mention to me that it seemed to him to be slightly excessive.' Alice was about to defend herself when Margery continued sweetly, 'And now... Do you have anything you wish to raise with me?' Alice considered for a moment and then described to Margery the ideas she had for the kitchen. She produced a scale plan which she had drawn on a sheet of graph paper taken from one of Edward-John's mathematics exercise books.

'It would make the preparation of food so much easier,' she said when Margery stared, baffled, at the plan, and was explaining the merits of her scheme when Rose knocked on the door, opened it and put her head into the room.

'Sorry to intrude, Alice,' she said, obviously delighted to have an excuse to interrupt the meeting. 'Only the meat's come and Tom says he could let you have a dozen best end of neck chops, if you want 'em...which means we could use them for a hotpot tonight and save the stewing steak to have with dumplings on Sunday...'

Having been complimented by Alice for her sensible planning, Rose threw a virtuous glance at Margery Brewster and left them. Margery was staring at Alice in astonishment.

'She called you Alice!' she exclaimed as soon as the door closed on Rose.

'Yes,' said Alice.

'D'you consider that wise?' Margery's attitude was clearly censorious.

'Yes,' said Alice. 'You use my Christian name and I yours and for the same reasons.'

'Which are?' Margery asked and Alice noted the raised eyebrows and was unsure whether Margery was irritated or amused.

'Because we work closely together and any distinctions between us on the grounds of class seem to me to be inappropriate.' Margery managed a tight smile while she considered whether or not her status as a bank manager's wife equalled or exceeded Alice's, whose husband was a civil servant of an unknown but possibly quite senior rank. Eventually she seemed to relax and, muttering benignly about war being a great leveller, allowed her attention to be drawn back to Alice's plans for the kitchen.

After Margery had left the farm, taking the plans with her and promising to show them to Roger Bayliss but warning Alice not expect him to welcome the prospect of spending yet more money on the refurbishment of Lower Post Stone, Alice lingered at the front gate. Some daffodils were pushing up through the overgrown border to the path, their sheathed heads a bright yellow-green in the sunlight. She could hear the far-off bleat of lambs. Sparrows were fighting over nest sites in the gable end of the farmhouse. She knew that she must soon pay attention to the situation between herself and her husband, realising suddenly how seldom she thought of him and that when she did it was with reluctance because he represented such a welter of negative feelings. He was sending her money. A small weekly amount was arriving in the bank account he had advised her to open in her own name. A bachelor uncle, having heard of her marital difficulties, had assumed responsibility for Edward-John's school fees and contributed generously towards the incidental costs incurred by his education. So, for the immediate future at least, Alice's financial needs were met. She had a home of sorts and her thoughts and her energies where fully occupied. It was easier to push her reaction to James's obvious indifference to her out of her mind. She could, after all, do nothing to change it.

'Reckon you should get out this afternoon,' Rose called

from the scullery as she washed Margery Brewster's cup and saucer. 'The hotpot's simmering. The 'tatoes is peeled and the cabbage chopped for tonight's dinner. Get yourself out and about for a few hours! Do you good!'

'Where would I go?' Alice asked, amused by Rose's tendency to organise everything and everybody who fell within her range.

'Bicycle into Ledburton! Only take you fifteen minutes! The pub'll be shut of course but you can get a nice afternoon tea at the Arms! Go on! Dare you!'

Alice enjoyed her nice tea, strolled round the square, bought postage stamps and some blurred postcards of Ledburton church at the general store and, noticing heavy cloud moving in from the west, mounted her bicycle for the ride back to the farmhouse.

The rain had begun as she negotiated the shallow ford. She had pedalled up the hill beyond it and was free-wheeling down the steep incline towards the farmhouse when a car, moving fast in the opposite direction, rounded a blind corner, appearing directly in her path. She braked too sharply, the wheels locked and the machine slithered forward depositing Alice, quite gently, on the bonnet of the car, which was by then stationary. She became aware of two men, both in naval uniform, their faces grave, their hands, as they helped her off the bonnet and stood her gingerly on her feet, both awkward and gentle. The first man, who was in his forties, was an officer. The second, who was older and had been at the wheel of the car, was crimson with embarrassment and shock and full of apologies. Alice, she repeatedly assured them both, was unharmed. She took responsibility for the accident which, she insisted, was caused by her haste to get home before the rain worsened. Having satisfied himself that neither Alice nor her machine was damaged, the officer introduced himself as Oliver Maynard, Adjutant at the nearby Fleet Air Arm training establishment.

'We was thinking this might be a short cut, madam,' the driver was explaining. 'Only we got lost...!'

Alice explained who she was and what she was doing and after helping the men re-establish their bearings, extended her hand to Maynard. He took it and shook it, looking appreciatively into her face, enjoying the grave eyes, the set of her mouth, the creamy skin and the colour and texture of her hair. She was exactly the sort of woman he most admired.

'Perhaps... Sometime... Your land girls would care to visit the camp? One of my responsibilities is to keep the lads happy...' He hesitated, seeing in Alice's response to this something which caused him to rephrase it. 'I mean... I organise events at which the young people can meet. Socially. Concerts. Sports of various kinds. Dances and so on.' Alice smiled and nodded. She became aware that her hand was still in his and withdrew it.

'I see,' she said, smiling at the commander's driver. 'Well, you know where we are.' She mounted the bike and, rather conscious of the two men's eyes following her progress down the lane, cycled away. Her left knee felt stiff and the front wheel of the cycle was slightly out of alignment so that she had to turn the handlebars a little to the left in order to achieve a straight line.

Rose met her in the cross-passage.

'A Mr James Todd telephoned,' she announced, her eyes watching Alice closely for her reaction to this news. 'I told 'im you was out and 'e said 'e'd ring again after four-thirty.' It was now twenty-five minutes to five and precisely as Rose finished speaking the two women heard the sound of the outside telephone bell.

Chapter Five

At the Bayliss farm father and son accepted their plates of breakfast from Eileen, the woman who had cleaned and cooked for them since she was a girl. Following the deaths first of her husband and then of his wife, Roger had been pleased to lengthen the hours Eileen spent at the farmhouse and had raised her wages to take account of her increased responsibilities. She left her cottage in the village at seven-thirty each morning and seldom returned to it before six at night, having cleaned the farmhouse, laundered the linen, shopped for groceries and prepared Roger's supper tray, his main meal, since the start of the war and except on special occasions, being taken at midday. When Christopher was on leave the two men ate breakfast together and Eileen contrived, whenever possible, to provide bacon and eggs, a fish kedgeree or devilled lamb's kidneys but on this occasion,

Christopher having returned home sooner than expected, rations were short and she had resorted to eggs from the farm's hens, scrambled in creamy milk and served on bread fried in bacon fat.

Christopher's hands were bandaged from knuckle to wrist and he winced as he tried to cut into his food. Eileen took his knife and fork from him and remembered, as she did so, numerous occasions on which she had done the same thing for him when he had been an infant and she, fresh from the village school, employed as kitchen maid and part-time nanny, had divided his breakfast into small portions. Christopher thanked her and, holding his fork between finger and thumb, began to eat. His father, keeping his eyes on his newspaper, read out several items concerning the progress of the war, remarking with satisfaction, as Eileen excused herself and left them, that the Eighth Army had at last penetrated the Mareth Line. He omitted to tell Christopher that in the casualty list, yet another of his school friends was reported killed in action.

'How goes your Land Army?' Christopher enquired casually, anxious to discover whether Georgina had survived the wretched weather or had sensibly decamped to a softer life in another service.

'The warden wants me to renovate the hostel kitchen!' his father answered, spreading Eileen's home-made strawberry jam on his toast and implying some unreasonableness in Alice's request. Christopher said he was not surprised and that it must be a nightmare trying to cater for ten thunderous young women in a kitchen from the Domesday Book. Roger smiled.

'I'm going to ride down there this morning,' he said. 'Come with me.' He hesitated and then, wondering whether Christopher's injuries would prevent him from managing a horse, added, 'If you feel up to it.'

Alice, about to shake Christopher's hand, drew back when she saw the bandages. The undersides of his fingers were pink and blistered where they emerged from the dressing. She guessed he was burnt and he saw the look that changed her expression from polite greeting to concern.

'Don't worry,' he said. 'It's nothing serious.' He turned the conversation to the subject of the kitchen.

Alice made a good case for her alterations and had even discovered a stack of disused marble slabs, once part of an old dairy, which would, she said, be perfect for her purposes. Christopher suggested using timber salvaged from the same dairy as framing and supports for the new work surfaces and Roger found himself agreeing that as soon as Jack had finished drilling the spring wheat he could be released from farm work for a few days and put at Alice's disposal. Rose, whose many useful ideas had been incorporated and credited to her in Roger's presence, was as pleased as Alice herself with this result.

'Us won't know ourselves, will us!' she crowed

triumphantly as she and Alice watched the men turn their horses towards the lane that led up the valley and back to the higher farm.

He found her at last in the farm office, bringing the land girls' worksheets up to date. Her colour was slightly heightened by exposure to the winter weather but her eyes were as fine and her hair as sleek as he remembered. He smiled and sat opposite her, offered her a cigarette and leant forward to light it for her, using the same match to light his own. Then he sat back, looking at her and exhaling gently.

She guessed at once that it was because of his injured hands that his latest tour of duty had been curtailed and she asked what had happened. He gave her an edited account of the incident that, two weeks previously, had killed Peter Fairfax, one of the few airmen from Christopher's intake who were still flying. The slangy, gung-ho, mess room language in which Christopher told part of his story would have offended Georgina if he had not looked so wretched.

It had happened on a raw day in early March. A flight of four Hurricanes had been scrambled in support of another which was responding to a heavy enemy presence over Portsmouth. Christopher's aircraft was still in the hands of the servicing mechanics so, at the last moment, he was pulled from the operation and only three planes were approaching take-off. Christopher, wearing his flying suit and leather helmet, was standing with his back to the service hangar, putting a match to a cigarette and watching the take-off when a Dornier broke through the cloud cover, came howling in from the south-west and released a stick of bombs, one of which struck the runway. The first Hurricane, which had already lifted off, climbed, banked and vanished into cloud, pursuing the attacker. The third pilot throttled back and managed to veer away from the mutilated strip, bouncing to a standstill on the tussocky grass. For the second man, Peter Fairfax, who was committed to take-off but had not yet achieved the necessary speed, no evasive action was possible. He forced the plane's nose sharply upwards but not before a wheel plunged into a crater. Instantly his starboard wing dropped, embedding itself in the ground with such force that the aircraft slewed and then cartwheeled, crumpling into an unrecognisable tangle of metal. Christopher's cigarette fell from his hand as he and several other observers began to sprint forward. The blast from the Hurricane's exploding fuel tank almost threw them off their feet.

Christopher could see Peter Fairfax struggling to open his canopy which appeared to contain a solid mass of fire and fumes. As the perspex slid back a sheet of incandescent flame shot upwards enveloping him as he hauled himself out of the cockpit and slithered down into the wreckage of the blazing fuselage. To Christopher it all seemed, as it had appeared frequently since in dreams, to take place in slow motion. Fire engine and ambulance were heading out across the airfield. But slowly. As he went into the flames, got a hold on Peter and dragged him clear, Christopher's flying suit protected him and at first he felt nothing. They had rolled the burning man on the ground to put out the flames. To make his breathing easier someone pulled off his leather helmet and oxygen mask. With it came most of the skin from his face. He was screaming. Only when the needle had gone into his lacerated forearm, and he had been floated off into the blur of agony and hallucination which was all he would know of the remaining four days of his life, did Christopher feel the pain in his own blistering palms.

'A mate's kite blew up,' he told Georgina, ashing his cigarette. 'Had to get him out in a hurry!' She stared at the bandages and at the damage in his eyes which he was unable to conceal.

'And did you? Get him out, I mean?'

'Yeah, we did. We got him out.' He paused and then abruptly asked her to have dinner with him that night. She looked at him. She would have preferred to decline but that, she sensed, would have been churlish, even unkind. Georgina was neither churlish nor unkind so she accepted.

He borrowed his father's car and, although, when he took the wheel, the pain in his hands made him wince, drove her to a favourite restaurant in Exeter where the chef managed to provide a dinner which was almost up to his pre-war standards. During the meal their good manners and similar backgrounds resulted in a steady flow of meaningless conversation in which each discovered a set of predictable facts about the other. On the drive home Georgina saw Christopher grit his teeth as he pulled the heavy car round a tight corner and persuaded him, since his injured hands were obviously hurting him, to let her take the wheel. He asked whether she was a licensed driver.

'Of course,' she said, putting the car smoothly into gear. 'Cars, tractors… And aeroplanes, actually!' She smiled at his astonishment and explained that her godfather, who was a director at de Havillands, having taken her up in his bi-plane on her tenth birthday, had been so charmed by her reaction and natural aptitude that he subsequently paid for flying lessons. She flew solo two days after her eighteenth birthday and got her licence on her first attempt. Christopher looked at her with open admiration. Then he sighed and shook his head.

'You could be having such a brilliant war, you know! If it wasn't for…' he stopped carefully.

'My convictions?' she finished for him and asked whether he considered that he himself was having a brilliant war, taking her eyes from the road just long enough to catch his expression. He did not respond and they barely spoke during the rest of the journey back to Lower Post Stone. He got out of the passenger seat and opened her door. In the moment they stood facing each other he kissed her mouth. It was a brief contact. Her lips felt warm against his. His, cold on hers. Then they thanked each other for a very nice evening.

He watched her negotiate the dark path, go through the porch and let herself into the dimly lit cross-passage, closing the door behind her.

Alice, waiting for Georgina, who, that night, was the only girl to have left the farmhouse, heard the sound of the door closing, called out, reminding her to bolt it and was surprised when Georgina came through the recreation room and tapped on the open door to her room. When Alice offered her a hot drink she declined.

'I had dinner with Christopher,' she said, standing in the doorway. Alice indicated the chair opposite her and threw a small log into the embers of her fire. They sat for a while, watching the flames lick round the dry wood. 'I think something awful has happened to him,' Georgina said at last. Alice waited but the seconds passed and Georgina remained silent.

'You mean…his burns?' Alice prompted, uncertain whether Georgina would continue.

'He didn't want to talk about it. No more than the basic facts, anyway. I could see that. So I didn't press him.' Georgina was thinking aloud and Alice hesitated to interrupt her. After a while Georgina began to speak, surprising Alice by launching into an exploration of her feelings about her commitment to Conscientious Objection. 'It seemed so simple – pacifism… But it isn't.' She paused. 'I mean, in principle war is wrong, obviously. But what do you do when the rules are broken? How do you defend people from other people's violence without using violence yourself? Innocent people get caught up and die of it. Like Chrissie did. Or their lives are wrecked. Like Andreis. And Christopher.' She paused, then turned, looking into Alice's face before adding hesitantly, 'I think he's cracking up, Mrs Todd.'

At the Bayliss farm Roger, as Alice had been, was sitting over a dying fire. An hour previously he had finished the whiskey in the decanter which stood on a low table beside his chair. He had decided not to broach a new bottle but, eventually, hoping that his son might, on his return from dinner, join him in a nightcap, he decanted a single malt, poured himself a tot and was rolling it carefully round his tongue when he heard the car, then the front door, then Christopher's footsteps on the staircase which led up to the first-floor sitting room where Roger spent his evenings. The old spaniel, which had been Christopher's since he was ten years old, got stiffly to her feet, greeted him and then flopped down with a sigh onto the tartan rug that Eileen always spread for her in front of the fire.

'Join me?' Roger said, indicating the whiskey. 'It's a rather good one. Christmas present from your Uncle Freddie.'

Christopher poured a generous three fingers of the gold liquid into a tumbler and added to it a very small amount of water. He sipped, tasted, nodded, swallowed, said, 'Not half bad. Good old Fred,' and dropped into the empty chair on the opposite side of the fireplace where he sat holding the tumbler and staring into the remains of the fire. His father watched as the young man appeared to drift off, not to sleep but to somewhere. Roger cleared his throat and asked whether Christopher's evening had been a success. For a moment there was no response and Roger thought Christopher had not heard him. Then he came back from wherever it was that his thoughts had taken him and answered brightly that yes, it had been 'enormous fun', and that Georgina was 'one hell of a girl'. His father watched for a while as his son sat sipping. Then Christopher announced that he intended going back to his base the following day. Roger asked why, since his hands were not healed.

'Oh, they won't let me fly, Pa. But I'm beginning to feel a bit useless here and they'll probably have something I can do...' Roger was about to speak. To make some obvious remark about regretting that Christopher felt he must go, but that if he considered he should, it might be for the best and so on, when Christopher continued, or rather did not continue but abruptly changed the subject. 'Tim Bretherton bought it the other day,' he said. 'A daylight raid on Brest. The announcement's in your paper.' Roger did not admit to having read the news. He watched as Christopher got to his feet and began to pace about the room. 'That Dornier pilot – the one that took Fax out – he died too, you know. Shot down by our chap. It seemed good at the time. When Fax was dying, I mean. Good to know that the bastard that did it to him had paid for it.' Christopher stopped pacing, wheeled round and stood motionless, facing his father. 'But what the fuck is it all about?' Roger was unprepared for this outburst. Years of reticence between the two of them made him incapable of a significant response. So he lifted the whiskey bottle, offering a top-up. Christopher shook his head, dropped back into his chair and closed his eyes.

'Sorry,' he said quietly. 'You must know what I mean though, after your experience in the First World War caper.'

Roger stiffened. 'What experience?' he asked sharply. 'I wasn't… I was too young for that one, Chris. I—' He stopped as Christopher cut in, interrupting him.

'I didn't mean you, personally, Pa. I meant, you know, losing the cousins and so on. Hearing the news, day after day, of the carnage in the trenches. Ypres. The Somme and everything…' Christopher failed to notice his father's reaction to this or how the tension seemed to leave him, allowing him to relax into his armchair as his son continued. 'I mean this tit for tat stuff. They blast Coventry to kingdom come so the next night we send a bunch of kids over to blow up Hanover or some other unlucky city. Fax gets incinerated but the bloke in the Dornier ends up spread all over a five-acre field in Hampshire, so that makes it all right! It's madness!' He paused. The last of a log collapsed into ash in the hearth. 'That girl…Georgina…'

'She's a pacifist, Christopher!'

He met his father's eyes and after a moment lowered his lids and downed the remains of his drink.

'Yes. I know.' What he was thinking was inexcusable.

Almost blasphemous, when he considered his dead and injured friends. He must be drunk. He would go to bed.

Roger sat over the last half-inch of his whiskey and heard his son moving between bathroom and bedroom. When the house was quiet the father raked the ashes, stood the guard in front of the fire and went to his bedroom.

By mid-April Edward-John was home for the Easter holidays, Andreis had reached the point in his painting when he no longer required Annie to model for him and one Saturday afternoon, her wavering intentions bolstered by Iris, Hester had boarded the bus to Exeter where she had undergone the trauma of the selection and purchase of a frock. Coupons had been snipped from her ration book and several pound notes extracted from her purse. She had worn her new dress at supper that night and, although pleased with the compliments she received, had refused to join the girls when they left for an evening in the pub.

Mabel's grandmother, together with the two-year-old Arthur, had visited for a weekend. To enable the Hodges family to sleep together in one room, Iris had moved in with Taffy, an arrangement which she preferred and which, with Alice's approval, became permanent.

Arthur, looking older than in Mabel's photograph, hurled himself into the embrace of his sister, whom he called May-May, and spent most of the weekend with his plump arms locked round her neck, her thick waist or one or other of her massive thighs. She took him to the Bayliss farm and persuaded Ferdie to give him a ride on the tractor and on the quieter of the two carthorses. She sat him astride the most placid of the milking cows and showed him how to throw corn to the chickens. On the Monday she wept when her visitors left for London.

Winnie and Marion had succeeded in re-organising their social life and now that their whereabouts were known, servicemen from the several military training establishments and airbases in the vicinity contrived to collect them in staff cars and return them in the nick of time to the hostel on Saturday nights and sometimes during the week. Occasionally whole lorry loads of the girls would be borne off to dance halls in Exeter or barrack messes where, to recordings of Glenn Miller and Duke Ellington and sometimes to live military bands, they jitterbugged and quickstepped, pirouetting at arm's length. Or they could be found locked in a close embrace but conducting themselves with caution for they were, most of them, sensible, well-behaved young women, aware of what was required of them if they were to avoid the disaster of besmirched reputations or, worse still, of pregnancy. They strutted and, to some extent, they teased but only because they were expected to tease and enjoyed it as much as the young men enjoyed being teased. If one girl or another drank too many gin-and-oranges, then one girl or another would take her in hand, sit her down with a cup of tea or remove her to the safety of the Ladies until the army truck arrived to convey them, hot, tousled, hiccuping, giggly but intact, back to the farm.

Marion and Winnie seldom spent their evenings with the main group of the Lower Post Stone girls and they, more than the others, received gifts from the servicemen and, according to Rose, more than gifts. Once, stripping their beds on laundry day, Rose had discovered a Post Office book under Marion's pillow. The account was, unusually, in the names of both girls. Each week there were entries which, confirming Rose's darkest deductions, exceeded their combined Land Army wages. She confided her suspicions to her son, Dave, who had recently been briefly home on leave. The sight of her boy in khaki turned Rose's stomach.

Early on a wet Wednesday afternoon towards the end of April the lorry brought Winnie and Marion back to the farmhouse.

'It's her monthlies,' Marion announced. 'She came on when we was having our sandwiches.' Marion watched as Winnie eased herself onto one of the kitchen chairs and doubled up with pain. Her face was white and beads of perspiration stood on her forehead.

'Reckon I strained meself,' she said between gritted teeth. In the yard Fred sounded the horn of the idling truck and Alice, filling a hot-water-bottle for Winnie told Marion to get back to her afternoon's work. Marion hesitated.

'I'm worried about her, Mrs Todd!' she said miserably.

'And well you might be,' Rose snapped and then, drawing Alice aside, continued in a lowered voice. 'That be more than "monthlies", Alice! She needs to see the doctor and fast!'

They put Winnie into Fred's lorry and, Alice beside her, drove her to Ledburton where the local doctor examined her and had her admitted to the cottage hospital.

That evening, with both Alice and Winnie conspicuously absent, the girls ate the meal which Rose, for the first time, had prepared single-handedly. She told the hushed table what she knew, but not what she suspected, finally drawing the girls' attention to her own culinary achievement on their behalf.

'You are a wonder, Mrs Crocker,' Gwennan said nastily, her face hardening when Rose retaliated.

'Kind of you to say so, missy, and since you'm so smart you can slice up that loaf for tomorrow's packed lunches!'

Hester, on her way through to the scullery with a load of dirty plates, heard the sound of the returning truck and peered out of the low window into the twilight.

'The lorry's back!' she called. 'Missus Todd's getting out… But Winnie bain't with 'er!'

They sat Alice down at the table and gave her a cup of tea because, Rose insisted, she must be famished.

'They're keeping her in hospital for a few days,' Alice said, confronted with anxious, though in some cases merely curious, faces. 'She was asleep when I left. Is everything all right here?' Rose assured her that it was and that, as a gesture of helpfulness, the girls had volunteered to do the washing-up. The girls groaned good-naturedly and Annie began to collect the used cutlery.

'We don't have to do this, you know!' Marion whined but it was a muted protest.

As soon as the girls were occupied in the scullery and she had the warden's ear, Rose whispered, encouraging her to confide, 'The doctors didn't say what the matter is then?' Alice sipped her tea for a moment and then answered quietly that they had not but that she supposed it was as Marion had suggested. Winnie had been moving heavy bags of swedes and the pulling and dragging had proved too much for her. Disappointed, Rose bit her lip and considered sharing her suspicions with one or other of the girls but the one most likely to enjoy a scandal was Gwennan, whose tight-laced Welshness irritated Rose. Also, there were ramifications to the situation which were beginning to nudge at Rose and to alarm her.

In the scullery Gwennan had sidled up to Marion.

'Bet you won't try that again, eh!' she muttered as Rose approached with the last of the dishes, her sharp ears picking up Gwennan's words.

'I don't know what you're on about, Taff,' Marion whined defensively.

'Yes, you does, Marion!' Rose muttered, adding, still quietly but loudly enough for the other girls to hear her, 'and so do the rest of you. But if you knows what's good for you, you'll keep it to yourselves!' Gwennan, in her sing-song voice, demanded to know why.

''Cos if Mr Bayliss found out he'd have Winnie and Marion out of here so fast their feet wouldn't touch the floor!' Rose hissed.

'Well, they shouldn't have done it! It's disgraceful!' Gwennan snapped back.

'Of course they shouldn't!' Georgina said coolly. 'But if Mr Bayliss finds out about it he would hold Mrs Todd responsible!'

'If you ask me,' Gwennan continued, enjoying herself, 'Mrs Todd don't know what happened! She thinks Winnie hurt herself lifting swedes!'

Hester was following the conversation as an observer follows a tennis match, her head turning from one speaker to another, eyes wide and mouth ajar.

'But she did…! Didn't she?' she breathed, confused, searching the girls' faces. They groaned and Gwennan told her not to be so stupid.

'Reckon you're right, Taff,' Annie said, 'about Mrs Todd not knowing. And she mustn't know, 'cos if she did she'd probably feel obliged to tell Mr Bayliss and—' Annie stopped abruptly as Alice appeared in the doorway with her teacup and saucer. 'Nearly done now, Mrs Todd!' Annie continued brightly, filling the awkward silence, lifting the last plate out of the suds and inserting it into the wooden rack, next to its fellows. Rose suggested that Alice might like to eat her dinner, which would be ruined if kept waiting in the oven for much longer.

The following Saturday was Edward-John's tenth birthday. As Iris's twenty-second had fallen during the previous week it was decided that the two occasions should be jointly celebrated with a cake and candles at teatime.

James Todd had sent his son a selection of additional pieces to add to the already comprehensive Meccano set with which the boy played in an attic directly above the bathroom. Here, after the evening meal, well muffled against the cold, Edward-John spent as much time as his mother would allow him, meticulously constructing bridges, cranes and towers while the pipes gurgled, the lavatory cistern hissed, the distant strains of the gramophone, the untuned piano and from directly beneath him, the rise and fall of the girls' voices as they took their shared baths and rinsed out their smalls, floated up through the ill-fitting floorboards.

As Rose carried the birthday cake through to the recreation room, its candles illuminating the gloom of the cross-passage, Margery Brewster delivered Winnie back from the hospital.

Alice greeted them and invited them to join the birthday party. But Winnie declined and Marion took her friend by the arm.

'I'll see to her,' she said, drawing her towards the narrow staircase.

'Light duties for a week,' Margery brusquely informed Alice. 'Then she should be as good as new. I'll let Roger have the certificate.' She smiled at Edward-John and agreed to stay long enough to eat a slice of his birthday cake.

In their room Marion and Winnie exchanged glances.

'You OK, Win?' Marion asked, lighting their cigarettes. When her friend nodded she continued anxiously, 'At the hospital… Did anyone…?

'No. No one guessed what happened. When they told me I'd lost it,' Winnie said, exhaling, 'I made out it happened natural.' There was a pause.

'I'm ever so sorry, Win.'

'Not your fault.' Winnie said dully.

Marion stared at the floorboards. 'What bugs me is that sergeant! Struttin' around, not knowin' what he's done or what's 'appened!' she said bitterly.

'Well, nothin' 'as, 'as it! Well, not to 'im any road!'

'And here's you, looking like you've been hit by a Sherman bloody tank!'

Winnie drew in smoke. She was safely back in their room. She felt tired and her legs were a bit wobbly but she had survived. She felt almost magnanimous.

'It might not have been the sergeant…' she murmured, ashing her Woodbine in a saucer on their overcrowded dressing table. They sat, one on each of the two beds, and looked at each other. They heard a burst of applause from the recreation room, then, to a piano accompaniment, the girls sang 'Happy Birthday'. There was a tap on the bedroom door and when Marion asked who was there it was Mabel who pushed it open with her foot. She carried two plates of raspberry jelly, each decorated with a blob of Devonshire cream but her usually sunny face was overcast.

'Mrs Crocker said I was to bring you these,' she announced flatly. 'And Edward-John and Iris says do you want some of their cake...'

'So why the po-face, Mabel?' Marion's tone was defensive. 'Aren't you going to say you're sorry Win's been poorly?' There was a pause while Mabel struggled to hold her tongue and failed.

'She hasn't been poorly though, has she!' she said, her fleshy face colouring as her feelings revealed themselves. 'I weren't born yesterday! I know what went on! We all do!'

'Nosy bloody parkers then!' Marion snapped, dragging on her Woodbine, while Winnie, unable to withstand Mabel's accusing eyes, lowered her own and stared at the floorboards.

'You should of kept it! Not done that to it!' Mabel blurted.

'Who says?' Winnie demanded but her voice was fragile.

'I does! Poor little beggar... You got no right!' But Mabel's anger was dissolving into grief, leaving her with brimming eyes and the image of the small twist of gory tissue that should have been a child. Marion's shrewd eyes were narrowing.

'What's it to you, Mabel, eh?' she said. ''Ow come you're in such a state about it? Unless...' She saw Mabel blanch. 'Unless that "baby brother" of yours...!' Mabel's reaction confirmed her guess. 'Little what's-his-name...'

'Arfur!' Winnie breathed, her attention caught.

''E does look like you, Mabel! Very like you! 'E's your kid, in't 'e!' Mabel protested that she didn't know what Marion was on about. 'Wonder what your new fella would make of that then, eh?' Marion continued spitefully. 'Your Ferdie? Told him about it, 'ave you? Have you, Mabel?'

Mabel was blundering towards the bedroom door when she was confronted by the warden who had come up to check on Winnie. For a moment the three girls stared at Alice, who suggested that Mabel and Marion should go and join the birthday party. Closing the door behind them she sat on Marion's bed and regarded Winnie who seemed, understandably Alice thought, to be on the verge of tears.

'D'you reckon I done the right thing, Mrs Todd?' she blurted out and suddenly, before Alice could react, continued, the words tumbling out. 'Mabel thinks I done wrong!' For a moment Alice wondered what Mabel had to do with it. 'It's OK for her though!' Winnie went on, 'she's got her gran to look after her Arfur! But I ain't got no one, see!' She paused, registering Alice's astonishment as she suddenly, at last, understood the situation. 'Oh Gawd!' Winnie moaned as she identified the cause of Alice's surprise. 'I thought you knew, Mrs Todd! Mabel said everyone knew!

But you didn't, did you! All that stuff about me lifting the swedes...' Winnie began to laugh shakily. It could have developed into hysteria but she managed to stifle it. In the silence Alice recovered fast. She took Winnie's hand and stroked it saying quietly that it was not for her to judge and that with hindsight it is all too easy to be wise. 'I feel rotten about it, Mrs Todd, I do! Like I did the other time!' Winnie, blowing her nose and wiping her eyes, failed to see Alice's reaction to this last statement.

In the recreation room the girls were singing, 'For He's A Jolly Good Fellow' to Edward-John and Iris.

Later, while her son amused himself with his Meccano set, Alice took Rose into her room and told her what she had discovered about Winnie that afternoon. 'She is the first person I have ever really spoken to who has led that sort of life!' Alice said and noticed Rose's lack of surprise. 'You knew, Rose, you knew all along that Marion and Winnie were...'

'On the game?' said Rose and then hesitated, reacting to Alice's expression. 'S'pose I shouldn't say that, should I? But they was billeted in the village, see, and word gets around.'

'Gossip, Rose?'

'Bit more than that I reckon.' Rose paused. 'Anyhow, what are you going to do?'

'Do?'

'What will you tell Mr Bayliss and Mrs Brewster?' Before Alice had to answer this they were interrupted. Marion wanted a word in private with Mrs Todd. Rose left them.

Marion held out a Post Office book.

'It's mine and Win's,' she said. 'Look inside, Mrs Todd.' Alice took the book, turned the pages and scanned the columns of entries which were mostly in the same hand, which was that of the village postmistress. 'There. On the last page. That's what Win and I have saved since we come 'ere.' The balance was two hundred and fifty pounds, seventeen shillings and ninepence. Alice stared. 'It's more'n we could ever have saved from our wages,' Marion said. 'See, Win and I – from way back when we was in school...we knew we could never get what we want from just savin' our pay and it wasn't like we was pretty or clever or nothing. And our families couldn't give us a leg up like some... There's no future for girls like us, Mrs Todd. It were just factory work till someone wed you – if they wed you – and then a struggle to make ends meet for the rest of your life. Win and I didn't want that, see? There was only one thing we could do as would earn us the sort of money we need. And it'll only be until we get it. So we started doing that. Mostly all we done is sell the presents the boys give us... stockin's and scent and stuff...to the other girls for a bob or two... You're shocked, I suppose... I'm not makin' no excuses but everyone has to make some sacrifices to get what they want and it wasn't hurting no one, leastways not till Win got caught out... We put every penny we earnt in that book, Mrs Todd, and we reckon, in a couple of years, we'll have enough.' She stopped and searched the warden's face for her reaction.

'Enough…? Alice asked. 'Enough for what?' She found herself considering the possibility of Marion and Winnie as the joint proprietresses of a house of ill repute. 'What exactly are you saving up for, Marion?'

'A pub,' the girl answered firmly, her face hard with determination. 'That's what we want. That's what we're aiming for, Mrs Todd. Our own pub.' Alice felt very slightly relieved. 'Five hundred quid we'll need for a down payment,' Marion elaborated enthusiastically. 'Win's uncle'll apply for the licence 'cos they don't like givin' 'em to women.'

Alice was dumbfounded, uncertain whether her reaction was simply shock and disapproval or whether it contained a trace of admiration for the enterprise and determination of these two underprivileged girls. She was, however, incredulous that such a situation could have been running undetected, under her nose in the hostel she was hired to supervise. She stared at Marion, forcing herself to concentrate on the girl's next words. 'You see, Mrs Todd, most of the girls here are "good girls", right?' Alice smiled and heard herself say that she certainly hoped they were. 'I'm not sayin' as they don't enjoy theirselves,' Marion added. 'But, when it comes to it they…well…they draw the line, don't they… Which means there's a lot of fellas out there as is desperate for…well…for a girl who'll go a bit further, if you take my meaning, Mrs Todd.' Alice concealed a fleeting inclination to smile and Marion continued. 'There's Tommies from the camp and the Navy lads over at the Fleet Air Arm place and now there's the Yanks... They give us loads, see – candy and fags and stockin's and scent and undies – in return for a kiss and a cuddle! And sometimes...well... if they're nice fellas, for a bit of the other.' Marion glanced nervously at Alice. 'They know what our wages are, see, and the GI boys are that generous! They slip us a few quid. Sort of... as a present. But mostly it's the stockin's and make-up and ciggies and stuff – that we flog to the other girls. Not only the Post Stone girls, Mrs Todd, there's lots more land girls round about here. We're known, see, for having the things they want. It were dead easy when Win and I was living at the pub... But we manage... You didn't know nothing about it, did you!' Alice admitted that she had not.

'If I tell Roger Bayliss,' Alice said to Rose the following Monday morning on returning from a visit to Exeter, 'he'll dismiss Winnie and Marion and they'll go from bad to worse... Probably take rooms in some boarding house near an army base. At least while they're here there's some sort of safety net if anything goes wrong. They're amateurs, Rose. Their payment seems to be more in the form of gifts than professional fees.' Rose was unmoved.

'You're not hoping to reform them, by any chance?' she asked coldly.

'Do you think that's a possibility?'

'I do not!'

'Nor do I.'

'The place is crawling with servicemen,' Rose went on, peeling the last of a pile of carrots. 'All after one thing. There's some as seems to reckon a uniform gives 'em a licence to go on just as they please. What's to stop Winnie or Marion falling pregnant again? I'm surprised that staff nurse at the cottage hospital swallowed Winnie's story! She won't get away with "lifting swedes" a second time!

'I tried Doctor Strong,' Alice said and Rose laughed scornfully.

'For preventives?' she scoffed. 'He'll be no help on that score!'

'No. He wasn't. But I had a word this morning with the matron at Edward-John's school and she's put me in touch with a woman who runs a clinic in Exeter and has agreed to provide Marion and Winnie with contraceptives.' Rose was impressed. She stared at Alice with a respect that had now been growing for several weeks. 'Diaphragms, since it's obviously useless to expect the men to take precautions.'

'I thought only married ladies was allowed them things!' Rose exclaimed with a hint of disapproval.

'Officially,' said Alice 'But, on compassionate grounds, there are those who are prepared to bend the rules.'

'Stupid rules is meant to be bent,' said Rose who, although disinclined to condone Marion and Winnie's morals, enjoyed a suggestion of subversion.

'And as "cure" seems unrealistic,' Alice continued, 'we

shall try prevention. I've made appointments for them.'

'You reckon they'll keep 'em?'

'It will be a condition of my silence!'

Rose grew pink with approval of Alice's deviousness.

'So you'll not be tellin' Mr Bayliss, then?'

'Everyone believes I fell for Winnie's story. Having a reputation for naivety carries its own advantages, Rose! And it gives Marion and Winnie another chance here.'

'And you!' said Rose.

'And me.'

'I'm surprised at you!' Rose said, impressed.

'Me too!' said Alice.

It was not until later that night when Alice sat drowsing beside the ashes of her fire, Edward-John sleeping soundly at the far end of her still warm room, the farmhouse quiet in the long night, that she suddenly remembered Winnie's words, recalling them vividly, as though the girl was in the room with her. 'It's OK for her though,' Winnie had said, meaning Mabel. 'She's got her gran to look after little Arthur!' Suddenly Alice was wide awake. Mabel's resemblance to the little boy, her overwhelming affection for him and her distress at their parting, were suddenly explained.

Alice was now in possession of several new pieces of information about the young women in her care. Added to the fact of Winnie's abortion was her admission that this had not been her first. Another was that Mabel, huge, ugly, foul-smelling Mabel, was a mother, had been somebody's lover, however brief the liaison. Then there was Georgina's concern for Christopher and her increasing doubts about her own pacifism. Alice felt her sense of responsibility deepened by these complexities but, despite herself, smiled. Ten land girls, she had been informed. Only eight to start with. 'You just have to run the hostel,' Margery Brewster had said encouragingly. 'Order the food, see that it's cooked, make certain the girls are in by ten. And report any problems to me.'

With the completion of the sowing of the spring wheat, Jack arrived sullenly at Lower Post Stone having been instructed to take his orders from Mrs Todd regarding alterations to the kitchen there. For three days the farmhouse reverberated with hammer blows and the sound of sawing. The preparation of meals was disrupted and suppers were late.

Alice was unused to dealing directly with tradesmen. Previously her experience of plumbers, carpenters or gardeners had involved referring them to her husband or, in his absence, relaying to them his instructions. 'Mr Todd wants…' 'My husband thinks…' When work on the farmhouse kitchen was completed Alice realised with a pleasing frisson that it had been she alone who had decided on the precise position and height of the work surfaces, she who had thought of ways of utilising space and incorporating existing features. She had referred to no one apart from Rose whose input had in some instances been useful but the initiative and the responsibility had been hers, as was the credit for the final result.

The kitchen was transformed. Wide expanses of dapple-grey marble supported by solid oak framing provided surfaces where cabbage could be chopped, meat sliced, pastry rolled, sandwiches cut, bread buttered, fruit peeled, potatoes mashed and onions skinned. Below, on wide shelving, the huge pans and baking trays were stacked close to where they would be used, together with sieves, colanders, steamers and marmites. The dining table, its surface no longer required for the preparation of food, was moved to a position that not only allowed more space for the distribution and consumption of the land girls' meals but gave better access to both scullery and larder. Roger Bayliss inspected the work and was hugely impressed. He told Alice that he had been unaware of the importance of the layout of a kitchen and that he believed his neighbour, a woman who owned a small private nursing home, might be interested in picking Alice's brains regarding the organisation of her own kitchens. Flattered, Alice agreed to meet with the woman. Margery Brewster was also impressed, hinting that the kitchens in some of the other hostels under her supervision might benefit from Alice's ideas.

Before the transformation had been completed, and while the kitchen was in a state of turmoil, Alice had received a visitor.

'A Commander Maynard has come,' Rose had announced and Alice, overalled and with her hair tied up in a scarf, couldn't recall where or in what circumstances she had heard the name. It was not until the commander stepped, smiling, ducking his head under the low lintel of the kitchen door, that she remembered the incident of the confrontation between his staff car and her bicycle.

On this occasion he was here on official business and, after enquiring politely after her health, and having had the chaos of the kitchen explained to him, he stated it. Rose, from the scullery where she was scraping turnips, listened as attentively as Alice herself. As Camp Adjutant it was Oliver Maynard's responsibility to organise social events at which his men might meet with local civilians.

'Oh, yes,' said Rose and then lowering her voice. 'Local girls more likely!'

The commander continued, outlining his immediate project, which was the planning of a cricket match, his men versus Alice's girls.

'So…' he concluded persuasively, using every ounce of his considerable charm, 'do you think your young ladies would be interested, Mrs Todd?' In the background Rose's comment made both Alice and the commander smile.

'There's some that's interested in anything in trousies!' she announced curtly, intending to be heard.

'The third Sunday in May has been suggested,' the Commander continued. 'About three? Simply a bit of fun, you understand. We'd give them tea in the mess afterwards.' Ignoring Rose's disapproval, Alice said she thought the girls would love it.

One day, towards the end of her son's Easter holidays, Alice left Rose to prepare the evening meal and went with Edward-John to Exeter. James Todd had travelled down by train from London. He met his wife and his son in the foyer of the Rougemont Hotel, where he gave them lunch. The slices of roasted lamb were thin, grey and tough, the peas had come out of tins and the trifle which followed was watery. Nevertheless, Alice found herself charmed by the fact that she was eating food which she herself had not had to prepare. Afterwards they made their way through bomb-damaged streets to the cathedral close. James put a pound note into Edward-John's hand, pointed to a toy shop and suggested that the boy went to spend his money there, joining his parents when the cathedral clock struck three.

They found a secluded bench.

'You're looking well.' James sounded surprised. Almost, Alice thought, disappointed.

'I am well,' she said.

'I rather got the impression, when you started this job of yours, that you...' He paused, uncertain how to continue.

'That I was scared stiff of it?' she suggested, smiling. 'I was. I didn't think I'd be able to cope. But it seems I can. In fact,' she added lightly, 'I'm rather enjoying doing something more than simply taking care of you and Edward-John. Something useful. For the war effort, I mean.' She did not look at him but she sensed the indulgent smile and because of it, continued. 'I've become interested in the design of kitchens, James.' 'You've done what?' He half turned towards her.

'It was part of my Domestic Science syllabus, of course, but it isn't until you're really up against things in terms of the time and labour available for the preparation of meals that you realise how essential it is to organise space and surfaces and access to equipment.' She was aware of James's stunned silence and this drove her on. 'I redesigned the kitchen at the hostel, you see, and my boss was sufficiently impressed to recommend my services to a friend of his. And the Land Army rep has suggested to the Ag. Office that I visit a couple of quite large local hostels to streamline their kitchens. If they use my ideas I'd be paid for them. As a sort of consultant, I suppose.' Her husband appeared to be so taken aback that she heard herself asking him whether he minded her being employed in this way. He was astonished and said so. Alice laughed. 'I know!' she said. 'I was amazed, too! I seem to be rather good at it… And with the current labour shortage… What I'm doing could be quite important…' There was a silence. James was smiling again.

'Well…' he said eventually, 'I'm delighted you've found something that interests you, even if it is…' She guessed, correctly, that he was going to add 'only kitchens', and he apologised for sounding patronising. There was a silence. Then Alice said that she didn't know what had possessed her to ask him. 'Ask me what?' he said.

'Whether you minded… About me doing the consultancy work. Almost as though I have to have your permission! Why would I do that, do you suppose! Habit, perhaps.' James did not respond. A pigeon strutted up to them and regarded them quizzically with one, sharp bright eye. Unlike some of the people seated around the square, they had no food with them. Registering this, the bird moved off and Alice spoke again. 'I'm hoping that it might lead to…well, who knows…some sort of career. Anyway it should make it easier for you to say what you have come to say.' She waited.

James admitted that he had come to tell her that he needed his freedom to remarry and was about to elaborate when she interrupted him and said she would prefer not to be given the details. She told him that her cousin, whom he had met at their wedding and who was a solicitor, would handle the divorce. She took from her handbag a neatly folded sheet of paper on which she had previously written down the name and address of the cousin's firm. James took it from her and looked at it. 'I imagine he will ask you for details of whatever evidence he needs.' Alice glanced at her husband and smiled. 'You look surprised. Did you imagine I would make a scene? There wouldn't be much point, would there.' James did not reply and they both, at the same moment, caught sight of Edward-John, cheerfully making his way across the bright green grass towards them. Before the boy reached them James said, 'Alice...I'm so sorry.' Alice got to her feet. Smiling at her son, she asked James to spare her his apologies.

That night, after the girls were fed, the dishes washed and the next day's sandwiches cut, Rose brought a cup of cocoa through into Alice's room where she found her filling out a Ministry of Agriculture form. In response to Rose's inquisitive glance, Alice told her that having been encouraged to do so by Georgina, Annie Sorokova was going to attempt the Women's Land Army Forewoman's course. 'Mrs Brewster has asked me to endorse the application,' she said. 'I feel a bit like a headmistress!'

'Pretty rum sort of school!' Rose murmured and, hearing the clock striking ten, told Alice that all the girls, with the exception of two who had gone to the village pub, had returned. She challenged Alice to guess which two were still absent. When Alice named Winnie and Marion, Rose said, 'Who else!' adding, 'Come to think of it, I don't believe Mabel's in either.'

'She borrowed my bicycle again,' said Alice. 'She said Ferdie had invited her to play Monopoly.'

'Monopoly, eh!' said Rose, her inflection delivering precisely the element of suspicion needed to arouse Alice's concern. At that moment the sound of a car arriving at the garden gate heralded the boisterous return of Winnie and Marion, whose arrival coincided with Mabel's. Alice called out to the girls to lock the front door, wished them goodnight, confirming that all three of them responded and then, as they clattered up the staircase, she relaxed and sipped her cocoa. Rose replaced her own empty cup on its saucer and regarded Alice.

'Without wishing to pry,' she began, 'you look like a person what's got something off of their chest.' She saw Alice suppress a smile.

'"Without wishing to pry", Rose?' Rose had the grace to blush and asked Alice not to laugh at her. 'I'm not laughing at you,' Alice said and she paused, adding easily that it had proved less difficult than she had expected to discuss things with her husband. 'I had the advantage, I suppose. I knew what was coming! He was quite taken aback when I agreed to a divorce without the tears or the scene he'd been anticipating.'

'You're a bit upset though, I can tell,' Rose said, divorce, in her book, being every bit as serious as several, if not all, of the seven deadly sins. Alice admitted that of course, in a way, the afternoon had depressed her.

'But, when something you've been dreading actually happens you have this little space, don't you, before you have to face the next hurdle.' She drained her cup and smiled firmly at Rose. 'I think we should get to our beds now,' she said.

Chapter Six

At the end of April, which had been cold, windy and unusually wet, the wind backed suddenly to the south drawing mild air from the Azores and bringing with it the first swallows and house martins. Within days the girls had discarded their woolly vests, consigned their waterproof jackets to the linhay, pulled their sweaters off over their heads and were wearing their shirts unbuttoned at the neck. Winnie, Marion and Annie even went so far as to scissor the bottoms from their oldest dungarees and with these rolled up and their thick socks rolled down as far as their leather boots, exposed, from thigh to ankle, legs which quickly acquired a tan as matt and rich as the shells of the farmyard fowls. The sudden heat sent them home in the evenings with raging thirsts which Rose quenched with her home-made cordial, sharpened with citric acid in place of the unattainable lemons and flavoured with the young leaves of apple-mint which was bursting through the old grass under the orchard trees.

'I'm gonna strip off,' said Annie, trailing into the kitchen, boots and damp socks in her hand, bare feet relishing the cold stone floor, 'and lie on me bed starkers!'

'You'll do no such thing, miss!' Rose told her.

'It's sweated labour, that's what it is!' Marion grumbled, sitting heavily at the table. 'Hoeing those rows of turnips in this heat! Bloomin' endless they are! You wouldn't believe it!' She glared at Alice and Rose as though they were personally responsible for her exhaustion.

'Wouldn't I, now!' Rose snapped back. 'And if 'oeing upsets you just wait till 'ay-makin'! It'll be even 'otter then! When I was a nipper us all had to 'elp with turnin' the 'ay and then loadin' it! Soon as us could walk they'd put us to it! Mr Bayliss's father were boss in them days! Worked us till us dropped he did! Sixpence a day he give us kids! So stop your grumblin', Marion, and cool off with a nice sip of my cordial!' She ladled the liquid into half a dozen tumblers. 'And a thank you wouldn't come amiss neither!' Rose was only slightly mollified when the girls obediently, if grudgingly, chorused their thanks.

'Needs a drop of gin to liven it up, Rose,' Marion said, pulling a face but pushing forward her glass for more.

'Mrs Crocker to you!'

'Always gets the last word, does Mrs C!' Winnie murmured.

'And I'm not deaf, Winnie!' Rose called over her shoulder as she went into the pantry for more cordial. The girls smirked.

'She does, too!' Annie smiled, lowering her voice. 'Always the last word, our Sergeant Major!'

Soon everyone became used to the warm days and balmy evenings. Until darkness fell, later each succeeding night, groups of girls took to sitting out on the coping stones of the garden wall, their voices rising and falling in the twilight, the smoke from their cigarettes lifting and fragrant, while bats dived and scattered as sunset after sunset silhouetted the familiar hills. In the recreation room, to a Glenn Miller record, Annie was teaching Hester how to waltz: 'left, two three, right, two three...that's it! You're coming on a treat...'

One morning Alice encountered Andreis sitting in the sunshine, his back to the barn wall, his pale eyes squinting into the light. This was unusual. Despite her urging him to get more fresh air, Andreis had always shaken his head, saying he must use all his time to work on his painting. Now he caught her quizzical look.

'It is finished, Missus Todd. It is all done. Everything I have to say is painted!'

'Bravo, Andreis!' He responded to her smile with a shrug and Alice sensed that the completion of the painting marked the onset of a crisis for Andreis. Until now it had occupied him totally. Both physically and emotionally he had driven himself to this point, beyond which the future fell away and his mind, occupied for so long by the demands of his work, ran uncontrollably back to the situation that had inspired it. To Amsterdam. To his occupied country. To his family and friends, some in hiding, most transported to who knew where. Many, almost certainly, dead.

'This calls for a celebration,' Alice announced, her warmth briefly irresistible to him. 'Come to supper!' He smiled and Alice realised she had never before seen his face lose the grave, preoccupied look that haunted it. 'Come tonight! The girls would love it!' From the kitchen window she saw him, in the afternoon, stripped to the waist and with his head under the yard pump. He arrived, scrubbed and wearing a clean white shirt, carrying small posies of wild flowers, one for each girl, the stems bound together with twisted grass stalks. They sat him at the head of the table and watched as he relished a large helping of Rose's hotpot. This was followed by a wedge of suet pudding with raspberry jam spooned over it and decorated, in honour of the occasion, with a dollop of Devonshire cream. When Rose offered him the last slice of the pudding he leant back, smiling, in his chair.

'Thank you,' he said graciously. 'But no. I am absolutely fed up.' When the girls, and even Alice and Rose, collapsed into laughter he looked from face to face in smiling confusion and apologised for his poor English. 'Baint your

English that be poor, Andreis! 'Tis their manners!' Rose said, controlling her own laughter sooner than the rest while Marion struck her plate with her pudding spoon and shouted, 'Speech!'

Andreis got to his feet, smiling and nodding his thanks to the circle of bright faces round the table. The girls were young and tousled. Their suntanned skin was glossy. Their eyes clear. There were freckles and a few pimples. Dark roots were visible in Marion's bleached hair, Rose's ageing skin was weather-beaten and Alice, despite her smile, showed signs of the strain under which her situation had placed her. As he looked at them Andreis's expression changed and they, seeing this change, reacted to it, their smiles slowly fading as he began to speak.

'I have decided something,' he said, his face now so grave that the girls immediately sensed something which altered the mood of the evening and sobered it. 'You see…I came here from cowardice,' he began and when the girls murmured and shook their heads and Alice said, 'No, Andreis!' he silenced them. 'Yes,' he said, 'it is true. Cowardice. My excuse is that I did not know – no one did then – what was to happen to Jewish people when the Gestapo came into the Netherlands. There were rumours, yes, but by the time it was known what their orders were, those Jews that had not left – had not run, as I ran – were trapped. I do not know what has happened to my family and my friends! There are no letters, you see! Nothing! Only stories of doors kicked down in the night. Of people taken. Put onto trains to God knows where and then…nothing,' The girls sat, barely breathing as they listened. 'So I must go back. I do not know what will happen. Whether I can fight…or maybe I can only die… But I cannot stay any more here, in this peaceful place. I cannot!'

When, on the following morning, Roger Bayliss arrived at the hostel, Alice was uncertain of the reason for his visit. Usually he had some query or other, regarding the day-to-day affairs of the hostel. But on this occasion he seemed preoccupied and unable to communicate his concerns. Was he, Alice wondered, worried about Christopher? She was surprised to discover that the object of his concern was not his son but Andreis.

'He came to see me this morning,' Roger began. 'I gather you know about this plan of his to return to Holland?' After Alice had provided a cup of coffee and Roger was sitting in her room, drinking it, he continued. 'It doesn't make a lot of sense, you know. I mean… What does he think will happen to him? His family are missing. Amsterdam, as I understand the situation, is crawling with Gestapo and there are some pretty ugly rumours about, regarding their treatment of the Jews.'

'Doesn't he intend to fight?' Alice, it had to be said, had not given a lot of thought to the details of Andreis's plans.

'I assumed it was his intention to join the Resistance,' Roger continued, 'but he seems consumed with a desire to return to Amsterdam. If he does he would be walking into almost certain arrest. Probably transportation to one of these labour camps we hear about. Possibly death. He must know this but he doesn't seem to care. Have you any idea when he plans to leave us?' Alice said she hadn't but would try to find out.

It was a week before the cricket match that a girl arrived, appearing, during supper, in the doorway that opened from the yard into the kitchen and which, that night, because of the warm weather, was standing open.

Her Land Army uniform was clearly too large for her. The breeches were held up by a belt and the short sleeves of her aertex shirt reached almost to her elbows. The hat sat too low on her head, constraining her shoulder-length blonde hair, the jacket was slung over one shoulder and she carried a small suitcase. The girls stopped eating and stared. Rose, ladle in hand, hesitated over the pan of rice pudding.

'Nora Fuller,' the girl announced in the silence. 'I was told to come.' Alice was baffled. 'By the rep,' the girl concluded, firmly.

'Mrs Brewster sent you?' Alice asked.

'That's right,' the girl said, 'Mrs Brewster.'

'It's most odd,' Alice went on. 'She was here earlier in the week. We are expecting another two girls soon… But she didn't say anything about… It must have slipped her mind… Not like her, though… And I haven't had any paperwork…'

'They…she…said to tell you it would follow,' said Nora.

'The paperwork, I mean. In the post.' She spoke clearly and without a detectable regional accent. This immediately provoked a low level of hostility from Marion, Winnie and Gwennan. Alice invited the girl to take a place at the table and Rose produced a plate of shepherd's pie and a knife and fork to eat it with.

'Best get that inside you, dear,' she advised. 'Those breeches'll drop off of you else!' The girls giggled.

'They're much too big, I know!' said Nora. 'There's a shortage of small sizes. They're going to send me a replacement set as soon as they can.'

The introduction of the unexpected arrival inhibited the girls and they spooned up their rice pudding, their eyes on the newcomer, in an unusual silence.

Mabel who had several times during the course of the meal opened her mouth to speak (although no one had noticed) and then thought better of it, finally took the plunge.

'Mrs Todd,' she began uncertainly, catching Alice's attention and then continuing in a rush. 'It's me brother, Ernie.' She stopped, unsure how to proceed.

'Your brother?' Alice enquired vaguely, her mind on the decision she was going to have to make regarding which of the available beds would be the most suitable for Nora.

'E's got leave. And 'e's comin' down to see me next Sat'day.'

'That'll be nice, Mabel,' Alice responded, brightly.

'Yeah. Only 'e ain't got nowhere to stay and 'e can't afford the pub and please can 'e kip down in the 'ayloft? 'E's due back at Caterham on the Sunday. Please, Miss. Just the one night. 'E won't be no trouble, honest.' It was against the rules of course and Alice knew that Rose would not have allowed it. But Alice had seen Mabel's photo of her brother, a scrawny boy, lost in his army uniform and looking barely older than Edward-John.

'Very well,' Alice said and everyone heard the sharp intake of Rose's breath and saw the smile spread across Mabel's shiny face.

'Ta,' she breathed, pushing back her chair and rising from the table in a cloud of warm, pungent air, for she had not yet taken her bath and the day's sweat was still salty and sweet on her skin. 'That's ever so nice of you, Mrs Todd!'

'He may not come in the house after supper, Mabel!' Alice called sharply after her. 'And he must be on his way by seven on the Sunday morning.' Mabel promised no and yes. Rose rolled her eyes. Alice ignored her and decided that Nora could have the room which had been Taffy's before she had moved in with Iris.

With the exception of Georgina, who had been forced into games of cricket by her brother Lionel and his schoolfriends, none of the girls had ever bowled or batted before. So the match between Alice's land girls and Oliver Maynard's young Fleet Air Arm trainees was much more of a social occasion than a sporting one. The girls, unsuitably dressed in frocks or blouses and skirts, stepped doubtfully up to the crease when Georgina won the toss and chose to bat and although she raised everyone's expectations by hitting two fours and a six in the first over their hopes were dashed when Gwennan, to cries of 'Come on, Taff! Give it a good belting!', saw the ball moving fast in her direction, flung aside her bat and ran, screaming from the pitch. Annie proved a better partner for Georgina but after she was dismissed for three and Winnie had ducked instead of addressing a moderately fast delivery and Marion had been caught without scoring, the innings was soon over. The young men played gallantly, allowing Georgina and Annie between them to take three quick wickets. But the girls' score was soon reached and overtaken and the players gratefully trooped into a Nissen hut where afternoon tea was to be served.

Alice was sitting in dappled sunlight, at a small table outside the hut, enjoying a second cup of tea and the company of Oliver Maynard, when Rose, delighted to have been invited to join the occasion, excused herself for interrupting but needed a word with the warden.

'It's Nora,' she said. 'She come over funny just before the match. So Fred's drove her back to the hostel. On'y I thought I should tell you. Fred says as he'll be back for the rest of us as arranged. All right?' Alice said it was all right but she knew Rose well enough to perceive that there was more to this situation than she felt inclined to divulge in front of Captain Maynard. While Alice sipped her tea and responded to her host's conversation, wondering what the complication could be, a young officer approached.

What is it, John?' Oliver asked him. Alice paid little attention to the murmured conversation until she heard the young man asking about an Eleanor Fullerton whom he was certain he had seen among the party of land girls but who was no longer with them.

'It's just, well…it's just that I thought she was someone I know. The cousin of a chap I went to school with, actually. Could have sworn it was Eleanor. Then, when I went to speak to her, they said she'd gone. Headache or something…' The boy caught the blank looks passing between Alice and Oliver. 'Sorry, sir. A case of mistaken identity probably. Didn't mean to interrupt your tea!' He smiled at Alice, excused himself and left them.

In the Nissen hut, which served as a mess and was shared with a contingent of American GIs, Hester Tucker and Reuben Westerfelt were standing at opposite ends of the long, narrow building, their eyes locked. A slow blush was colouring Hester's cheeks. She stood, stock still, lips just parted, as Reuben made his way down the length of the space between them, in his left hand, a doughnut on a cardboard plate, in his right, a glass of lemonade and on his face a sweet, diffident smile.

Reuben, the eldest of three brothers, had been due to leave school the day after the recruiting officers arrived in the small town of Bismarck in the state of North Dakota where Reuben senior, a third-generation immigrant, owned a modest general store. He sold petrol from two pumps out front and, in a garage next to the shop, ran an auto repair business. As the township grew and his sons reached manhood, Reuben senior planned on overseeing a rewarding expansion of this family enterprise and was less than pleased when his namesake announced that he had enlisted in the US marine corps. There had been a certain amount of patriotic pride in evidence when, together with half his high school year, and while the town band played a Souza march, Reuben junior boarded an army bus and was driven off towards the highway. It was only when familiar landmarks fell away that he and his fellows began to comprehend the enormity of the decision they had made that day. At times, over the succeeding weeks, Reuben junior had longed for home. His throat had swelled at the thought of his mom and even his pa. But mostly he had been kept so busy with training, eating or sleeping that he barely noticed that he was being changed from a homesick boy into a robust young man, able to operate the machinery of war and to run, a two-inch mortar plus its ammunition strapped to his shoulders, for as many miles as he was ordered to and to obey instructions, whatever they were, without questioning them. Reuben Westerfelt was, by the start of his nineteenth year, an infantryman, his existence bounded by the life he was living and the men he was living it with. They were shipped to England, crossing what they boldly referred to as 'the pond' in a convoy harassed by German U-boats. Then, on a fine English summer afternoon, after watching the Fleet Air Arm boys play this crazy, British game they call cricket against a bunch of girls, he saw her. She was wearing a blue frock that matched her eyes. Her hair framed her small face in a pale gold haze. She was standing at the far end of a Nissen hut and she was looking at him. As he stood, transfixed, he knew that that image of her would stay with him for as long as he lived. Everyone and everything in the hut dissolved into a vague blur as he made his way towards her, lemonade in one hand, doughnut in the other. Marion, her make-up slipping slightly, what with the exertion of the cricket match and now the clammy warmth of the Nissen hut, watched Reuben and Hester for a moment, her expression briefly softening, then, smirking, she nudged her friend, 'Look, Win! Love's young dream!'

That evening the girls were so full of the buns (which their GI hosts had called 'muffins'), biscuits ('cookies') and cakes ('pastries') that they were unenthusiastic about the light supper – two slices of spam and a leaf or two of limp lettuce with bread and margarine – which Rose produced for them.

Alice watched Nora clear her plate and sip her cup of cocoa. She was, when Alice asked her, quite recovered from her headache.

'I'm fine now, thank you,' she had replied to Alice's

enquiry and she went, with Edward-John, up into the attic where the two of them had taken to playing for hours at a time with his Meccano set, constructing bridges and towers and fortresses until Alice insisted that it was way past her son's bedtime.

'Reckon there's something funny going on with that girl,' Rose announced when she and Alice were alone in the kitchen. 'Don't it seem queer to you, how she seems happier playin' with your Edward-John than spendin' time with the girls? Bit young for her age, wouldn't you say.' Alice said that Meccano was quite educational and in her opinion it was rather nice that Nora and Edward-John shared an enthusiasm for it. Rose, unconvinced, continued, 'And there was something going on at that cricket match. One of them young officers kept starin' at Nora. Couldn't take his eyes off of 'er. Then she comes up to me, "Oh, Mrs Crocker," she says, "I am feeling unwell and I think I should go back to the farm and lie down." Unwell my eye,' said Rose. 'It was him starin' as upset her! That was obvious!'

'Perhaps she was shy,' Alice tried. 'Some girls don't like being stared at by strange young men!' Rose shrugged but seemed prepared to accept Alice's explanation for Nora's behaviour.

'Not like our Hester then!' she said and when Alice looked at her in surprise, went on, 'Didn't you see 'er with that GI? Nice-looking lad. She introduced me to him. "This is Reuben, Mrs Crocker," she says, all pink and smiley.

"Bismarck, he comes from. In North Dakota, USA!" That proud of him, she were and very pleased with 'erself, too! Would you believe it! Our little Hester! A few months ago she wouldn't say boo to a goose!'

The Sunday morning following the cricket match proved a difficult one for Alice. During the course of it there were three unconnected incidents, two of which reflected badly on Alice herself and a third, which cast a terrible and lasting gloom on the farm and its occupants.

The first incident involved Mabel.

'Though I'm not one to tell tales,' Gwennan began in her clipped, self-righteous Welsh voice, 'I thought you should know that I saw Mabel and her brother come out of the barn about an hour ago. Her hair was all mussed, Mrs Todd, there was bits of straw stuck to her jumper and she was carrying one of the blankets off her bed!'

Mabel was contrite. 'After we got back from the pub I showed 'im where 'e was to sleep, Mrs Todd. But it was ever so dark in that loft and the wind was 'owlin' somethin' 'orrible and there was things scuffling about in the straw!'

'You slept out there with him?' Alice was aghast at this breach of her trust.

'He was that scared, Mrs Todd. I said as I'd just stay with 'im for a bit and then we got chilly and I fetched a blanket. We was warmer then and I must of nodded off. Next thing it were mornin'. He left before seven, like you said, Mrs Todd. He'll be well on 'is way back to camp by now!'

Alice had been grateful for this last piece of news and as the girls appeared in the kitchen, helping themselves to cereal and toast and relishing the prospect of a Sunday to spend as they wished, she considered what she should do about Mabel's breach of discipline. She was inclined to let the incident pass unreported to either Margery Brewster or to Roger Bayliss himself but Gwennan was unlikely to hold her tongue about what she had seen and would almost certainly be unable to resist the temptation to stir up trouble for Mabel as well as for Alice herself, as the person who was, after all, responsible for keeping the girls in order.

Alice was sipping a second cup of tea and making a list of things which needed to be done in preparation for the evening meal when a car nosed down the lane and drew up outside the farmhouse gate.

Moments later Alice was surprised when Margery Brewster came briskly into the kitchen. She was followed first by a stout, middle-aged woman in a tweed suit, then by Oliver Maynard with the young officer who had interrupted their tea on the previous afternoon. A chair scraped back and Nora, white-faced, was on her feet.

Alice took the visitors, together with Nora, through to the recreation room, leaving the half-dozen girls, wide-eyed, in the kitchen and Rose, who was radiant with the pleasure of having been right all along about Nora, happily stacking the dirty breakfast plates.

In the recreation room they seated themselves awkwardly

on the old sofas and easy chairs, Nora glowering at John and the tweed-suited woman, who was introduced to Alice as a Miss Singer, headmistress of Nora's boarding school, glaring at her pupil.

'How could you, Eleanor?' Miss Singer demanded. 'Have you any idea of the anxiety you have caused? Your parents have been desperately worried about you and I, as the person responsible for you, have been up all night, trying to find you! If it hadn't been for Captain Howard,' here she smiled tightly at John, 'who knows how long it would have taken us to track you down!'

'Why did you do it, Eleanor?' John Howard asked more gently. 'There's been a hell of a panic, you know?' Eleanor looked at the floor.

'Because I hate school!' she said. 'I'm useless at lessons!' She nailed John with accusing eyes. 'Why did you have to be at that stupid cricket match! And why tell on me! I just thought I could be a bit useful, working on the land and you have to see me and blab and ruin it all! Everyone but me is having such fun in this war!' She hesitated, looking from one to another of her audience and sensing their extreme disapproval. 'I mean… I didn't mean…' she fumbled on into silence.

While Eleanor fetched her belongings, Margery Brewster asked Alice to explain how it had been possible for the girl to arrive and to remain at the farm for almost a week without Alice contacting the Exeter office.

'She was very plausible, Margery,' Alice began. 'She told me the paperwork from your office was in the post. She was in uniform. She—' Here Alice was interrupted by Miss Singer.

'I can explain that!' she snapped. 'We have a land girl who cultivates the kitchen garden at the school. While she was on leave Eleanor must have taken her uniform from the shed where it's kept! Stolen it, in fact! Then she told us she was expected at home for the weekend and by some clerical oversight...' Here she blushed with embarrassment. 'We assumed that was where she was... Until John Howard, here, telephoned her parents and told them he thought he'd seen Eleanor with a bunch of land girls! Appalling behaviour! Her family are quite distraught to discover that she had, in fact, been missing for almost a week!'

As the car moved off, Eleanor, wedged in the back seat, searched Alice's face for signs of forgiveness.

'I'm ever so sorry, Mrs Todd,' she said. 'I didn't mean to get you into trouble. I just didn't think!'

'Well, perhaps, now,' Alice said soberly, 'you understand that "not thinking" is a very foolish thing to do. Particularly when there is a war on!' Alice glanced at Margery and saw, to her surprise, a trace of a quickly suppressed smile.

'Silly child!' Margery said, almost to herself as the doors of the car were slammed. 'How on earth did she think she was going to get away with that!'

'Thanks to me she did get away with it!' Alice had been

right. Margery was trying not to smile.

'Poor kid,' she murmured, making her way towards her own car and settling herself into the driving seat. 'Anything else I should know about, Alice?'

Alice shook her head, smiled and closed the door of Margery's car. Margery wrestled with her gear lever and told Alice she'd pop over during the coming week.

It was around midday that Georgina's brother Lionel arrived on his motorbike to take her home for a family lunch. He found his sister sitting on the garden wall with Annie.

'You two have met before, haven't you?' Georgina asked, remembering her arrival at the farmhouse three months previously. Lionel propped his motorcycle.

'Only very briefly,' he said, pulling off the gauntlet gloves, leather helmet and goggles he wore when riding his Royal Enfield.

'Well then, let me introduce you properly,' his sister said, becoming aware of her brother's reaction to Annie and hers to him. 'Hannah-Maria Sorokova, known as Annie, meet Lionel Horatio Webster, known as Li!' They shook hands and then stood, smiling. 'Got a problem with the bike, Li?' Georgina asked and when Lionel assured her he hadn't, she said she thought she had heard it backfire as it approached the farmhouse.

'No,' Annie said, 'that was a gunshot from somewhere behind the barn. Probably someone shooting rabbits.' She smiled at Lionel, conscious of his attention to her.

'Not Andreis, though,' Georgina said. 'He's leaving here tonight. Must go and say goodbye when I get back.' She was buttoning her jacket and climbing onto the pillion seat. 'Come on, Li. Mother'll kill us if we're late for her lunch!'

It was evening when Georgina returned, the bike purring down the lane. She knew at once that something was wrong. A cluster of the girls were standing near the porch. The south wind had veered north. The girls looked cold and miserable. As Georgina dismounted Annie ran down the path towards her.

'It's Andreis,' she said flatly. 'Oh, Georgie, he shot himself.'

They should have known something was wrong. Some of them had known. Roger Bayliss had been aware of the circumstances of Andreis's desertion of his family and his homeland and that he was temperamentally incapable of joining an allied army and fighting for his country. Winnie had once seen him, when a stray Messerschmitt had swooped low over the farm, fling himself onto the ground, wrap his arms round his head and lie, quivering, long after the sound of the plane had faded to silence. Annie, posing for him while he painted onto the whitewashed partition in the barn his reaction to the Nazi's treatment of the Jews, had seen him possessed by a desperation which had alarmed her. And Alice, preoccupied as she was by her responsibilities, had sensed that his ambitions to return to

Holland and in some way to involve himself in resistance to the German occupation were no more than a fantasy. True, she had counselled him to reconsider but she had not done enough, none of them had, to recognise the impossibility, or the obvious consequences of his decision, or to predict and maybe even prevent this tragic outcome of it.

Fred, checking his rabbit snares, had found him, at about three o'clock that afternoon, in the field behind the barns. By then he had been dead for several hours, all his blood having seeped out of a wound that had shattered the femoral artery in his left thigh. The sound that Georgina had thought was her brother's bike backfiring was, almost certainly, the shot that killed him.

Wartime protocol meant that his body had, initially, to be collected by the military police. In a few days' time, after an inquiry into the circumstances of what was referred to as 'the accident' and of his presence on Lower Post Stone Farm, his remains would be released to his sponsor, Roger Bayliss, and could then be returned to his native land for burial.

The girls lit the fire in the recreation room and sat, stunned, watching the flames. Edward-John slept soundly in his mother's room. In the kitchen Alice and Rose prepared Monday's sandwiches in silence.

It was dark when Annie came into the kitchen.

'We're going over to the barn, Mrs Todd,' she said. 'We want to look at Andreis's painting. You and Rose can come with us if you want to.' At first Alice was reluctant.

But the girls, even Winnie, Marion and the cold, detached Gwennan, were gathering in the cross-passage and moving through to the linhay for their boots and galoshes.

A fine rain, lit by wavering shafts of light from their flashlights – the use of the outside light was forbidden because of the blackout – drifted between the farmhouse and the barns as they crossed the yard. One by one they climbed, hand over hand, up the ladder and into the loft which had housed Andreis for almost two years. The blind across the skylight was drawn so they were able to light the three oil lamps. They stood them on the floorboards under the painting. With the illumination from the lamps augmented by the roving pools of concentrated light from their half-dozen flashlights, the picture swam into focus.

The girls, flanked by Alice and Rose, stared at the huge creation and fell silent in the face of the intensity of Andreis's depiction of the driven people. Jackbooted soldiers herded abject civilians across a landscape of blitzed towns and pillaged farmland, the refugees, some clutching young children, raised their arms in gestures of fear, eyes straining for last glimpses of neighbours, homes and family. The piece was slightly surreal and largely symbolic. The land girls were bewildered by the fact that all the women resembled Annie and the men Andreis himself. Unused to paintings, they learnt, some of them, how to understand what Andreis had spread before them and even those whose intellect remained challenged by the work were at some level affected by it.

There was a loud gulp from Hester and, as Alice looked from one to another of her charges, she saw several pairs of brimming eyes and wet cheeks.

'Right,' she said, her voice less steady than she intended. 'We should go now.' She turned Hester and moved her towards the ladder. While Rose extinguished the lamps, the girls, one by one, their eyes lingering on the now almost invisible colours and shapes of the painting, lowered themselves down the ladder and into the gloom of the cowshed where the old mangers and stalls stood, disused since Roger Bayliss had moved his dairy herd up to the higher farm.

Rose filled mugs with milky cocoa which the girls carried into the recreation room. They pulled the old sofas closer to the fire and, together with Alice and Rose, sat sipping, united by the disaster of that day.

Then Annie was on her feet, her hands tight around her mug of cocoa.

'That painting,' she began, in a clear, firm voice. 'It can't stay there. The barn is collapsing and the roof is starting to leak. It must be taken somewhere where it will be safe and where people, lots of people, can see it. We have to do this...for Andreis. And for all the people in his picture... And everyone in this war who have... People like Chrissie... who...' Her throat closed and she turned to Georgina for support, sitting down suddenly, as Georgina began to speak.

'That's a brilliant idea, Annie! There's a War Artist's

thing, isn't there? Some of the big names are already commissioned, people like Stanley Spencer and John Minton and John Nash...to paint the war! To...sort of...record it, for the future.' She got to her feet. A wing of glossy dark hair swung forward and was hooked briskly back behind her ear, revealing wide eyes which, in the firelight, glittered with energy and determination. 'My brother's godfather is a sort of curator at the Victoria and Albert Museum. He'll know what we should do! I'll write and ask him! Now!'

Taking her cue from Alice, Rose heaved herself to her feet and began collecting the empty cocoa mugs.

'Tomorrow, Georgina, my dear,' Alice said firmly. She was aware that her immediate duty as warden was to move the girls on from the tragedy of Andreis's death and to restore, as quickly as possible, the rhythm of life at the hostel. 'It's late and everyone's exhausted. Bed now. For everyone. Goodnight, Hester. Goodnight, Gwennan.' She spread the embers across the hearth and stood the guard in front of them. The girls, calmer now and each dealing in her own way with the day's disaster, stretched and yawned, wished Alice goodnight, their voices fading as their footsteps began to thump up the wooden stairs. 'Night, Mrs Crocker!' 'Night, Georgie!' 'Night, Taff.'

Annie remained at the fireside, staring at the glowing ashes. Alice sat down beside her.

'It's hardest for you, Annie,' she said quietly. 'You knew him better than any of us.'

'Yeah. I did. And I probably knew better than anyone how sad he was. More than sad. More like tortured. Tormented, even... He felt so guilty, Mrs Todd. And ashamed of not being how he thought he should be. Or doing what he thought he should do. And now... Well, it's all over, isn't it. And in a way, I'm glad, Mrs Todd. Know what I mean? All his unhappiness has stopped. I reckon that's what people mean when they say "rest in peace". Well, I hope he is. In peace, I mean.'

Rose became aware of Oliver Maynard's feelings for Alice long before Alice herself did. He had taken to dropping in at the farmhouse with phrases like 'just happened to be passing', or 'thought I'd look in on you on my way to...' But Rose knew only too well that Lower Post Stone Farm wasn't 'on the way' to anywhere, nor would anyone who hadn't lost their way 'be passing' it. Unlike Rose, Alice was unaware of the way Oliver's eyes followed her as she moved about the farmhouse kitchen making him a cup of tea or coffee, depending on the time of day. Nor did Alice see how appreciatively his gaze lingered, taking in the narrow waist and the slender legs and ankles which were visible now that the weather was warmer and she wore blouses and skirts instead of her winter trousers, bulky jumpers and thick boots. Rose saw him watching her elegant hands as she poured milk into his teacup and slid it across the surface of the kitchen table towards him.

On the day after the shooting Oliver arrived at midday, solemnly offered his condolences to both Alice and Rose and suggested that, in view of the depressing time they were all having, he should take Alice out to lunch.

'You go,' Rose had said, when Alice had hesitated. 'Do you good.'

The pub was a low, thatched building with wooden tables set out on a terrace overlooking the water meadows of the River Exe. In spite of the war, or perhaps because of it – gamekeepers where in short supply – there was salmon on the menu. Poached and dressed with dill and cream, it arrived at their table with a crisp Hock and a bowl of tiny new potatoes and was followed by freshly picked strawberries still warm from the midday sun. Alice was enchanted. Oliver, like most naval officers, had exquisite manners. He was assured, attentive and witty. Alice rediscovered, as she sat enjoying his company and the delightful food and wine he was giving her, the sense of her own self-esteem which James's desertion had threatened to destroy. In easier times she had known how to respond to the good things in life. She had been witty and self-confident. Now, these half-forgotten qualities were returning. The sunshine and the wine were warming her, making her skin glow and a sense of well-being flow through her. What if her husband had left her in favour of a younger – but in fact, rather mousy – girl? What if she was overworked, underpaid and almost constantly exhausted? What if her hair needed properly cutting, her fingernails were broken and her once smooth hands had become reddened by hard work in the hostel kitchen? This man, sitting opposite her, treating her to a splendid meal, was finding her – at the very least – good company. She sipped her wine and made him laugh at her account of her first meeting with Roger Bayliss but, if anyone had suggested to her that Oliver, if not already in love with her, was becoming seriously attracted to her, she would have been astonished.

'Tell me about your wife,' she said suddenly and was slightly surprised by his reaction. His face seemed to stiffen and his smile became fixed and tight. 'At the cricket match,' Alice continued innocently, 'you told me about…Diana, was it?' His charm seemed to slide back into place. He smiled at Alice. It was a warm, reassuring smile. They had finished their strawberries. Oliver shook the cigarettes forward in his pack of Capstans.

'D'you mind if I smoke?' he asked smoothly and when she shook her head, offered her a cigarette, spun the wheel on his lighter, leant forward to light hers and then his own, inhaling deeply and then blowing the smoke carefully to one side.

'Well?' Alice persisted, almost playfully. He was a married man, she a married woman. What could be more natural than for her to enquire about his wife? 'Tell me about Diana!' Then Alice saw a hardness in his face that she had not noticed before. Or perhaps it had not been there before.

He ashed his cigarette and with his eyes lowered, said, 'Forgive me, Alice, but I don't want to spoil our perfectly lovely lunch by talking about my wife.' Alice felt suddenly chilled.

'I'm so sorry!' she said. 'I didn't realise...'

'Didn't you?' He continued to avoid her eyes. 'I would have thought you might have considered it odd that, with a permanent posting down here, Diana did not feel inclined to join me? Just as it seems odd to me that your husband doesn't appear to want you with him in...where is it?'

'Cambridge,' Alice said dully.

'Yes. Cambridge. I remember now.' Their eyes engaged and held. She searched his face and found nothing more sinister, now, than a frank vulnerability. 'It wouldn't be unreasonable would it, Alice, to assume that both of us have – what these days are described as "marital problems"?' He paused, blowing smoke. 'Probably would never have happened to either of us if this war hadn't barged into our lives. But it did barge in. And problems have developed.' He paused again. 'Haven't they, Alice.' It was a statement, not a question. Alice nodded and swallowed the small amount of wine that remained in her glass. 'So what I would like to suggest, my dear, if I may, is that we, you, Alice and me, Oliver' – he made it, Alice thought, sound rather like a wedding ceremony – 'form an innocent alliance designed to make life more pleasant for both of us. No strings. Just a simple friendship involving occasions such as this, visits to the cinema perhaps, a drive to the coast maybe?' He smiled. 'What do you say?'

What could she say? There was no question here of an emotional entanglement, no hint of any form of infidelity to their respective spouses. The sun was shining, the food and wine had worked their simple magic leaving Alice feeling at ease and confident. Her son was safe and well. She had surprised herself by achieving and enjoying a modicum of independence. Oliver met her smile, poured the last of the wine into their glasses, lifted his and proposed a toast which took the form of a question.

'To us?' he asked as the glass rims chimed.

'Us!' Alice agreed, laughing.

Life in the hostel rolled on, leaving the trauma of Andreis's death in its wake.

Mabel's brother Ernie was slightly injured in a training accident.

Lionel's godfather agreed to send someone from the War Artists' Commission to assess Andreis's painting and Alice, on several evenings, left the hostel in the company of Oliver Maynard. This caused a certain amount of nudging and winking among the girls when his Navy-issue car arrived at the farmhouse gate to collect her.

Lionel rode over on his motorbike, ostensibly to visit his sister but Georgina soon realised that it was Annie, not she, who was the attraction. So she left them to themselves, sitting on the garden wall as the light faded, making hesitant conversation until Lionel plucked up the courage to ask Annie if he could take her for a ride on his motorbike.

It had been almost two months since Christopher's last leave. Roger Bayliss had been vague when Georgina had enquired whether the burns on his hands had healed and whether he was flying again and had muttered something about Christopher spending a leave with a cousin in Sussex. Then the subject had been dropped.

Alice heard no more from Gwennan about Mabel's inappropriate behaviour with her brother and assumed she had decided not to take her complaint to Margery Brewster who, on her regular monthly visit to the farm, had surprised Alice who caught, as she passed her a cup of tea, an unmistakable trace of alcohol on Margery's breath.

Marion and Winnie had to be admonished for repeatedly flouting the curfew. One more offence, Alice had warned, and she would be forced to report them. Winnie had been chastened by this threat but Marion had tossed her head in defiance of it.

Mabel ran a pitchfork through her foot and had to be driven to the hospital in Exeter for a tetanus injection.

Reuben, who was training on the south coast, visited Hester several times and wrote to her each week.

'Has my letter come from Reuben, Missus Todd,' she would enquire, blushing and beaming with pleasure when Alice said, 'Yes! Regular as clockwork, Hester!'

The days had lengthened and reached the midsummer solstice when, for a few weeks, the sun hesitated before beginning to track slowly back towards the shortening days of late summer and early autumn. The hay had been mown a second time, turned, dried and the ricks thatched. Barley heads, heavy and whiskered, began to droop and fade from green towards gold. The lambs had grown plump and the ewes parted happily with their fleeces in the July heat.

The water in the valley stream was low but there was enough in the pool below the bridge for the girls to plunge in on hot evenings or on sunny Sundays, sometimes wearing only their brassieres and knickers.

Before the onset of harvesting the farm seemed to gather itself for the coming burst of activity. Ferdie Vallance impressed Mabel with his clever assessment of the signs in the skies and in the hedgerows of the sort of weather they might expect at harvest time. 'If the Old Man's Beard be too thick and clustery and the squirrels be already at the 'azel nuts and the magpies 'as gone quiet, then you've to worry see, 'cos them's the signs of August storms!'

'Oh,' Mabel said. 'And are the squirrels at the nuts? And 'as the magpies gone quiet, Ferdie?' She was wide-eyed in the face of this wisdom.

''Tis too early to say yet, my lover,' Ferdie responded cleverly. 'Ask me in a week or so and I'll be able to tell for definite.'

In the meantime there was work to do. The harvester,

which Roger Bayliss shared with a neighbour, must be oiled and fired up. Sickles must be sharpened, carthorses shoed and wagon wheels checked. Drinking troughs, thick with the green slime that flourished in warm weather, had to be emptied and refilled with sweet water. The low, granite byre, up on the high pastures, known as The Tops, where the sheep flock spent the summer and which was used each year as a shelter at lambing time, had to be mucked out, the fouled and mouldering straw piled up outside and its earth floor swept bare, ready for the layer of fresh bedding on which next January's lambs would be born. It was this job that, one hot afternoon, fell to Annie and Georgina.

Chapter Seven

It was noon when Georgina and Annie left the Bayliss farm. With their packed lunches stuffed into their dungaree pockets and long-handled shovels over their shoulders they set off. Ignoring the circuitous route of the track which wound its way up to The Tops, they struck directly uphill. It took almost an hour of hard climbing to reach the summit. Just below it, on the leeward side, they could see the lichen-covered slates which roofed the byre. Out of breath and sweating after the steep climb, they spread themselves on the wiry grass. When they had regained their breath, first Annie and then Georgina unwrapped and hungrily ate their sandwiches and drank the milky tea in Annie's flask, saving Georgina's for later.

'Reckon we owe ourselves a kip,' Annie said, settling back, closing her eyes against the sunlight and relaxing her aching muscles. Soon her even breathing suggested to Georgina that she was already asleep.

Georgina lay on her stomach, elbows bent, chin in cupped hands, her eyes on the sweep of land dropping away to the east. To her left the foothills of Dartmoor blurred off into a blue haze. To her right there were distant glimpses of the sea.

The sheep which had lifted their heads and stared when the two girls had first arrived on The Tops, had resumed grazing, cropping their way down the slope towards the byre. Georgina, eyes narrowed against the strong light, saw one and then another of the sheep hesitate and then stand alert, heads lifted, ears focusing on some small sound that only they could hear, eyes fixed on the shadowy interior of the byre which was visible through a wide opening in the crumbling wall. Then the ewe nearest the byre turned suddenly and bolted away, followed immediately by the rest of the flock. Georgina sat up. Obviously something inside the byre had startled them. A fox perhaps. Or a sick sheep which had limped into the byre to die.

Georgina could never quite remember what it was that created the frisson of alarm that she experienced when, leaving Annie sleeping, she approached the byre. As she stood in the doorway, her eyes slowly adjusting to the dim interior, she knew for certain that something or someone was inside. There was a faint sound, a movement in the straw. Then a crouched shape solidified beside the dripping water trough in the far corner. A lark, in the bright sunlight behind Georgina, sounded unusually loud as it began a noisy ascent. Then, for some inexplicable reason, against all logic and without any practical explanation, Georgina knew what the shape was. Who the shape was. And she spoke the name of the person she somehow knew was there. She heard herself say, 'Christopher?'

He made a sound that was something between a sigh and a groan. Enough to confirm to her that she was right. He was there. She could see him now. He got slowly to his feet. He looked like a wild creature. His clothes were tattered and filthy. His hair was matted, tangling into his straggling beard. What was visible of his face was almost unrecognisably gaunt, the eyes sunken and huge. He stretched out a grimy hand, the nails broken and stained and he said, 'I can't do this any more,' and then again, 'I can't do this any more!' His knees buckled and he slid down the rough stones of the wall. She went over to him and knelt in front of him, unsure whether or not he knew who she was.

'You're all right now,' she said. And then, 'You're all right. You don't have to do this any more.' She reached forward, took his hand and they sat, his one hand gripping both of hers. Then he said, 'Georgie?… My God… It is! It's you! Oh God, Georgie.'

That was when they heard the sound of the lorry labouring up the track from the farm. She felt his fingers tighten their grip.

Annie, woken by the sound of the truck, was already on her feet as it came lurching over the crest of the hill. She stood, astonished, looking for Georgina. Calling her name.

There were four uniformed military policemen in the lorry. Two in the cab and the other two standing in the back, holding onto the roll-bar. They were all armed.

One of the less pleasant traits in some of Alice's girls was the way they relished any misfortune that befell those whom they regarded as their superiors. The news that Margery Brewster's car had broken down halfway across the ford and that she, making her way to safety, had slipped and sat down heavily in three feet of muddy river water, had kept Marion, Winnie and Gwennan amused for days and when Roger Bayliss's hunter had stepped on his master's foot there had been an 'ah' of disappointment when news arrived that no bones were broken. But that night, while, over supper, Annie gave her account of the arrest of Christopher Bayliss, the girls' attention was more on Annie's words than on the supper they were eating. Georgina's plate of fish pie lay untouched and she sat staring into space as Annie described the events of the afternoon.

'Like a tramp he looked! Some old coat, he had on, Lord knows where he got it… Filthy it was and his trousies—'

'That boy,' Rose interrupted, 'used to look the bee's knees in his uniform!'

'Stiff with dirt, 'is clothes was!' Annie went on, her

voice low. 'And his hair all mussed and matted and his face looked…well, not like himself at all! Not like Christopher Bayliss looked!' She glanced at Georgina, hoping that she would join in the telling of the story. But Georgina did not respond and didn't appear to hear Rose when she said – quite gently for her – 'Eat up your supper, Georgina, dear.'

'Did he make a run for it then?' asked Marion with her mouth full.

'Dunno,' Annie said. 'I couldn't see. The MPs wouldn't let me go inside the byre.'

'I saw,' Georgina said. The girls turned and looked at her. 'He didn't run. He could barely stand. They hauled him onto his feet and they spun him round and shoved him against the wall and then they handcuffed him!' Georgina's chair scraped back across the slate floor and she stood up. 'And this was a fighter pilot who'd done more ops than he should have done…and been burnt…and seen his friends blown apart…and…' She stood gulping. 'If you'd seen him! If you'd heard him!' Then she turned suddenly and faced Alice, almost accusingly, 'And where was his father?' she demanded, shouting now. Alice went towards her but Georgina lifted a hand as though to hold her off. 'He must have known Christopher had gone AWOL, Mrs Todd! He's been on the run for five weeks! Five weeks!'

'Hang on!' Mabel said suddenly, a forkful of pie halfway to her mouth. 'That was about when the MPs turned up at the Bayliss farm! You lot was all off turnin' 'ay and Ferdie and I was doin' the milkin.' Two of them there was and Mr B took 'em into his office. When they comes out they 'as a quick gander round the yard and then they gets in their truck and goes. They must of bin lookin' for Christopher then! And 'is farver never said nuffink to no one! Blimey!'

'He was quite lucid, Mrs Todd. He knew who I was. He just kept saying he couldn't go on. Couldn't do it any more. I suppose he meant he couldn't go on running and hiding. He had no strength left. I think he'd been made to be too strong for too long and it was more than he… More than anyone…'

Alice had invited Georgina into her sitting room and, without consulting her, had poured a tot of brandy and was now watching her as she sipped it. The night was warm and the windows at each end of the room were open, the curtains just stirring in a breeze that carried with it the humid scents of the summer countryside.

'Aren't you having one, Mrs Todd? I don't like drinking alone.' There was, in Georgina's voice, a thin hint of her humour. Alice smiled, poured a finger of the brandy into a second unsuitable tumbler and sipped, wincing slightly at the sharp taste. The twilight colours outside the window were fading into monochrome.

'Do we know where they've taken him?' Alice asked after a few moments of silence. Georgina said she did not know but believed that, initially at any rate, he was to be detained in a military prison.

'The police wouldn't talk to Annie and me. So we refused to confirm that it was Christopher Bayliss they had arrested. They made us tell them our names and which farm we were from and they wrote them down in a notebook. I told the one who was knocking Christopher about to leave him alone and he said if I didn't keep quiet he'd arrest me as an accomplice. They said Christopher was a deserter and deserved all he got.' Georgina swallowed the last of her brandy. 'I'm going to see Mr Bayliss tomorrow. I'm going to ask him why he pretended not to know what was happening.'

'Perhaps he didn't know, Georgina.' Alice was finding it difficult to justify Roger's behaviour but felt obliged to question the girl's condemnation of it.

'Of course he knew! Where did he think Christopher had been all that time?'

'Didn't he tell you he'd been spending his last leave visiting relatives in Sussex?'

'Yes he did! But that was weeks ago! Obviously he was lying!' Georgina put down her glass. She got to her feet and from the doorway reaffirmed her intention to confront Roger Bayliss on the following day.

Upstairs, in the small room above the porch where Georgina slept alone, Annie was waiting for her, thumbing through one of the textbooks Georgina was studying for her Ministry of Agriculture exams.

'This looks ever so hard compared with the course I've signed up for.'

'By the time you get to this one you'll be OK.'

'I doubt it,' Annie said. 'I 'aven't got the brains!'

''Course you have! You've read the first twenty pages already! Anything you didn't understand?'

'No!'

'Well then!'

They smiled and a silence formed.

'Rotten day, Georgie.' Annie spoke quietly. Georgina nodded. 'You mind, don't you,' Annie said, picking at a broken fingernail.

'What d'you mean, "mind"?'

'You mind about Christopher. What happens to him and that. You care about him.'

Since the evening, months ago now, when Christopher had taken her to dinner and she had driven his car when his burnt hands had hurt him, Georgina's concern for him had been slowly pushed into the background by the everyday pressures of life at Lower Post Stone – a succession of minor but nevertheless compelling incidents, some as trivial as the arrival and then the swift departure of Eleanor, the runaway schoolgirl, and others, like the death of Andreis, sobering and provocative. Since Chrissie had been killed in Plymouth by a stray bomb and Christopher Bayliss had described to her the horrors he was witnessing on a daily basis, Georgina had found herself questioning her convictions regarding pacifism. Mostly she controlled the doubts that rose in her mind, excluding them by immersing herself in the physically exhausting work of the farm and using any energy she had left at the end of each day to swot for the looming Min. of Ag. exams she was soon to sit. But today, confronted by the tragedy of Christopher's situation, she found herself seriously doubting the logic or the justification of turning the other cheek. Annie's low voice brought her back to the present.

'Go on, Georgie,' Annie said. 'Admit it!' But there was nothing to admit. She wasn't in love with Christopher. She was defensive of him. Enraged on his behalf. Even protective. But not in love. When they had first met, his arrogance had irritated her. She had agreed to have dinner with him on that chill, April evening, when his mouth, briefly against hers, had felt so cold, not because she found him attractive – although he was attractive – but out of a feeling of responsibility for the way he was. So obviously stressed and exhausted by the hours of tension spent flying in combat and by the split-second life or death decisions he was constantly forced to make. His shaking fingers and the brittle state of his nerves had not escaped Georgina, nor had the fact that he had been drawn into this situation by the pressures of a society of which she herself, like every other civilian, was part. Every man, woman and child, every father, commanding officer and politician, demanding courage, bravery and sacrifice.

The girls may not have been certain why Georgina was so determined to involve herself in their employer's relationship with his son but they were in no doubt about her intentions. There was a certain ambiguity about their own reaction to Christopher's situation. He was, after all, a deserter. He had run away from a war that other men were still fighting and would continue to fight until the enemy was defeated. A lot of them would die. But, as Annie pointed out to them, they hadn't seen the state Christopher had been in when he was arrested.

'More dead than alive, poor fellow,' Annie had said.

'But not shot!' Gwennan snapped back at her, crisply self-righteous. 'Not blown to bits and bleeding! Like my cousin who come back from Dunkirk with half his leg clean gone! I don't see young master Bayliss missing a limb, do you?'

Mabel's culinary involvement with Ferdie Vallance had, by this time, become established. By mid-afternoon each Saturday she would have borrowed Alice's bicycle and be pedalling up the lane towards Higher Post Stone Farm where Ferdie would greet her with a display of the ingredients for the meal they would cook together that evening. Sometimes it was a pair of rabbits, occasionally a pheasant, feloniously procured, or a salmon filched on a moonless night from a privately owned stretch of the Exe.

On the day of Andreis's death, and at that point unaware of it, Mabel arrived, sweating and eager, at the door of

Ferdie's cottage, propped the bike against the wall and found her host flourishing a large lump of meat. It was a bit jagged round the edges and only just recognisable as a leg of lamb but Mabel was suitably impressed. Even at the hostel, when the village butcher was feeling generous and Rose had presented him with the correct amount of meat coupons, such a pink and splendid offering had rarely been slipped into the farmhouse oven.

'Where d'you get it, Ferdie?' Mabel was round-eyed with appreciation. Ferdie, squirming with pleasure, tapped the side of his nose and said she mustn't ask him that. She glanced nervously round. 'But did you kill 'im?'

'No! Fred and me found 'un. Some of the flock got through a break in the fence above the quarry. This young 'un must of fallen and got hiself caught up in the brambles. Danglin', he was, poor varmint! 'E'd choked to death when us found 'un. Still warm though…' A lesser woman than Mabel would have shuddered.

'So what did you do, you and Fred? Did you cut him into pieces there and then?'

'Lord no! Us stuck 'un under some sacks in the tractor! And us dropped 'im off, after dark, in Fred's shed! No one seed us! Didn't do much of a job with the butcherin',' he said, eyeing the jagged bone and gory flesh, 'but you can't have everything, can you!'

'Where's the rest of him, Ferdie?'

'Fred's missus 'as got the other leg and one of the

shoulders. The rest we give to 'er cousin Doris over at Stoke Cannon. Three kids she got and her bloke's at sea so us takes 'er a bit of this and a bit of that from time to time.' This act of charity seemed to have absolved Ferdie of any sense of guilt regarding the procurement of the lamb.

They rubbed the ungainly lump of flesh with salt and pepper and laid it in a wide pan loaded with onions, potatoes and some of the young turnips which were just coming into season in the Bayliss fields. While the cottage slowly filled with the intoxicating smell of roasting meat, Mabel made a suet pudding that, garnished with golden syrup and Devonshire cream, would round off their feast. By the time the onions had collapsed into soft mounds, the potatoes turned golden-brown, the fatty skin of the lamb was blistering crisply and the pan was running with meaty juices, Ferdie and Mabel could barely control their appetites. Hacking off thick slices of the tender meat and piling their plates with vegetables, they ate noisily, if wordlessly, for an impressive length of time, exchanging, now and then, greasy smiles of mutual satisfaction.

Like Marion and Winnie, returning to the hostel at curfew-time that night, Mabel had been confronted with the bleak news of Andreis's death.

On the morning after Christopher's arrest Georgina watched until she saw his father make his way as usual to the farm office and enter it. She crossed the yard and knocked on his door. 'Come,' he said.

He was already at work, checking through a sheaf of invoices and delivery notes. He glanced at her.

'Ah, Miss Webster. What can I do for you?' He still held some of the sheets of papers in his hands, implying that, as Georgina was interrupting his work, she had better have a good reason for doing so.

'I just wanted to say,' she began and then hesitated. This didn't look like a man in the throes of a domestic crisis. A man whose son, after being missing for five weeks, had been arrested for desertion and despite being in a state of mental and physical collapse was being held, pending an investigation, in a military prison. He was looking at her. The resemblance between father and son, which had previously eluded Georgina, struck her now and added to her confusion. 'I just wanted to say how sorry I am… How sorry all of us at the hostel are…about Christopher.'

There was a pause. Roger Bayliss regarded Georgina steadily. 'Yes,' he said, eventually. 'Well, these things happen.' There was another pause. Georgina was unable to tell whether he had so much to say that he couldn't begin to speak, or whether, and this seemed to her to be more likely, he had nothing at all that he wanted to say. 'But it is most kind of you…you and the other girls…to express your…your concern.' These words, Georgina realised, were intended to conclude the interview. She was, she understood, being dismissed. But she remained, standing straight and motionless in front of him.

'How is he?' she asked and when he didn't immediately reply, repeated, 'Christopher. How is he?' A flicker of what Georgina perceived as irritation crossed Roger's face.

'As well as can be expected, they tell me,' he said at last.

'Are you going to visit him?' Georgina's heart was racing. Colour flooded her face. While she was becoming heated, Roger Bayliss seemed so cool. There was no hint now of the polite smile with which he had greeted her. His face was expressionless. She was prepared for his eyes to be hard and intimidating when she steeled herself to engage them and was faintly surprised when he avoided hers.

'I have no immediate plans to do so,' he said, flatly.

'Then I shall go,' Georgina said. 'Tell me where he is and I—'

'All I can tell you,' he interrupted, 'is that he is shortly to be moved from...from where he is now, to an appropriate hospital.' He would, he said, let Georgina know when and where that would be. It was, he repeated, most kind of her to take such an interest but now she would have to excuse him as he had work to attend to. But at this point Georgina, having already gone too far, found it impossible not to go even further.

'Are you ashamed of him?' she heard herself demand and was surprised by how harsh she sounded. Whatever feelings her question created in Roger Bayliss failed to reveal themselves in his expression.

'That's enough,' he said in the restrained tone of voice that her own father had used when she was young and he was teaching her how to behave. She apologised without meeting Roger Bayliss's eyes and let herself out of the office.

'I shouldn't have said it,' she confessed to Alice when, after supper, the two of them took a turn round the cider orchard behind the farmhouse. 'It was what my father would have called "out of order". I don't suppose he is ashamed of Christopher, do you? I mean how could he possibly be...? But to keep quiet about him going AWOL and now say he's not even going to see him! How can he do that?'

'It does seem odd,' Alice murmured. 'There has to be a reason for it. Shock perhaps? Refusing to admit that anything was wrong with Christopher until it was too late to help him? Guilt affects people in different ways, Georgie. No one understands what goes on between family members – or why.'

Above them, cider apples, still green, clustered tightly. The light, under the trees, was thickening into dusk and the toes of their shoes were already picking up moisture from the grass. They walked in silence for a while and then Georgina said that as soon as she knew where Christopher was to be hospitalised she would visit him.

Weeks passed. Alice, intending to relay any news about Christopher to Georgina, asked Roger more than once how his son was. He told her that as far as he knew, he was improving but he did not volunteer any details regarding Christopher's whereabouts and Alice sensed that he did not wish to be drawn on the subject. It was Oliver Maynard who, on one of their evening excursions to a local inn, told Alice that while visiting one of his own charges who was experiencing a breakdown, he had seen Christopher in the grounds of Axmount House, a country estate which had been commandeered by the Ministry of Defence for use as a psychiatric hospital. A phone call confirmed that Christopher was a patient there and on the following Sunday Lionel rode over on his motorbike, collected his sister and transported her the ten miles to Axmount, leaving her at the manned gate and arranging to collect her an hour later.

She saw Christopher with his back to her, sitting near the tennis court, watching a group of players. Not wishing to startle him she approached him slowly and stood in front of him. He still looked gaunt. But his hair had been cut and was short and trim, as it had been when she first met him. The tangled beard was gone. His hands, hanging loosely between his thighs, were clean, the nails scrubbed. He looked at her for a long time and then got to his feet. Then he clicked his heels and saluted. A perfect RAF salute. He gave a little bow, said, 'Good afternoon, Miss Webster!' then sat heavily down again on the seat, dropped his head into his hands and cursed. When he stopped swearing he sat in silence with his head turned away from her.

'I don't want you here, Georgie. Really. I don't. It's sweet of you to come but I don't want you to see me like this. With the shakes and everything. And blubbing. I can't stop! It's pathetic! I'm so ashamed!'

She sat beside him with her thigh just touching his.

'Were you ashamed when your hands were burnt?' she asked him. 'Would you be ashamed if you had been hit by shrapnel? Or crash landed? Or bailed out?' He smiled and shook his head.

'Bless you, Georgie,' he said quietly. 'But I've thought of all that. And the shrink here says the same thing to me every day.'

'Because it's true!'

'No it isn't, you see.' He had turned and was facing her, looking hard into her eyes. 'Those things are out there!' He held out his hands, palms up. The scars from the burns were still visible. 'This…other stuff,' he said, placing both hands against his temples, 'this is in here. In my bloody head!'

'But it's the same thing, Chris! It's damage! It's a wound! Caused by fighting! Caused by the war! Not by something you have done or haven't done! You were pushed too far! Anyone could see that.'

'Everyone in the squadron was pushed, Georgie. They didn't all crack up.'

'You don't know what they did! There are unexplained

crashes, ditchings, mid-air collisions. Pilots crack up in different ways!'

While Georgina was only vaguely aware of these facts, Christopher knew them to be accurate. He had known men so exhausted and so consistently overexposed to danger that their basic instincts of self-preservation had become non-existent. He had seen them climb into fighter planes and fly like lunatics. Some had survived – so far. Many had not. He got to his feet.

'Let's walk,' he said.

The once beautiful gardens of Axmount House, having been deprived of the team of gardeners who, until the outbreak of the war, had tended them, were rank after three years of neglect. The lawns were tussocky. Shrubs needed pruning and the herbaceous borders and the rose gardens looked almost surreal, draped and choked by rampant convolvulus. Hollyhocks and delphiniums lay flattened by the last gale while the autumn flowers, the marguerite daisies, dahlias and chrysanthemums, struggled through a tangle of brambles. An ornamental pool, embellished by its neo-Gothic bridge and its clustering mass of waterlilies, looked much as it had done in peacetime although the wild Dartmouth daisies, pushing through cracks in the paved terraces, would not have been tolerated by the men who were now in various uniforms and serving their country.

'It's supposed to be soothing, all this,' Christopher

said, staring across the pool and into the trees and green spaces of the parkland beyond it.

'It's probably doing you more good than you think,' Georgina said. 'You will get well, Chris. You know that, don't you.' But he had suddenly stopped. He took her by her shoulders, turned her to face him.

'Let me look at you!' he said, holding her. 'Let me just have one long look at you!' Her eyes, wide and steady, were inches from his. 'I get these dreams, you see. The medics give me stuff to stop them. But it doesn't stop them and they seem to come in the day as well as at night. They are the worst dreams, Georgie! You have no idea how awful! All the most horrific things that have happened since I've been flying. Over and over. And what I do, you see… What I do when the dreams start…is this!' He was looking intently into her face, his eyes moving from feature to feature. 'I conjure you! I put your face together. The shape of it. Eyes. Nose. Mouth. Until you are complete! And I hold you there, like I'm holding you now! So that you are between me and the dream! Between me and a cockpit full of flames in a plummeting plane. Between me and the flier I'm pulling out of an airstrip pile-up with his body coming apart in my hands and his eyes seared…' To silence him she put her fingers briefly against his mouth. Then he continued more quietly. 'Blocking it out… D'you see?'

Neither he nor Georgina had been aware of the approach of the white-coated male nurse.

'It's me, sir,' the man said steadily, aware of his patient's outburst. 'John, sir. I've brought your medication.' He held out the pill and watched as Christopher washed it down with a sip of water from the tumbler the man was holding out to him. 'And it's time for your afternoon nap, sir.' John turned to Georgina. 'Best come again another day, miss,' he said evenly. 'We're a bit tired now.'

She repeated her visit after a fortnight. He seemed more rested and had regained some of the weight he had lost during the frantic weeks when he had been on the run. He told her about the day when he'd been scrambled and had been unable to move from the mess table where he had been sitting over an uneaten lunch. It hadn't been that he had consciously refused the orders that were being shouted at him. He had simply found himself incapable of carrying them out.

'I remember a medic being called,' he told Georgina. 'My pulse and blood pressure were checked and a torch beam was shone into my eyes. I just knew I had to get away. Anywhere so long as it was away. The next thing I remember was being amongst trees. I slept a lot and then I was hungry and then I was cold. I only had a few quid on me and by then I was in such shit order I couldn't go into pubs or shops. I got chased a few times by the MPs. I found my way back home. God knows how. I got into the house at night and I stole food but I knew if I kept doing it I'd get caught. So I went up onto The Tops. There were mushrooms after the rain. I ate those.

I walked about at night to stop the dreams. Then I couldn't walk any more and I lay down in the straw in the byre. I was ready to die. The dreams took over. And then you were there. And that other land girl, Annie, was it? And the MPs of course. That's all I can remember.'

They were sitting on a garden seat, the afternoon sun on their backs and shining full on the graceful face of Axmount House. 'This place seems to be some sort of hospital. Did you bring me here?' She told him she hadn't and she realised that he had no recollection of what had happened to him since his arrest. Almost three months of his life had been obliterated, initially by the trauma and now, probably, by the drugs which were designed to stabilise him.

'They tell me that my father will be coming to see me soon. He may have come before but I don't remember. Have you come before? I think you have, haven't you. I suppose I talked lot of gibberish. Sorry.'

She told him she had been to see him and that it hadn't been gibberish. They entered what had been an orangery and sat down at a small table covered by a gingham cloth. An orderly brought them tea. Christopher held his cup in both hands. A woman from the local WVS went from table to table, offering a plate of scones and little cakes which she had obviously baked herself. When Georgina thanked her, the woman looked past her, smiled at Christopher and said it was the least she could do.

'Everyone is very kind here,' Christopher said. He was,

it was true, very much calmer now than he had been on her earlier visit. But it was also true that the person sitting across the table from her, eating cakes and carefully lifting his cup of tea, bore little resemblance to the arrogant and dashing young man he had been six months previously. This depressed and scared Georgina. What she did not know was that Christopher's drugs were being slowly withdrawn and that soon his doctors would begin to allow him to face the problems which the next phase in his recovery would deliver.

By now the harvesting of the arable crop was in full swing. Both Higher and Lower Post Stone farms were alive with activity. The weather was kind in the sense that it was dry and hot with no threat of the storms or damp weather which could have ruined the crop. Barley, wheat and oats went under the harvester and as it spewed out the bound sheafs the girls gathered them and propped them in rows of stooks, up and down the lengths of the fields to dry out in the warm wind, ready for threshing. Edward-John, now on his school holidays, joined in, working alongside the girls and, to his mother's consternation, enjoying the pursuit of the rabbits, which, finally trapped in the last remaining acres of standing wheat, made frantic bids for freedom and were, only too often, clubbed to death by Fred and Ferdie and even, occasionally, by Edward-John himself.

The dry heat, which ensured the swift and safe gathering in of the harvest, took its toll on the girls who, dusty, hot, dehydrated and scratched by thistles, were, by the end of each long day, so exhausted they could barely speak. Even Rose was sympathetic when they limped and reeled into the farmhouse as dusk fell.

''Twon't be long now, my pretties, till it'll be over,' she soothed, pouring cordial and then ladling onion gravy over plates piled with sausages and mashed potato. 'Mr Bayliss allus give us a day off once the threshin' be done and the ricks thatched! So that'll be nice, won' it!'

'Only one rotten day?' Gwennan's voice was an agonised wail. 'I'll need a month in the cottage hospital after this!'

It was rare for Marion and Winnie to decline invitations when army trucks drew up outside the farmhouse and sounded their horns as the girls finished their supper. But on several nights during the harvesting, the trucks had driven off without them.

'It's not so much the goin' out,' Marion sighed wistfully, stretching out in her dressing gown, across a sofa in the recreation room, her sunburnt skin pink after her bath, her hair still dusty with chaff and several of her fingernails torn. 'It's the gettin' dolled up ready for 'em I can't be doin' with!'

Hester, who in spite of Reuben's continuing attention, wore very little make-up, remained fascinated by the fact that Marion, before she transformed herself with mascara, pancake foundation, crimson lipstick and powdered rouge and had rolled her hair into solid mounds which gave onto cascading curls and had caged her body in waist-cinching belts, above which frilled blouses suggesting irresistible roundnesses and softnesses, was an entirely different person from the frowsy, angular, pale creature with lank hair and thin lips who, at breakfast and during working hours, was familiar to all of them. 'What you gawpin' at then, Hester?' Marion would demand as Hester stared spellbound when she tottered dangerously down the steep stairs in her high heels and what Annie called her 'warpaint'.

'Nothing, Marion. I'm not staring,' Hester would smile. Winnie relied less heavily on the jars and tubes and bottles and brushes that crowded the dressing table she shared with her friend. Not because she disapproved of Marion's complicated ritual but because, being an altogether prettier girl, she was more easily transformed into something eye-catching. Also, she knew better than to compete with Marion, who needed to be recognised as the more dazzling of the two of them and consequently the rightful recipient of the lion's share of any available male attention that was on offer.

Annie, with encouragement from Georgina, had embarked on her studies for the series of Ministry of Agriculture certificates, which, if she was successful, would eventually qualify her for employment as an assistant farm manager.

'What d'you want to waste your time on that for?' Gwennan had asked curtly, when she heard about Annie's plans. 'That's for posh girls, in't it? An East Ender like you's never going to get work as a farm manager!'

'Why not?' Georgina asked on Annie's behalf.

''Cos she's common, that's why! 'Cos of the way she talks! It's obvious, "Miss Webster"!' Calling Georgina Miss Webster was Gwennan's way of reminding her of the class difference between them. The girls were sitting over the cups of tea that rounded off their evening meal. Gwennan, leaning forward, reached for the pot and drained it into her cup.

'Ta, Taffy,' Marion said wearily, clattering her empty cup in its saucer. 'I *would* like another cup, thanks very much!' While Gwennan and Marion glared across the table at one another Georgina went to fill the kettle.

'You're talking rubbish, Taff,' she called from the scullery, hoping to ease the tension by using the Welsh girl's nickname. 'Almost the only good thing about this war is that it's kicked all that class rubbish out of the window!'

'Rubbish, is it?' Gwennan snapped back. 'Then why is it that girls who get into the WRNS and the WRAF is all lah-di-dah and the ones in the munition factories or up to their necks in muck, like us, is board-school kids?'

Georgina stood the kettle on the stove and returned to the table. This was not the first time that the question of class had been raised in the hostel and would not be the last. Her own status as a pacifist also caused tension.

Annie had confided in Georgina that, after delivering his

sister back to the farm after her second visit to Christopher, Lionel had drawn her aside and invited her out.

'And are you going?' Georgina had asked, smiling. Her brother's obvious attraction to Annie had not escaped her and now, seeking Annie's reaction to it, she scanned the girl's face. She was easily the best looking of the Lower Post Stone girls. Her dark hair framed striking features. The lustrous eyes were huge and solemn, the jawline delicate, the mouth lush. Georgina had heard Annie speak of a boyfriend, Pete, with whom she had been 'going' since they were both at elementary school. His father ran a market stall off the Mile End Road where Pete, from when he quit school at fifteen until the day he was conscripted, had worked alongside his dad, in his shirtsleeves in the summers and blowing on mittened fingers in the winters as he weighed out the fruit and veg. Now he had progressed to a trainee aircraft mechanic in the RAF, writing letters to his girl and sometimes sending her small gifts. A pair of mother-of-pearl earrings had been his latest offering. But Georgina had sensed in Annie a desire to move on from Pete, just as she had yearned to move on from employment in her uncle's garment factory.

'Well?' Georgina asked again and, when Annie hesitated, repeated the question. 'Are you going out with my bro?'

'I dunno, Georgie.'

'Don't you like him?'

''Course I like him. He's…well, he's lovely, isn't he! Good-looking and funny and everything, but…'

'Then what's the problem?'

'I'm not…well, I'm not the sort of girl a bloke like him goes out with, am I? It's no good you looking at me like that, Georgie! Or goin' on about there being no class system!'

'There isn't! Well… Not as much as there was, anyhow.'

'Enough though,' Annie said. It was evening and the two girls were sitting on the garden wall. Bats were diving and wheeling above their heads and the August full moon, a soft rose-pink globe, was just clearing the eastern horizon.

'Shall I give you a for instance?' Annie offered and when Georgina nodded, paused for a moment before continuing. Then she said, 'You remember that Sunday we got volunteered for church parade?' Georgina nodded. A few weeks previously Margery Brewster had coerced a group of the Post Stone girls into attending morning service at Ledburton church.

'It's good for the Land Army's image,' she had explained to Alice over morning tea. 'We need to be nicely represented from time to time, in public, in uniform and in church. There will be coffee and cakes in the vicarage afterwards. Don't encourage Mabel Hodges to volunteer, Alice. And if she does, make sure she's… Well, you know what I mean!' Alice did know. Even after a bath and dressed in a clean uniform, Mabel was not quite the image of a land girl that Margery Brewster wanted to offer for public scrutiny. Fortunately for Alice, Mabel was not in the least inclined to spend the morning of her precious day off sitting in a church. So it was Alice herself, accompanied by Edward-John, Gwennan, Georgina and Annie who sang the hymns, sat through the sermon, said the prayers and afterwards filed across the churchyard and into the parsonage where they were introduced to the vicar and his wife.

'Pleased to meet you!' Annie had said and, 'Ta very much,' as she helped herself to a fairy cake.

'So?' said Georgina. 'What was wrong with that?'

'What was wrong, Georgie, was that you and Mrs Todd said "how d'you do" when you was introduced. And "thank you" when you took your cake!'

'They're only words, Annie!'

'Yeah, but the ones I use is the *wrong* words!'

'But the meaning was fine! You *were* pleased to meet them and you *were* grateful for the cake!' But Annie was not convinced.

'Then there was that time you and me had tea at the Rougemont!' The two of them had, Georgina recalled, entered the prestigious hotel and, amongst the potted palms, ordered afternoon tea in the formal lounge. Annie, attempting to summon the waitress for more hot water, had called 'Miss!' The girl, immaculate in black dress, white apron and frilled cap, had approached their table and deliberately ignoring Annie, very pointedly addressed her 'yes, madam?' to Georgina. 'I should of said "waitress", shouldn't I! "Miss" is what common people call waitresses, isn't it!'

'It doesn't matter, Annie!' Georgina laughed.

'That waitress thought it did! If I went out with your brother I'd be scared to open me mouth lest I embarrassed 'im! You could give me lessons, Georgie! Teach me to say "how de-do" and hold up my hand, like you did, with your forefinger raised and your other fingers curled and say "Waitress! May we have our bill, please"!' Annie's faux accent, delivered falsetto and with a po-face, sounded so much like Margery Brewster's when she summoned the girls to the recreation room for the regular six-weekly meeting, which always concluded with her looking from face to face and enquiring shrilly whether any of them had any questions, that one or two startled faces appeared at the hostel windows.

Annie did go out with Lionel. On Saturday afternoons she hauled up her skirt and climbed onto the back of his motorbike, wrapped her arms tightly round his waist and leant against his broad back.

'I'm not being forward or nothing!' she explained to Hester, who witnessed her arrival back at the hostel one evening, her face flushed by the rush of wind and her hair tangled. 'But you has to hold tight like that, Hes! You'd fall off else!'

They made love among gorse bushes on cliffs above Branscombe Beach. It was not her first time. Pete had taken her virginity the year before. But it was Lionel's. Annie taught him how to avoid making her pregnant by withdrawing from her before he ejaculated. He managed it, apart from the first time and after that was always equipped with what Annie called 'preventatives', which he had procured with only a minimum of embarrassment when his barber tactfully enquired whether he needed 'something for the weekend, sir?'

For Alice the summer passed quickly. The routine she had established, together with the new layout of the kitchen, made her heavy workload at first possible and then tolerable. Edward-John's uncle had visited the boy and his school and, being impressed by both, had offered not only to continue to pay the fees but to make funds available for other expenses. Letters passed between Alice's solicitors and James's but no date had yet been set for the divorce hearing. Oliver Maynard was attentive and charming though there had been a couple of occasions when she had to remind him that their relationship was one of friendship only. He was careful not to embarrass her, understanding, correctly, that to do so at this stage would be to lose her.

She was concerned about the welfare of a few of her girls and unsure how far she should take her attempts to influence them. Since the crisis over Winnie's abortion, she and Marion were, presumably, using the contraceptive devices with which they had been fitted but, although the results were under control now, their relationships with Tom, Dick and Harry continued to raise eyebrows and to encourage widespread attention from soldiers in the many camps, barracks and training establishments where British, Commonwealth and American troops were being prepared for the next major offensive of the war, the invasion of France, which was to become known as the D-Day landings.

Hester, when Reuben's courtship had intensified, had taken him to Barnstaple to meet her family and had returned to the farm in tears.

'I'm not to go home no more, Missus Todd,' she had sobbed. 'Marryin' outside our faith is a mortal sin. They never want to see me again! Reuben says I'm not to think of them as my folks no more. He says, one day, his mother will be my ma and his dad my pa! I didn't want it to be this way, Missus Todd! I love my mum and my brother Zeke. But I love Reuben more! I won't part with him! Not for no one!' It concerned Alice that Hester and Reuben were both still very young and that with the most violent fighting of the war still to come, their future was, at best, uncertain.

Margery Brewster had expressed her concern regarding Mabel Hodges' relationship with Ferdie.

'I understand that she spends a great deal of her free time in his cottage. What do they do, d'you suppose?'

'They cook, Margery,' Alice replied. 'And sometimes she washes his clothes and darns his socks. She tells me all about it and it seems quite innocent and very constructive to me.' Margery considered this and then conceded that Ferdie was certainly looking cleaner and fitter than he had done since his poor mother had died.

'So he's probably doing a better day's work than he used to – and that has to be good for the war effort!' she said and made a note to this effect in her six-weekly report on the occupants of Lower Post Stone Farm.

Gwennan's mean streak continued to provoke Marion and Winnie and no one was very sympathetic when the Welsh girl was stricken with a succession of physical misfortunes. She seemed always to have a headache or a sore throat or an upset stomach. Despite spraining her ankle, being stung by a hornet, breaking a tooth on a swinging gate and being chased and very nearly gored by a bull, she received very little sympathy from the other girls who found her unfriendly, critical and spiteful – which she was.

'They doan like me here,' she announced to Alice one evening in the kitchen when she came asking, not for the first time, for an aspirin to ease today's discomfort. 'But I doan care what they think o' me, so there!'

'Well, you are rather hard on them, Taffy. And a bit critical, don't you think, sometimes?' Alice shook the tablet out of the bottle and onto Gwennan's palm. Rose had joined them in the kitchen and Alice had made a sign to her, suggesting that she should keep out of this particular discussion.

'I speak as I find, Mrs Todd,' Gwennan said, with a sideways glance at Rose. 'Some of them girls are just plain stupid and one or two are downright immoral if you ask me!'

'Well, the thing is, Taffy, we don't ask you, do we!' Alice spoke with a good-humoured smile. 'And until we do, you might find things were happier for you if you waited until then to give us your views.' Gwennan washed the tablet down with a sip of water and stared morosely at Alice.

'I should have thought, Mrs Todd, that part of your job here was to make sure they behaved themselves!' Before Alice could think of a reply that would not provoke a stronger exchange, Gwennan, limping heavily on her still slightly swollen ankle, left the kitchen.

Rose exploded, deliberately pitching her voice so that her words would be audible to Gwennan as she hobbled up the stairs. 'Why you put up with her cheek, Alice, I do not know!'

Because of their similar backgrounds and education it had always been easy for Alice and Georgina to converse and exchange opinions. With the other girls they had to choose their words and references carefully in order not to sound 'posh' and stuck up. While Alice and Georgina kept themselves informed about the progress of the war by listening to the news on the BBC, to the girls it was simply something happening somewhere else and to other people.

It was while they sat, Alice on one side and Georgina on

the other side of the wireless set, trying to interpret the words of the news bulletin reaching them through the crackling, hissing static, that Alice began to be aware of Georgina's changing views on pacifism. This had begun, Alice realised, with the raid on Plymouth that had killed Chrissie, made a widower of her twenty-year-old husband and brought sharply home to Georgina the impact of an uncompromising war on innocent individuals who barely understood what it was about. The tragedy of Andreis, and the effect of the legacy he left in the form of his powerful and disturbing painting, had fuelled Georgina's questioning of the convictions she had inherited and accepted from her parents. Christopher had initially been fiercely dismissive of her pacifism yet it had been the onset of the condition which finally resulted in his catastrophic breakdown that triggered her conversion to something approaching militancy. For a while she had kept this to herself, only occasionally confiding her increasing doubts to Alice. Then Christopher, who had seemed, when Georgina first met him, to be a walking embodiment of her opposition to war, had, over a period of months and before her eyes, been virtually destroyed by it.

Chapter Eight

Georgina's work on the farm, although physically exhausting, left her mind free, initially to analyse her waning convictions regarding pacifism coupled with her increasing need to take a more active part in the war and then to consider how she could achieve this. At the back of her mind lay the fact of her ability to fly. She knew that women pilots did not take part in combat missions in the RAF but the man who had paid for her flying lessons – she called him her de Havilland godfather – had told her of the group of women flyers who served in an organisation called the Air Transport Auxiliary. Known as Ferry Pilots, they were responsible for moving planes between the airfields where they were needed, often to replace those which had been destroyed by enemy action, and for transporting damaged aircraft to repair workshops which were scattered up and down the country. Georgina wrote to her godfather, announced her intentions, told him enough to account for her rejection of pacifism and asked him not to mention the fact to her parents until she had made her decision and discussed it with them. He told her where to apply to the ATA and, without her knowledge, contacted an influential colleague who was connected to that organisation. Georgina received an application form, filled it in and sent it off together with copies of her flying certificates. Weeks passed and the procedure proved to be a lengthy and complicated one. Details of her birth and education had to be verified and references to her health were cross-checked with Land Army records. The final stage in the selection process involved a visit to the headquarters of the ATA and a long day of interviews and tests which culminated in Georgina being required to take the controls of a Tiger Moth and, under the eye of a daunting RAF instructor, to execute a take-off, two circuits of an airfield and a landing. All of these commitments were carried out on Georgina's days off together with one long weekend, which she had earned by working several of Gwennan's shifts. A week later she received a letter telling her she had been accepted by the ATA and asking when she would be available to attend a week's training course at the airfield at White Waltham. At this point she confided her plans to Alice Todd.

With the grain harvested and the straw ricks thatched, the focus of the girls' work – apart from the on-going duties with the dairy herd, the pigs and the poultry – moved to maintenance tasks in preparation for the coming winter. The last of the potato crop was lifted during a period of wet weather when the girls themselves, their dungarees and their waterproofs were caked in rich, red Devon mud. Swedes and mangel-wurzels, which would provide winter fodder for the cattle, were heaved into long mounds and strewn with straw to protect them from frost. Ditches, clogged with summer growth, were cleared ready for the autumn rains and Ferdie was commissioned to teach the girls the basics of hedge layering.

On a sunny Saturday afternoon Pete visited Annie and when Lionel arrived unexpectedly the two young men eyed each other warily until Georgina managed to persuade her brother to take her for a spin on his motorbike. They went to a tea shop in Tiverton.

'Who is this fellow, anyway?' Lionel demanded sulkily as Georgina poured their tea.

'He's her boyfriend, idiot!' Georgina explained. 'Well, he was. Before the war. Want a scone?'

'Thanks. But hasn't she told him about me?'

'Oh, come on, Li! Why on earth should she? Have you told her about Mary Box? Or Susan French? Or little Drusilla, who admires you so?' His sister reeled off the names of a few more of the girls who had received attention from her brother. Lionel had the grace to smile. By the time they arrived back at the farm Pete had departed and Annie was in the recreation room, busy swotting for her Ministry of Agriculture exams.

Lionel sat astride his bike revving it slightly in order to draw Annie's attention to his presence. There was no response.

'D'you think she gave this Pete fellow the old heave ho?' Lionel asked his sister hopefully. Georgina shrugged. She was unsure of Lionel's feelings where Annie was concerned and considered that a little uncertainty on his part would do him no harm.

'I've no idea,' she said blithely. 'You'll have to ask her!'

Lionel dropped the clutch and accelerated away down the lane.

'But you believed so strongly in pacifism!' Alice had said when, one Sunday evening, Georgina first confessed her doubts to the warden. 'This is a complete…' Alice hesitated.

'Volte-face,' Georgina said, 'if you want to get all Latin about it. Yes, it is, Mrs Todd. But you know why.'

'Well, I know there've been things that have upset you since you've been here.' They were in Alice's sitting room, Georgina watching as the warden sewed name-tabs into her son's school uniform. 'First Chrissie,' Alice said, 'then Andreis and now Christopher, but…'

'You think I'm being too easily influenced by what's happened here, don't you? This isn't a sudden thing, Mrs Todd. I've been worrying about it for months now. I was blinkered, you see. I accepted my parents' opinion because I respect them but I never really thought for myself about what was happening or bothered to find out why. Working in the Land Army and being involved in the war, even in the small way we are here, has made me realise how complicated it all is – the decisions I mean, about what you do – what a country does, about aggressors.'

'So if someone asked you now, whether you are a pacifist…?'

'I'd say no.'

Alice snipped her thread, folded her son's new shirt and smiled, assuming that now the declaration had been made, Georgina's mind would be at rest. But a glance at the girl's face suggested otherwise.

'So… What now? You're not going to rush off and enlist, are you?' Alice was joking but Georgina's reaction instantly sobered her. 'Oh my goodness, Georgie, you are, aren't you!'

'I shall give Mr Bayliss my notice at the beginning of December,' she said, watching Alice's reaction, 'and leave here after Christmas. My training with the ATA starts in January.'

'But your parents! Whatever will—'

'There'll be huge arguments. But you see I shan't be actually fighting, Mrs Todd. The ATA is what's called a support facility. Not involved in combat. Oh, I know! I know! They'll be horrified. Probably throw me out onto the streets!'

Christmas was approaching. Unless lambing began early, Roger Bayliss, after consultation with Margery Brewster, was proposing to run the farm on a skeleton staff from early on Christmas Eve until the day after Boxing Day. This would allow the majority of the girls four days in which to visit their homes for the festivities. When he asked for volunteers to work over the holiday Gwennan swapped the four days at Christmas for five in January. Mabel offered to stay and work, providing her gran and her young brother could spend Christmas in the farmhouse. This was agreed. Hester, banned from home but promised a visit from Reuben, who was now stationed in Wiltshire, was happy to stay at the farm and work shifts alongside Fred and Ferdie, who, together with Gwennan and Mabel, would be able to manage the milking and the distribution of fodder for the cattle, pigs and poultry. Other duties would be put on hold for the four days, leaving all the other girls free to travel home on the morning of Christmas Eve.

As for Alice, she resigned herself to the fact that this Christmas would be very different from the last one. She would roast the goose Roger Bayliss had promised. She would eat it with Edward-John, Gwennan, Mabel, Mabel's gran and little Arthur, Hester and Rose – and if he managed to get a forty-eight-hour pass, Rose's son Dave. She thought of Roger Bayliss, alone at Upper Post Stone and invited him to join them.

'You never!' was Rose's reaction to news of his acceptance of the invitation. 'Mr bloomin' Bayliss? Sittin' down at that table with us lot?'

Alice was unsure of her reasons for inviting Roger. On one level she felt sorry for him, isolated in the big farmhouse at a time when it is considered essential to have company. On another level and one which she was too preoccupied to explore, she found him oddly challenging. His unexplained treatment of his son was incomprehensible to her but she was too intelligent to imagine that there was a simple explanation for it. The melancholy tension, which she had hardly noticed when she had first met Roger, seemed over recent months to have increased. At their infrequent meetings, the subjects of which were always various problems and queries relating to the hostel and the group of girls who lived in it and worked on his land, he was always courteous and attentive. She sensed that he had grown to respect her. Far from being the liability he had feared she might be when he first, reluctantly, agreed to her appointment as warden, she had proved to be not only diligent and committed but, on the one or two occasions when they had disagreed, surprisingly courageous, standing her ground when necessary against both him and Margery Brewster. Unlike some of his neighbours, the conduct of his group of land girls had, so far, not seriously embarrassed or inconvenienced him. There had been no bad accidents and the one or two unfortunate incidents which had occurred, Alice had handled skilfully. He visualised her moving purposefully about Lower Post Stone, level-headed and focused on whatever task she was engaged upon, her grey eyes clear, her skin smooth and her glossy hair swept charmingly back from her forehead. He found himself wondering what she would look like dressed as a youngish woman of her class would dress for, say, a cocktail party.

'I'm inviting a few neighbours in for a drink on the Sunday before Christmas,' Roger announced one morning when, riding past Lower Post Stone, he had hitched his horse's reins to the gatepost and called in to see how things were. 'Very much like you to join us, Mrs Todd, if you'd care to?' Alice accepted. Roger smiled a rare, faint smile and stood tapping his riding crop against his booted calf. He would, he said, pick her up in his car at about six on the night of the party. Alice decided that on that night Rose could manage the girls' supper, which on Sundays was always a light meal, dinner having been consumed at midday.

'Why is it,' Alice mused, 'that I think of everything in terms of the girls' food? I get invited out – do I wonder what to wear or whether I shall have time to go to a hairdresser? No, I worry about who will feed the girls! My mind is full of groceries! Have I got enough of this? Are we running out of that? Is there something I've forgotten to order? No wonder I've no time to consider the future!'

Alice's future was, in fact, taking shape almost without her being aware of it. Over the past few months she had been asked for her advice on the layout of the kitchens of several local establishments. She had proved to be astute when assessing what those kitchens needed in order to facilitate the smooth and efficient production of meals.

Lower Post Stone and a neighbouring – and much larger – Land Army hostel were early beneficiaries of her skills and subsequently a nursing home, two hotels and an officers' mess had been added to her list of credits. She had received small but significant cheques in payment for her new-found talent for making the best use of space, studying the work practice of employees and advising on the selection and installation of kitchen appliances. Oliver Maynard had insisted on helping her to draw up a scale of fees for future consultancy work and her notion of one day supporting herself in this field seemed likely to become a reality. But all of this lay in the future. In the distant region of 'after the war'. For the present her time and her energy were focused on the hostel and its occupants and on Edward-John, who, his hair bleached and his skin tanned by summer sun, was growing tall and strong, working alongside the land girls, as hard and in some cases at least as willingly as they.

On her third visit to Christopher at Axmount, Georgina found him looking physically recovered. He had been working in the gardens, clearing the overgrown shrubberies and with the help of the two young sons of a gardener who was now serving in North Africa, had undertaken some serious lopping and even the felling of one or two of the large trees that needed attention. He walked Georgina round the parkland, pointing out to her what he had already achieved and outlining what he planned to do.

'I've always been fascinated by trees,' he told her. 'When I was a kid I spent a lot of time with my father's woodsmen. I'd go up into the forest with them and work alongside them. Great blokes, they were!'

'I didn't know your father owned a forest!'

'How should you?' He smiled and went on to describe the five hundred acres that, before her marriage, had belonged to his mother's family and had passed to Roger on her death and which lay on rising ground between the Post Stone Farms and the moor. 'Mostly hardwood,' Christopher told her. 'But we do a lot of coppicing. On the lower slopes there are firs which go for pit-props. Then there are the poplars and bat willows and so on. It's all been badly neglected since war broke out. Which is where I come in.'

'You?' Georgina realised suddenly that she had never imagined Christopher in any other role than as an airman. It had simply not occurred to her to wonder what his youthful ambitions might have been before the war had scooped him up.

'Yes,' he continued. 'Me. I suddenly have a very clear idea of where I'm heading and what I want to do with myself. Which is just as well, as I'm no longer any use as a flyer!' He laughed at her shocked expression. 'Don't look at me like that, Georgie! You know it, I know it and more importantly they know it.' He fished a crumpled piece of buff paper from a pocket and held it out to her.

It was not a personal communication. His name, as the

recipient, and the scrawled signature of the sender had been added in ink to a printed page. Georgina had to read it twice before its precise meaning and implications registered.

'Where did this come from?' she demanded. 'How did you get it?' Christopher was smiling, his hands were deep in his pockets and he was rocking, in a very relaxed way, back and forth on his heels.

'My father came to see me,' he said. 'He brought it with him.'

The document in Georgina's hands was notification of the discharge from the RAF of Flight Lieutenant Christopher Alexander Bayliss. In the column giving the reason for the discharge, the letters LMF were printed in ink.

'What does LMF mean?' Georgina asked at last.

'It stands for "lacking moral fibre", Georgie.' He saw her expression twist suddenly into an incredulous mix of anger and anguish. She stepped back, almost as though what she had heard had knocked her off balance. He took her by the shoulders and steadied her.

'Hey,' he said gently. 'It couldn't matter less. It really couldn't.'

She pulled away from him.

'Of course it matters! Your father brought you this…? How could he? Who wrote it?' She shook the paper at Christopher. 'How dare they?'

'It's what happens, Georgie. Nothing personal.' She knew it was true. It was the form war took, the style of it. It had always claimed the young and courageous and killed them, or seen them destroyed, and when they were of no further use as fighting men, discarded them. But these were facts with which Georgina was familiar and her anger dissipated until it began to refocus on Roger Bayliss himself. He had failed, for months, to visit Christopher and then when, finally, he had arrived at Axmount he had entered through the locked gates, made his way past the nurses, the orderlies and their blanched and damaged patients, found his son and put into his hands a piece of paper which accused him of cowardice.

'But your father… How could…?'

Christopher, still smiling, shook his head.

'Poor old Pa,' he said amiably. 'I'm a bit of a disappointment to him, you see. Perfectly understandable when you think about it.' Georgina stared, incredulous. But an attack on his father was, she sensed, not what he wanted from her. 'Anyway,' he said easily, 'it's sorted now. I'll tell you all about it. Let's walk.' They moved off, side by side, along a slippery pathway and he began to unfold to her his plans.

Christopher's recollections of the late spring and the summer of 1943 were hazy and confused. He retained little more than fragmented memories of his last weeks of flying or of the sequence of events that followed the day when his nerves went to pieces and he ran. No one would ever know the details of the five weeks that elapsed between that day and the moment Georgina entered the byre and when, despite his shattered physical condition and the vivid hallucinations that possessed his mind, he had recognised her. There were people who might have recalled the sight of a bedraggled man sheltering in a cart shed or loping along a lane in the half-light but they would have been unaware that a few weeks previously that same man had been way above their heads, attacking a Junkers Eighty-Eight, shooting down a Dornier, fighting for his life – and for theirs. In the days following his capture he was questioned by a psychiatrist and put through a series of physical examinations. When left alone he slept, sedated and only vaguely aware that his skin, hair, the pyjamas he was wearing and the blankets that covered him, were clean and that his hunger and his thirst were quenched.

His attraction to Georgina, which began when, even before he acknowledged it, he was starting to buckle under the extreme pressure he was under had, from the moment he set eyes on her, been profound. It was as though, on every level, he had recognised her as a significant and abiding presence in his life. Her appearance pleased him. The level grey eyes, the way her hair fell, dark and sleek when so many of her contemporaries wore theirs in frizzy curls. The general impression she created was that she was striking, rather than beautiful. She was straight and strong, moving easily and with an unselfconscious elegance. He liked her fiery spirit and the way she had the grace to apologise when a flare of temper put her in the wrong. Even in the small number of hours which she and he had spent together the impression of her was burnt into him so that as he slid into and moved through his breakdown he had retained the image of her. When all other sensations and emotions had been stripped from him he had held onto Georgina, using her, as he had subsequently confessed to her, to form a shield between him and his demons. Then she had become the personification of his gradual recovery. She was his talisman. She, he now believed, had been right to denounce war as futile and destructive.

At Axmount, under the care of his doctors, he was slowly being restored. He had been weaned off his medications, fed, rested and slowly brought back to life. He had accepted the news of his discharge from the RAF with an ironic gratitude because it relieved his future plans of the complication of having to refuse to take any further part in the war. He would tell Georgina about his conversion to pacifism and his plans for a future which he hoped, even expected, that she would want to share.

'You were right,' he announced.

'I'm glad to hear it! About what?'

'About war being an inappropriate way of dealing with aggression. About how it damages the very people it is supposed to protect, turns innocent men into killers and encourages psychopaths!' Georgina had stopped in her tracks. 'What?' Christopher demanded, half smiling into her astonished and bewildered face. 'It's what you said, Georgie! It's exactly what you said!'

'It was awful, Mrs Todd!' Georgina wailed to Alice that night. 'He was so disappointed in me! I explained why I feel like I do! But you can understand how he feels! He'd listened to me. Thought about what I'd said about war and it had made sense to him! But I'd listened to him, too! And I understood what he had meant about war and then... then when he himself became a victim of it...' She paused, remembering Christopher's disintegration. 'I suppose I expected him to be pleased with me for wanting to fight – or if not actually fight at least to help defeat the Germans. But he behaved as if I had betrayed him – and in a way, I had, hadn't I!' She paused. Alice remained silent. 'He's planning to live in a building which was used by his father's woodsmen before the war. He says it's a ruin but he's going to repair it and when it's habitable he wants me to join him there! And be his wife!'

'And you don't want to?' Alice asked.

'No!'

'I thought you loved him!'

Georgina sat in silence for a while. When she spoke it was quietly. Almost reluctantly.

'I don't think I do, Mrs Todd. I'm fond of him. But I don't love him. At least...not the way he seems to love me.

He makes me feel protective. I want to defend him. But defending and protecting are not...not...' She stumbled into silence and then began again. 'When I first met him and he was so arrogant and self-opinionated... He was...sort of...challenging. I know it must seem peculiar to you but although I almost hated him, he was more attractive then. More than now, I mean. Now that he's...' She searched for the right word, shook her head and said, 'broken,' adding, 'I'm not making any sense, am I!'

Although Alice had not had any personal experience of Georgina's situation, she was aware of the sexual pull of men whose fascination lies in the fact that they are dangerous and possibly damaging. She had, like many women of her generation, watched *Gone With the Wind* and been more attracted to the wild, wilful and unprincipled Rhett Butler than to the gentler, sensitive and altogether more admirable Ashley Wilkes. So she nodded sympathetically and told Georgina that she thought she was making perfect sense and asked what had happened next.

'We should have been able to agree to differ but of course we didn't. Or couldn't. So we argued. And pretty soon it was almost like when we first met. Toe to toe. Eyeball to eyeball. He said I had misled him into thinking I was in love with him. Why else would I have visited him in hospital and been so angry over his discharge? I said it wasn't my fault if he'd misread me and that I'd been angry on his behalf and then I said something I should never have said. I said I had been sorry for him.'

'Oh dear,' Alice murmured. 'And how did he react to that?'

'He just stood there. Then he said he had an appointment with one of his doctors – he calls them his "keepers". He excused himself, very politely, and left me. I had half an hour to wait before Lionel collected me from the main gate. And it was raining.' Alice suppressed a smile.

'Poor Georgie!' she said.

'I 'eard from Mrs Fred,' Rose confided to Alice, several days later, 'that young Christopher 'as bin discharged from that Axmount place.' Alice said she was glad to hear it. 'But 'e's not come home, Alice! Leastways 'e did, but o'ny for as long as it took 'im to load up the old truck – the one Mr Bayliss don't use no more – with stuff. All sorts there was, Mrs Fred says. Bedding and pots and pans. Books an' that. The old table and chairs from what used to be the servants' parlour in the old days. Piled it all in the back of the truck 'e did and drove off!'

'Where's he gone?' Even as she asked, Alice thought she knew the answer to this and Rose confirmed her guess.

'First off no one knew!' Rose said. 'Then Ferdie says as Master Christopher 'as took the woodsmen's axes and saws and ropes an' stuff with him. So us put two and two, Alice, and come up with the woodsmen's cottage. 'Cos 'e used to like it up there, Christopher, I mean, workin' the timber, when 'e were a lad. But 'tis years since it were lived in!'

Historically, there had always been a building on the site of what became known in the twentieth century as the woodsmen's hut. Its origins were lost in time but its four stone walls, chimney stack, slated roof and cobbled floor had, from time to time, been maintained and when, a century ago, the forest began to be managed and men needed shelter when they worked there, a couple of windows had been put in and a door to keep out the worst of the weather. There was a fireplace inside, in which a huge and now rusted wood burner had been installed. Outside was a well with a pump beside it, a lean-to, a couple of small, derelict stone outbuildings and that was all.

The first thing Christopher did when he arrived at the cottage that late November afternoon was to light a fire. The neglected forest was littered with fallen branches and he had soon collected enough dry wood to keep the wood burner going for several days. Then he swept the accumulated leaves from the floor and removed the cobwebs from the two low windows, working fast as the short winter afternoon passed and the light faded. He moved his furniture inside as a drizzle of rain began, lit two of the three oil lamps he had brought with him, carried in the boxes and the bedding and assembled the camp bed.

Outside the darkness was complete. The wind had risen and was roaring through the tops of the trees. His father's housekeeper had prepared a stew for him. He had set the huge cast-iron pot on the top of the wood burner which, with its doors closed and a strong draught making the flames roar, was filling the cottage with a moist and musty warmth.

Since Roger Bayliss had been widowed and Eileen had taken on the role of housekeeper at Higher Post Stone Farm, she had considered herself responsible for Christopher's well-being. He was a small child when he had lost his mother and it had been Eileen who prepared his clothes for boarding school and nursed him through his childhood ailments. It had been she, more than his father had appeared to, who saw the first signs of the impending breakdown and was shocked by the news of his capture, arrest for desertion and incarceration in what, to her, was nothing short of bedlam. She had baked cakes and sent them through the post to Axmount. Whether or not he received them she did not know and thought it best not to enquire. She had hoped, when he recovered enough to come home, to nurse him back to health and strength. But he had gone, within hours, to the forest, to live in what she remembered as little more than a pigsty, five miles away, halfway up the moor and in the middle of a wood. So she had prepared a hamper for him and, just before he left the farm, heaved it out to the truck.

'There's a few bits and pieces,' she said breathlessly, and went on to list the pies, cakes, tins of ham, fish and rice pudding, pots of jams, side of cured bacon, home-made loaves and boxes of hens' eggs which she had filched from the farm pantry. Christopher, having forgotten to include supplies in his immediate plans for departure, was both touched and grateful. He hugged her as he had always hugged her, enjoying the softness of her bosom and the faint, familiar smell of her perspiration.

'And you'll need this,' she told him, releasing herself and tucking his ration book into a pocket. 'You'll get nothing down the grocer's without it!'

Eileen's mutton stew was huge and would provide his main meal for at least two days. She had cooked it gently until the meat was ready to fall off the bones and the carrots, turnips, pearl barley and potatoes had all softened together into an aromatic blend of concentrated goodness. As it warmed in its cast-iron pot, the smell of it filled the small space and gave Christopher a misleading sense of well-being. The place was like a cave filled with warmth in the soft light from the oil lamps. He felt safe under the arch of wind that swept over his roof. Occasional gusts threw a spatter of raindrops hard against his window panes. He cut thick wedges of Eileen's bread, dipped them into the stew and let them soak up the gravy. Without knife or fork he ate with his fingers, lifting out lumps of the meat and pieces of carrot. He found a bent spoon on the floor, cleaned it and used it to scoop up the softened vegetables and more of the rich, fatty gravy. When he was done he made up his fire, closing the damper as he had seen the woodsmen do when they wanted to slow the fire's consumption of logs and keep it burning through the night. He rolled himself up in his blankets and lay down on the narrow camp bed.

His priority next day was to fill the lean-to with dry wood. The rain, during the previous night, had been light and the mass of fallen timber in the acres immediately surrounding the cottage was not yet affected by the penetrating dampness of autumn. He drove a short distance down the track, sawed fallen timber into six-foot lengths and heaved them onto the truck, drove back to the cottage and stacked them under the lean-to. Five times he made this journey. By the time the light went the lean-to was filled to its rafters and Christopher was exhausted.

The stew was waiting for him, gently heated by the low fire. He opened the iron doors and let the draught roar into it, feeling the temperature inside the cottage rise while he satisfied his appetite. That day and for the five that followed it, he worked every hour of daylight and with every ounce of his increasing strength.

On the morning of the sixth day, Roger Bayliss, using a bridleway that made a shorter journey from his farm to the woodsmen's cottage than the track offered, heard the thwack of his son's axe before catching sight of him through a stand of beech trees whose autumn colour had been finally stripped from them by the latest gale.

Christopher embedded his axehead in a log and stepped forward to greet his father. They shook hands. He took his father's reins and tethered his horse.

'Tea?' the son offered. 'Kettle's on but I've only got tinned milk, I'm afraid.'

They had sat on either side of the wood burner sipping the hot tea and, in the sort of silence with which both were familiar, smoked their cigarettes. Christopher watched as his father looked slowly round at the primitive living arrangements, at the murky stone walls and the low boards that formed the ceiling.

'Can't persuade you to come home, then?' he asked.

Christopher shook his head. 'Thing is,' he smiled amiably, 'this feels like home, Pa. I like it here. It needs some attention admittedly but, when I've done what I have in mind, it'll be fine. And out there,' he waved an arm in the general direction of the encircling woodland, 'there's enough work to keep me out of trouble for years!'

Christopher missed his father's reaction to the implication that his son's commitment to this situation was long-term. But the possibility had occurred to Roger and he had already devised a series of conditions which would rationalise and to some extent normalise it.

'This is true,' he said. 'It'll be a while before the forest could become financially viable again but, if you want to have a go at it, you have my blessing.'

Unknown to Roger, the state of Christopher's mind, which was still affected by his breakdown, had not led him to consider what his father's reaction might be to his retreat to the woodland or how he himself would have responded had his father opposed it. Because of this his father's apparent approval had very little effect on him and he merely smiled and ashed his cigarette into the fireplace.

'However,' Roger continued, 'you must allow me to put things on a proper footing.' Christopher looked baffled. 'Firstly,' Roger went on, 'you must be waged.'

'Waged?'

'Yes. Given a salary. Paid for your work. Secondly, you must allow me to make you more comfortable up here.' Christopher opened his mouth to protest but Roger raised a hand to silence him. 'There's not a lot that can be done with this place but I insist that you don't starve, that your bedding and your clothes are laundered, that you allow me to provide whatever supplies you need and that you keep the truck up here so that whenever, if ever, you have had enough of it up here, you can get home to the farm. I won't have you living like a tramp, Christopher.' Roger was prepared, if his son had refused his terms, to have him forcibly removed from the cottage and, if necessary, certified as insane. He was, therefore, relieved to see that Christopher seemed more than happy to comply.

'Thanks, Pa.' He smiled. 'That sounds great – as long as you're sure I'm worth it!'

Together they compiled two lists. The first consisted of the items which Fred would deliver by truck on a regular basis each week and the other of materials, tools and items of furniture with which Christopher would transform the cottage – as much as it would be possible to transform it – into the place in which he wished to live and where, when she eventually arrived, as he was convinced she would, he would welcome Georgina.

Alice took some time over deciding what to wear to Roger Bayliss's party, eventually settling on a well-cut black jersey dress, which she had worn once or twice when she had accompanied her husband to Ministry receptions where she had been expected to make polite conversation with the wives of senior civil servants and other government officials. She had regarded these evenings more as a duty, when she was required to be an asset to James, than a pleasure and she had always sighed with relief when James appeared at her side, a welcome indication that it was almost time for them to leave. She had lost weight since she had been working at Lower Post Stone and the dress, when she tried it on and turned this way and that in front of the long looking glass in the cross-passage, flattered her figure even more than she remembered. With her mother's pearls, silk stockings and black court shoes she would, she considered modestly, do.

Being short of men for his party, and in view of Oliver Maynard's hospitality to the Post Stone land girls on the occasion of the cricket match and since then to several 'hops' at the camp, Roger had reluctantly included him on his guest list. Oliver, insisting that he would be practically passing Alice's door, talked Roger into letting him convey her to and from the party. Arriving together, their fellow guests assumed them to be 'a couple'. Oliver was, Alice felt, slightly overattentive to her, giving her little chance to talk to the other guests, most of whom were well acquainted with each other and included Margery Brewster and her rotund and florid husband. Eileen, aided by her niece Albertine, a robust schoolgirl whose capacious bosom resembled her aunt's, refilled sherry glasses, ladled out mulled wine and offered a choice between Eileen's cheese straws or, as the evening progressed, her mince pies and slices of the Christmas cake for which she had been accumulating ingredients throughout the year. At one point there was a slight disturbance when, flushed, overexcited and to the acute embarrassment of her husband, Margery Brewster fell off a chair and found it so amusing that it took both her husband and Oliver Maynard to get her back onto her feet.

Roger, who had been curious to know what Alice would look like dressed for an occasion such as this one, was enchanted with what he saw. He observed her as much and as closely as he could without his interest attracting the attention of his other guests. He saw her eyes explore his warm, well-furnished sitting room and when she moved closer to a large oil painting hanging above the fireplace, he joined her.

'My grandfather,' he said. 'Painted by a man called Pickersgill in the 1890s. And that's his wife – my grandfather's wife, I mean of course. Elizabeth Anne

Clifton.' They crossed the room and Alice stood gazing at the serene face framed against a dark background by a pale, ruched lace cap, its delicate ribbons tied under her chin. Oliver Maynard had joined them.

'Fine-looking woman,' he said but the woman he was looking at was Alice and Roger was aware of this.

'She is beautiful!' Alice said, turning to Roger. 'And I think I see a trace of a family likeness. Something about the set of the eyes, perhaps.'

'Interesting,' Roger said. His expression had for once lost its familiar closed, defensive look. 'That was exactly what my wife – what Frances – always said. If we'd had a daughter we would have called her Elizabeth Anne.'

Later, the interior of Oliver's car was cold. Condensation ran down the windows and frost glittered in the headlights.

'Nice party,' Oliver said and suggested that Alice might feel like 'going on' somewhere. 'Not that there's anywhere to "go on" to in this God-forsaken neck of the woods.' Alice said that anyway she needed to get back to the hostel. Oliver grunted, took a corner rather too fast, skidded on a patch of black ice and had to struggle to avoid slewing into the hedge. He was angry with himself and apologised profusely.

'That was unforgivable. Unforgivable. Reprehensible behaviour. Reprehensible…' For some reason, perhaps because it had been a pleasant evening, perhaps because of the warmth of Roger's smile and the attentive way in which he had helped her into her coat when it was over, she found Oliver's abject apology amusing.

'Don't apologise,' she laughed. 'It was rather exciting!' Oliver glanced at her. Reflected light from the dimmed headlights revealed just enough to confirm that she was smiling. The fact that she was pleased with him rounded off his evening. As they drew up outside the farmhouse he leant across and kissed her mouth. It was a light, unassuming kiss and, as such, Alice briefly returned it, getting quickly out of the car, closing its door behind her and calling out goodnight and thanking him for the lift as she picked her way along the icy path and into the porch.

On his homeward drive Oliver experimented with a few controlled slides which resulted in his arrival at the camp with a significant dent in his offside mudguard.

'I 'ear from Eileen as Mrs Brewster enjoyed 'erself las' night!' Rose said next morning, with a suggestion of disapproval in her sharp Devonian voice. 'Fallin' about a bit, Eileen says!'

'Mrs Brewster lost her balance, Rose.' Alice made a point of discouraging gossip where those in authority were concerned.

'Mrs Brewster should take a drop more water with it!' Rose said virtuously.

This was the first intimation Alice had regarding Margery Brewster's problem with alcohol. Rose's comment had the effect of reminding her that once or twice she had caught a whiff of spirits on Margery's breath and once she had brought a bottle into the hostel and insisted that Alice joined her in a sip of gin-and-orange at the kitchen table.

'Don't fret, Alice!' she had laughed, her face flushed slightly from the pleasure of the drink. 'Your charges won't be back for hours yet! Cheers, my dear! Down the hatch! Mud in your eye and all that!'

On the second of Fred's trips up into the woodland with supplies for Christopher, Alice had ridden with him, wedged into the passenger seat as the truck lurched uncomfortably up the uneven track. There were places where recent heavy rain had scoured its surface, leaving deep potholes and forcing Fred to make detours round them, the truck, with two wheels halfway up the steep bank, tipping perilously and causing his cargo to slide from side to side. In addition to the regular supplies of food, drink and clean laundry, Fred was today delivering an old sofa which had, years previously, been replaced in the Bayliss sitting room and had lain since in the attic, gathering dust and being nibbled at by mice. This, Christopher had decided, when spread with the half-dozen sheepskins which had accumulated in the tackle room, would provide a warm and practical place for him to relax and probably sleep, in front of his fire on cold nights in January and February.

Christopher's pulse had quickened when he saw that there

was someone sitting beside Fred in the cab of the truck. Almost at once he had realised it was Alice Todd who was Fred's passenger and not Georgina as he had at first hoped. He recovered quickly and approached Alice with the well-mannered charm she remembered from before he was ill.

'Mrs Todd!' He shook her hand. 'How very nice to see you!'

Alice confessed that everyone at Post Stone had heard so much about the woodsmen's cottage that she had been unable to resist an opportunity to inspect it so that she could report back to the girls. She presented him with the treacle tart that Rose had made for his supper.

What Alice saw as she entered the cottage was very different from the scene that had greeted Roger Bayliss two weeks previously. The walls and ceiling had been whitewashed. Cooking pots hung beside the wood burner. The camp bed was made up. There were books on the shelves and Christopher's old spaniel, sprawling across a worn rug in front of the fire, thumped her tail as Alice watched her master light the oil lamps.

'We'll bring in the furniture,' Christopher said. 'Then you'll have somewhere comfortable to sit while you drink your tea!'

The sofa, its broken springs barely audible under the skeepskins, was so comfortable and the warmth of the cottage so soothing that Alice, whose previous night's sleep had been disturbed by Gwennan, first asking for an aspirin and then for some warm oil to soothe an aching ear, almost fell asleep over her cup of tea while Fred unloaded the rest of Christopher's supplies.

'Youse'll be comin' 'ome for Christmas, I s'pose?' Fred enquired on Eileen's instructions. Christopher answered evasively and deliberately inaudibly. 'Eh?' Fred insisted and Christopher raised his voice slightly and said he thought probably not, in the circumstances. 'An' what circumstances be they?' Fred persisted. But he was retreating, lowering his head under the lintel of the door and muttering darkly to himself. 'A son oughta spend Christmas with his pa, I reckon...' Then he raised his voice. 'Reckon we should be on our way, Mrs Todd, if it's all the same to you.' He was in the cab with the engine running as Alice said her farewells.

'And the girls?' Christopher enquired, handing her into the truck. 'Everyone well?'

Alice assured him that everyone was very well indeed. She knew that what he wanted was news of Georgina and drew a deep breath.

'Georgina is leaving us,' she said, as lightly as she could.

'Leaving?' He was standing absolutely still, his face level with hers.

'Yes,' she said. 'She's joined some flying organisation – one that moves RAF planes from one airfield to another. They're called—'

'Ferry pilots... Yes, I know what they're called, Mrs Todd.' His interruption had been curt. Almost rude. 'I should have guessed,' he said flatly. 'Her flying experience. The de Havilland godfather, and so on.' He had a hazel switch in his hand and began striking the side of his wellington boot with it, thwack, thwack, thwack, just as his father did with his crop against the leather of his riding boots when he was irritated. There was a small, tense silence while Fred revved the engine of the truck.

'Shouldn't you talk, the pair of you?' Alice asked. 'Come and see her before she goes!' She was uncertain that he had heard her. He seemed lost in his thoughts.

'We did talk, Mrs Todd,' he said at last. 'And she knows where I am if she wants me.'

The Christmas break was looming. The girls bought presents to take home to their mothers and fathers, brothers, sisters and grandparents, they ironed their best frocks and washed their hair. As the preparations continued the weather became cold, then colder still until the frost lay thick and crackling all through the days, the ice in the drinking troughs was six inches thick and the yard pump froze solid.

'Us'll 'ave snow afore us sees the back of this lot,' Ferdie announced, eyeing the bleak grey sky and turning his back on an icy easterly wind. 'On'y needs for this wind to back round to the north and we'll cop it, you mark my words!' While Mabel spent her Christmas at Lower Post Stone with her grandmother and little Arthur, Ferdie was to visit his widowed sister, bearing with him a brace of pheasants and a salmon, all poached from his employer.

By the morning of Christmas Eve the goose was plucked, stuffed and waiting in the Lower Post Stone pantry for the moment, on Christmas morning, when Rose would slide it into the oven. The girls, their suitcases packed and lined up in the cross-passage, ready for when Fred would arrive to collect them and deliver them to the railway station, were hurrying through their morning tasks when the first flakes of snow shimmied down the wind. Ferdie lurched painfully across the yard; his damaged bones always hurt him more when the weather was foul.

'See that?' he roared, pointing north to where the sky was dark with lowering cloud. 'Didn't I say? Due north that wind be now! And the snow baint far behind 'un neither!'

By the time the girls had returned to Lower Post Stone, changed their clothes and, clutching their suitcases and parcels, were climbing, shivering, into the back of Fred's truck, the landscape was solidifying into a white blur. Lionel had already arrived and with Georgina, well wrapped, on the pillion seat of his motorbike, had ridden carefully away along the slippery lane and headed towards their home.

Alice, Hester and Mabel had waved goodbye from the porch and then run, shuddering with cold, back into the warm farmhouse. Gwennan, on the grounds that she thought she might be coming down with something but possibly simply to avoid being asked to help prepare the vegetables for Christmas dinner, went to bed with a hot-water bottle. An hour passed and a sort of peace descended on the farmhouse, broken only from time to time by squeals of pleasure from Arthur, who was playing on the recreation room floor with Edward-John's train set. The snow, spiralling down, the flakes huge and soft, now blanketed the landscape and, driven by the wind, was beginning to pile up into significant drifts. Alice, her larder stocked with enough food to feed her reduced household for at least two days, felt curiously safe and satisfied as, with her fingertips, she cleared the condensation from her window and peered out at the immaculate snowy scene.

Then, to her surprise, she saw Fred's truck labouring cautiously along the snow-filled lane towards her. Why, she wondered, had he returned to Lower Post Stone and not to the higher farm where his cottage stood, close to the byres and barns where his work lay?

She watched as the truck slithered to a stop outside the gate. Amazed, she saw her girls, one after the other, climb down from the rear of the truck and, clutching their suitcases and parcels, troop forlornly through the deep snow, up the path and back into the farmhouse.

'There's no trains runnin'!' Marion wailed.

'Some goods-wagons 'as got derailed up Taunton way and they've blocked the track! What with the snow and all, no one can do nothin' so they've on'y gone and closed the bleedin' line!'

'There's no trains runnin' in or out!'

'So we can't go home!'

'We can't go home!' they chorused in unison, their eyes on Alice as though she, by some miracle, could change things.

'I'm so friggin cold, Mrs Todd!' Annie hissed between chattering teeth.

Alice reached for the teapot. She ordered the weeping, shivering girls to go to their rooms and change into warm clothes. She decided to offer them hot buttered toast and it was when she went to the bread cupboard that the full implications of the situation hit her. She had food enough for those left in her charge over Christmas and, at a pinch, for a couple of days after it. But not enough to feed the girls who had been unable to make their journeys home. Gwennan, in her dressing gown and clutching her hot-water bottle, burst into the kitchen.

'Fred's got the truck stuck in a snowdrift, just along the lane, Mrs Todd! I saw him from my window! He tried to dig himself out, like! But then he left the truck and it looks like he's going to walk back to the higher farm! But will he get there, Mrs Todd?' There was a slightly unhealthy excitement in Gwennan's delivery of this news, as though, in her dark and Celtic way, she relished it. 'Or will he die in the snow like Captain Scott?'

With the girls warmed and sipping hot tea, Alice set about checking her supplies. The goose, sliced thinly, would feed them all on Christmas Day and there was no shortage of potatoes and swedes. She checked the pantry shelves and found tins of beans and of spam. There was a full can of milk but when that was gone it might be some time before any more arrived from the snow-bound dairy at Higher Post Stone. Bread would be the main problem. With no packed lunches to provide for four days, Alice had ordered only two loaves. Long and reassuring as they were, they would not last long now that she had her full complement of mouths to feed.

Rose, basking in the company of her son Dave, and enjoying the prospect of showing him off to Alice over Christmas lunch next day, had seen the girls return and knew, only too well, the implications of this where the hostel catering arrangements were concerned. Leaving Dave to sleep off the enormous lunch she had fed him, Rose waded through the loose snow of the yard and joined Alice in the kitchen.

'Whatever will you do?' she demanded dramatically – there was nothing Rose enjoyed more than an impending disaster. 'This could go on for weeks, you know! Coupla years ago we was snowed in for almost a month! Couldn't get in nor out! It's the steepness, see, of the lanes!' Alice had noticed the steepness of the lanes and was not comforted by what she heard.

'The first thing, Rose, is tonight's supper. We'd better open those tins of spam, fry some onions, chop up some potatoes and make a hash. The second thing is to let Mr Bayliss know that the girls didn't get away and that we're snowed in here and already short of bread and milk. I'll go and telephone him now.' Alice pulled on her waterproof coat and her rubber boots and, with her scarf wound tightly round her neck, made her way across the yard, her boots sinking into deep, soft snow. It was only half past two but because of the thick layer of leaden cloud it was already almost dark. Alice fumbled her way into the barn where the telephone was and shone her torch onto the dial. Roger Bayliss would know what to do. He'd dig out the stranded truck and send a tractor loaded with supplies down the valley to Lower Post Stone. She lifted the receiver. There was no dialling tone. The line was dead.

Chapter Nine

Roger Bayliss was settling a log of wood onto the fire in his warm sitting room when Eileen, with the briefest of knocks on his door, burst in.

''Tis Fred,' she said. 'E's at the kitchen door and 'e's froze!'

They brought him into the sitting room and sat him on a hard chair, which Eileen placed close to the fire. Melting ice pooled at his feet; his dripping coat, white with snow when he entered the room, was returning now to its original brownish colour. Blanched fingers protruded from wet, unravelling mittens as he clutched the tumbler of whiskey that his master had poured for him. He told how he had driven the land girls to Ledburton Halt only to find the railway closed and how he had returned them to the safety of the hostel and then, as he attempted to persuade the truck back up the hill towards the higher farm, it had slithered into a ditch and become firmly embedded in deep snow.

'Varmint of a thing,' he grumbled. 'So I 'ad to bloomin' walk, di'n I!' He sipped noisily, eyeing his master. 'Main thing is them girls is all accounted for – save for the Webster one. Went off earlier on the back of her brother's motorbike, she did. Lord knows where they got to!'

'Mrs Todd can telephone the parents to make sure the girl arrived safely.'

'Well, that's where you'm wrong, sir, with respect. 'Cos the lines be down. I seen the wires danglin' as I come up the 'ill.'

Since Fred's arrival Roger had been waiting for Alice's phone call. He had been preparing what he would say to her. First he would have asked her to confirm that all the girls were safely with her and that she had enough fuel and food for the immediate requirements of the additional mouths she had to feed. Then he would have instructed her to make a list of everything she would need to see the inhabitants of Lower Post Stone through the days or possibly even weeks of virtual isolation which might lie ahead. He would have asked her to telephone him in the morning to give him the list and he would have assured her that the supplies would be delivered by tractor without delay. He would have arranged for extra paraffin and more logs so that the fires could be kept burning round the clock until the thaw. The warden would have confirmed her instructions. Now, with the news of the damaged telephone lines, this imagined conversation could not take place though Alice would almost certainly have tried, unsuccessfully, to contact him.

Outside, darkness had fallen. Thick snow-clouds diffused what little moonlight there was. To attempt to take the tractor down to the farm in these conditions would have been hazardous and if it, too, had become stuck in the icy snow, it would have reduced the chances of getting supplies through to the farm on the following day. Fred's glass was empty.

'By jim'ny, sir,' he wheezed, 'that be a powerful drop! I can feel the blood just startin' to flow back into my frozen limbs!' Eileen could see that Fred's heavy hint had fallen on deaf ears.

'You're quite certain, Fred,' Roger asked, 'that all the girls are safely in the hostel?'

'Oh yes, sir. I saw every one of 'em go up that path an' in through the door afore I left 'em an' tried to get meself 'ome!'

'You best get back to Mrs Fred,' Eileen suggested, relieving him of the empty tumbler. ''Er'll think youm lost in the blizzard, else.'

Christmas morning, despite dazzling sunshine and a brilliant blue sky, was bitterly cold. The girls, having recovered from their disappointment, began to respond to the fact that this morning they were not obliged to pull on their cold, damp dungarees and face the elements. With fires blazing round the clock, the farmhouse, its thick walls and thatched roof retaining every joule of generated warmth, was positively cosy. Hot water gurgled dangerously in the pipes and the bathroom became a steamy, tropical delight. Some of the girls slept in, pottering down to the kitchen to toast slices of the dwindling supply of bread and brew pot after pot of tea. Others took it in turns to soak luxuriously in the bath until the skin on their fingers became wrinkled. With no rules to obey and no timetable to be adhered to, they wallowed in the freedom from the grinding routine of their work.

At Higher Post Stone Roger Bayliss, in the pitch-dark, icy cold of milking-time, had pulled on his working clothes and joined Fred and Ferdie in the byre where they relieved the cows of their milk, rolling the churns out into the snow, anxious about how long it would be before the milk-truck could get through to collect them.

Eileen, unable to return to the village on the previous night, had made up a bed in the room in which the servants used to sleep, risen early, helped with the milking and then cooked a robust breakfast for the men.

A dozen miles away at the Fleet Air Arm training camp, Oliver Maynard was experiencing a situation not unlike Alice's. While most of the men under his command had been given seventy-two-hour passes and had got away before the snow had closed in, he was left with a dozen or so of his own men and a similar number of Americans who, after a

Christmas dinner which they would eat at noon, had been planning to head off for Exeter or Taunton to find what pleasures they could in pubs and dance halls. This, because of the snow, had now become impossible. It was suggested that their Adjutant might make a Bren-gun carrier available to them but Oliver Maynard refused to permit the use of the military equipment under his immediate command for anything other than training purposes. It was this fact that gave him the idea that, within three hours, he had implemented and which was to transform Christmas day for everyone who became involved in it.

Underlying Oliver's plan was his increasing ambitions where Alice Todd was concerned. His own domestic situation had, over recent weeks, worsened. When, soon after the outbreak of the war, his wife Diana had miscarried, it had been decided that, because his postings were taking him further afield and for longer periods of time, they should postpone any immediate attempts to achieve a second pregnancy until after the war and that, in order to fill her time constructively, Diana should join the WRNS, where she soon became a busy and consequently happier young woman. The enforced separation took its toll on the relationship and Diana had recently written to her husband, apologising for various infidelities on her part and suggesting that he should consider their marriage over.

By ten in the morning and at approximately the same time as the goose went into the oven at Lower Post Stone and the succulent smell of it began to permeate the farmhouse, Oliver Maynard gave his men their instructions and began masterminding what he would later refer to, in the report he would submit to his commanding officer, as Operation Snowman.

In the silent cottage in the forest Christopher was woken when a shaft of low morning sunlight moved across his closed lids, penetrating a dream in which he was in the cockpit of a Spitfire and blinded by the beam of a searchlight. He woke gratefully and lay, while his pulse slowed, comfortably cradled by the undulating contours of the old sofa. The sheepskins over and under him were warm and his fire, well stoked at midnight, was still alight. He dismissed the dream and for a while let his mind drift back to the Christmases at Higher Post Stone when his mother was alive and cousins came to stay. Eileen's father, now long dead, would arrive on a farm cart, dressed as Father Christmas. The children would humour their parents by pretending not to recognise him. For a few minutes Christopher considered making the slippery journey down to his father's farm. But who, he asked himself, would it please if he did? Not him. He would rather be alone until Georgina came. She would come. Maybe not today. Or for some time. But one day she would. And not his father, whose eyes he could no longer meet because of the strange look in them, which he interpreted as accusation and disappointment but which, as he would one day discover, was something more complex and more forgivable. Eileen would be pleased if he arrived at the farm in time to enjoy the Christmas dinner she would undoubtedly be preparing. He did not know that, were it not for the blizzard, Eileen would have been alone in her cottage while his father ate roast goose with Alice Todd at Lower Post Stone.

The hamper of Christmas food which Fred had delivered to Christopher early on the previous morning, and just before the threatening snow had begun to fall, contained an impressive array of festive food. Eileen, despite the rationing, had excelled herself. There was a game pie, a Christmas pudding and a pot of brandy sauce, an apple tart, a jar of pickled herrings, a Christmas cake, and a large jug of chicken soup together with his usual supply of milk, vegetables, eggs and bread. Christopher had shot a pheasant, plucked it, stuffed it with sweet chestnuts that he picked up from the forest floor and wrapped it in rind from the ham, a section of which still hung from a hook above his fire. At midday he would flatten the embers and set the bird to roast. He broke the ice in the well and refilled his water pots and kettle. He carried in an armful or two of split logs. He had discovered an old hip-bath in an outbuilding and had hauled it into the cottage. A couple of buckets of water, heated on the wood burner and tipped into the bath, met his needs. He shaved, lathered his hair, sluiced himself with the warmed water, towelled himself down and dressed in the clean clothes that Eileen had sent up with his groceries.

Despite his near normal appearance, Christopher was not fully recovered from his breakdown or from the trauma that had induced it. He still had nightmares and far from addressing the future in the way most people would, even when recovering from a disastrous experience, he blotted it out, living his days one at a time and contriving to be so physically tired at the end of them that he would fall asleep, curled up on the old sofa amongst his pile of sheepskins, before provocative thoughts could form. When the nightmares woke him he would light a lamp, brew a pot of tea and focus his mind on the pages of one or other of the books he had brought with him, reading until sleep overtook him or dawn broke, whichever happened first.

At Lower Post Stone, Hester Tucker dolefully set the kitchen table for Christmas dinner. Reuben, currently stationed at a training camp on Salisbury Plain, had been expected to arrive by noon but because of the snow it seemed unlikely that he would arrive at all.

'This is my Dave,' said Rose, who, anxious to show off her son to Alice Todd, had encouraged him to cross the yard with her. In fact, Dave, now rested and full of his mother's good food, needed little persuasion and was anxious to meet the bevy of girls who, so promisingly for a young soldier on his first home leave, had been conveniently deposited across the yard from the cottage in which he had been born and bred.

Hester was the first girl he saw and, for him, she was more than enough. He stood transfixed, smiling into her wide blue eyes and lost in the curve of her unpainted mouth. She was the right height, the right width and her accent, when she said, 'Pleased to meet you, Dave,' was as familiar to him as his own. His mother did not for one moment miss her son's reaction to the girl. She had seen his eyes light up and something like a blush deepen the colour of his ruddy Devonian complexion. When Hester went out to the pantry to fetch the platter on which the roasted goose was to be carved, Rose leant close to her son and whispered urgently to him.

''Tis no good you lookin' in that direction, Dave! Hester be spoke for!' Dave seemed not to hear her. Even when Annie, Gwennan and Winnie joined them in the kitchen his eyes remained on Hester, or, when he sensed that his admiration was attracting attention, on the slate pavings of the kitchen floor, while he racked his brain for something to say to her.

'Bin a land girl long, then?' he managed at last.

'Feb'ry, weren't it, when you come 'ere, Hester?' Rose answered, butting in. Hester smiled and nodded.

'Like it, do you?' Dave tried again. This time it was Gwennan who took the question.

'Oh, yeah!' she said. 'It's great being up to your middle

in mud, with rain runnin' down your neck!'

Marion, in the bedroom she shared with Winnie, was still wearing a powder-blue rayon dressing gown which she had recently persuaded a young naval rating to buy for her in Exeter when, from the low window, she saw the Bren-gun carrier. It was, at that point, a quarter of a mile away from the snowbound farmhouse and was making a lurching descent into the valley. Marion had never seen anything like it before. She could see that it had tracks like a tank, which was why it was able to negotiate the deep snow. She could see the barrel of a gun and behind that the heads of a dozen men. Thinking that they might be Germans and that this was an invasion, she anxiously scanned the paintwork for a Swastika and was relieved not to find one. As it grew closer, Marion saw that the vehicle was towing a trailer and that on the trailer were more men. It was the fact that the vehicle itself was camouflaged with curious shapes in various shades of brown and green and that the men aboard it were wearing khaki that finally plunged Marion into action. By the time the Bren-gun carrier was idling outside the farmhouse gate, Marion was not only dressed in her most flamboyant frock, but had rouge on her cheeks, mascara on her lashes and lipstick on her mouth. She was rapidly fixing her hair as Oliver Maynard made his way up the path and knocked loudly on the door.

He had thought of everything. The turkey and the ham were both cooked to perfection and, being well wrapped, had, together with the roasted vegetables, remained piping hot during the half-hour transfer from the cookhouse at the camp to the farmhouse kitchen. Puddings, cakes and pastries were unloaded from the trailer together with kegs of beer, bottles of port, ginger ale and Coca-Cola. They had brought plates, glasses, knives, forks, spoons and tablecloths.

'All we need,' said a burly GI cook, settling his chef's hat over his crew cut, 'is a table! Can you guys manage that?' Alice and the girls thought they could.

Sergeant Marvin Kinski, US Marines, bearing a barrel of beer, swaggered into the farmhouse kitchen, the stump of a cheroot clamped between his strong, white teeth. His stocky build had earnt him the nickname 'Short-arse'. His beard grew so fast that within an hour of shaving he looked as though his chin had not made contact with a razor blade for many days. His deep-set, brooding brown eyes had a sharp, defensive look which conveyed an 'OK, lady, so you don't fancy me, well, guess what – who cares,' approach to women. And he was right. Most women didn't find him attractive. Except for Marion, who, much later and in the privacy of their room, confessed to Winnie that, although she didn't know why, because, let's face it, he wasn't her type, she'd felt quite peculiar when she was dancing with Sergeant Kinski – which she had been, exclusively and almost continuously, from the moment Christmas dinner was finished until well after midnight, when Oliver Maynard had ordered his men to bid the girls goodnight.

''E asked me if I'd write to him, Win and I said I would. 'E said 'e'd write to me... Don't suppose he will though. 'E's being posted to somewhere over Dartmouth way for training. Slapton Sands I think 'e said. Funny, isn't it! Usually I like 'em tall, don't I!'

'Yeah,' said Winnie, 'and dark and handsome!'

'Well, he is dark.'

'Yeah, he is dark... But not handsome, Marion.'

'No... But he's got something about him, Marvin has. If you'd spent all evening with 'im you'd know what I mean.' Marion was wiping her make-up off and with it, Winnie reckoned, the face Sergeant Kinski had fallen for. 'What was yours like, then, Win?'

'He was OK,' Winnie murmured vaguely. She had already almost forgotten the young corporal from Alabama who had attached himself to her for most of the evening. 'Just a bloke,' she said. 'With pimples.'

Winnie had never considered the possibility that the burning ambition to open a pub that she and Marion had shared for almost as long as she could remember could be jeopardised by one or the other of them becoming seriously involved with a man, or that any man who would be interested in either of them would be able to offer them the things they wanted from life. To Winnie men were a faintly threatening necessity. A source of what she needed. First money for a down payment on a public house and then permission to assume responsibility for it. It was unlikely, she knew, that she and Marion would be granted a licence. When they applied for one it would be Marion's uncle Ronald, a publican himself, whom they would need to approach for legal, if not financial support. The idea of either of them losing interest in their plan sent a shudder down Winnie's spine.

The kitchen table had been barely large enough for all the food. Everyone had loaded their plates more than once and carried them out into the cross-passage where a trestle-table, with every chair in the hostel, a couple of benches and even an old wicker seat from the porch, clustered round it, made an adequate dining table. When the meal was underway, with the gramophone blaring and thirty voices raised over it, no one heard the approach of the tractor.

Roger Bayliss had loaded sacks of potatoes and swedes, boxes of eggs and a churn of milk into a small trailer and carefully negotiated the slippery lane. He had guessed, as soon as he saw the Bren-gun carrier, that Oliver Maynard had seized the opportunity of the blizzard to further his obvious interest in Alice Todd. Roger experienced a pang of frustration that it had not been he who had arrived first with practical support for his warden.

Alice was sitting at the head of the table in a wicker chair that had once stood in his own conservatory. When, on the arrival of the servicemen, the land girls had put on their best frocks, Alice did the same. The garnet velvet of her dress suited her. Oliver Maynard was sitting on her right. As Roger ducked his head under the lintel and stood, amazed by the scene, Alice and Oliver were sharing a joke. As soon as she saw Roger, Alice rose and made her way round the crowded table to greet him.

The noise of boisterous conversations interrupted by bursts of hearty laughter, all of this competing with the music of Glenn Miller at full volume from the gramophone in the recreation room, made it almost impossible for Roger to hear Alice as she explained how the day had developed for her and her girls. She invited him into the slightly quieter kitchen, encouraged him to help himself to the food and led him back into the cross-passage where everyone moved up enough to make room for him at the table. Oliver poured him a glass of wine and, in the manner of a victor, raised his own glass and proposed a toast to Alice, who responded with a short, charming speech of thanks to Oliver and his men for helping to give her girls such a splendid Christmas feast.

With the table cleared from the cross-passage and the sofas in the recreation room pushed against the walls there was space for some serious dancing. Dave took Hester in his arms and carefully circled the floor with her. Gwennan stumbled through a foxtrot with the cook, who, thanks to his chef's hat, equalled her lanky height. Annie, much in demand, moved sociably from one partner to another, while Winnie smiled politely for her GI Joe and watched Marion and Marvin jitterbugging as though their bodies were designed exclusively for that purpose. Mabel and her gran led the Lambeth Walk. Dave organised the hokey-cokey and Alice tried, without much success, to teach everyone the steps of Sir Roger de Covelly.

At ten o'clock, when most of the food and almost all the drink had been consumed, Reuben arrived. He had been walking for nine hours and stood, breathing hard, snow in his hair, packed ice falling off his boots, his skin glowing with exertion and exposure, his eyes scanning the room for his girl. Dave, waltzing with her, felt her pull away from him, watched her weave through the dancers and fling herself, to whoops of delight and applause from everyone, into Reuben's arms.

''E needs feedin', Mrs Todd,' Hester said happily and taking Reuben by the hand, led him into the kitchen, closing the door behind them.

The Webster home, when Georgina and Lionel had reached it, looked much as it always had on Christmas Eve. The tall spruce standing in the hallway was decorated with familiar gilded fir cones, tinsel and lights, topped with the now bedraggled fairy that Georgina had made in kindergarten. The house was warm and in the kitchen festive food was being prepared. The snow, which had barely begun to fall when Lionel had collected his sister from Lower Post Stone, had become a wind-driven blizzard and by the time they reached their destination they were chilled to their bones.

Their father had led them into the warm sitting room and administered mulled rum-and-orange, watching them as they sipped. Later, after Georgina had lain for some time in a hot bath and was now wrapped in her dressing gown, Lionel wandered into her bedroom and sprawled across her bed.

'Seen your chap lately?' he asked her.

'Which chap is that?' she countered, adding, 'If you mean Christopher Bayliss, no. Not lately.' She had washed her hair and was towelling it dry.

'Why not?'

'Because he's taken himself off somewhere and become a lumberjack.'

'I heard that much from Annie. But it doesn't explain why you—'

'Why I what? You're being very nosy, little brother! Stop it!'

He ignored the second part of her response and repeated his question.

'Why, after visiting him in that hospital place, have you suddenly dropped him? Doesn't make any sense to me!'

'That's because you don't know—'

'I know I "don't know", woman!' he interrupted. 'That's why I'm asking!' Georgina laughed, went to her bedroom door and opened it.

'Can I have some privacy, please?' She was teasing him. 'I need to get dressed now. I promised our mother I'd help her in the kitchen.' As Lionel went past her onto the landing she added, 'I will tell you all about it, Li… But later… OK?'

Georgina was grateful that the family had company for Christmas dinner, which they were to eat at three o'clock. It gave her a valid reason for not broaching the awkward subject of her future plans until most, if not all of the day's festivities were over.

Alan and Pamela Marshall farmed nearby and the two families were well acquainted. The Marshalls put chains on the tyres of their car and safely managed the two-mile drive to the Webster house, bringing with them their younger daughter, Drusilla. An older girl was with the WRAC at Caterham. Drusilla, still at boarding school, was a pretty seventeen-year-old and had been in love with Lionel since she was twelve, a fact of which he remained unaware.

The afternoon and evening passed pleasantly. The two families played their own familiar versions of some Christmas games. At eight o'clock everyone went out into the garden and pelted each other with snowballs, returning to the warm house for a light supper followed by dancing to gramophone records. Lionel dutifully partnered his mother, Pamela Marshall and then his sister. After that, it was noticed, he danced almost exclusively, with Drusilla.

By midnight, with the guests departed, the house was suddenly quiet. Georgina had decided that rather than spoil the happy atmosphere, she would keep her difficult news until the morning. She was about to switch off her bedside light when Lionel knocked on her door.

'You said you'd tell me later, why you've dumped your mad airman.'

'He's not—!'

'I know!' Lionel interrupted her interruption. 'I know he's not mad and I've found out something about these guys… these pilots that crack up. Want to hear it?' Georgina nodded and patted the bed, inviting him to sit, as he always had, for as long as either of them could remember, when they had something important to discuss. 'It's not always that they lose their nerve, you know, or even that they get traumatised by what they have to do – although that would account for some cases, but…' He paused, trying to formulate the information he had for her. He told her about a friend of his who had been at university reading psychology when the war broke out. Because of this he had been given the opportunity to work with a group of consultants on cases where servicemen suffered breakdowns caused by what, in earlier conflicts, had been classified as 'shell shock'. Frequently, brave men, having exhibited acute symptoms of distress, had been condemned to death and shot as deserters. Georgina said she knew this.

'But did you know, Georgie, that front-line guys, like pilots, are regularly dosed with amphetamine these days?' His sister was not absolutely certain what amphetamine was. 'Stimulants, Georgie. Stuff that keeps you awake and fired up when you're exhausted but you need to keep going. You've heard of pep pills?' She had. 'Well, like that only more so. Now, some guys can cope with it. Others can't and they get all sorts of problems with side effects. Black outs, breakdowns, hallucinations – a whole range of psychotic symptoms. I thought of your Christopher. I thought that could be the reason he's, you know… Not…how he was. And maybe that's why you feel…' Lionel, watching his sister's face, realised suddenly that this could not be the reason for Georgina's rejection of Christopher Bayliss – if it was rejection. She had a more compassionate and sensitive nature than that. He fell silent, feeling foolish.

'The thing is, Li,' she began, 'it's not that I don't want to see him, exactly. It's that he doesn't want to see me. He's… well, he's cross with me. He thinks I let him down. And in a complicated way…I did.'

'What on earth are you talking about?'

'It was the pacifism thing. We used to argue about it. After what happened to Chrissie – you remember? The girl who got killed in a raid on Plymouth? – and then Andreis and then Christopher himself – you didn't see him, Li, when the military police arrested him… All of those things made me realise just how awful war is… What it had done… To just three individuals that I happened to know!' She paused, scanning her brother's face. 'Anyhow, at the same time as I'd decided that pacifism is not the answer, Christopher decided that it is – and when I told him, he…'

'When you told him what? That you'd stopped believing in pacifism?'

'It was more than that, Li. I told him I was leaving the Land Army and joining the ATA. That's the Air Transport—'

'I know what the ATA is!' He was staring at her. 'God Almighty, Georgie! What will Ma and Pa say!'

'It's not the RAF, Li. It's not exactly fighting! I shan't go on missions! I'll only be delivering planes to airfields—'

'From which someone else does go on missions!'

There was a long pause. 'You won't believe this,' he said at last, 'but I've been having the same arguments with myself as you've been having. And I decided, the other day when I was watching the Pathé news in the cinema in Taunton and it showed people trying to escape from some French village while Jerry blew it up because the locals had been hiding members of the Resistance in their houses… And I thought… To hell with this turning the other cheek stuff! I need to have a go at those swine!' He paused and then added quietly, 'I've decided to enlist.'

'No!' Georgina's voice was loud in the quiet house. 'You can't, Li! You mustn't!'

'Shush!' he said, smiling. 'You'll wake the parents!' Georgina's expression changed from shock to controlled determination. She shook her head and lowered her voice.

'You can't enlist! You're not to. There must be some other way you can—'

'Fight? Without actually fighting? We're not all as clever as you, Georgina Webster, with your "non-combatative" involvement!'

At the farmhouse Alice was dancing with Oliver Maynard while Roger Bayliss, having paid his respects, eaten some of the excellent food – his own plump goose having become somewhat lost amongst the mountainous contribution from the Fleet Air Arm kitchens – was wondering how soon he could decently make his farewells and leave the party. He would have very much liked to dance with Alice but she seemed always to be circling the floor with Oliver Maynard or attending to some domestic duty or other. From time to time she sought him out, making sure he had all he needed to eat and to drink but each time, just as Roger gathered himself to invite her onto the dance floor, Oliver Maynard appeared at her elbow and led her back into the jostling dancers where, eventually, Roger saw him put his lips to her ear and whisper earnestly.

'I need to talk to you, Alice.'

'You are talking to me, aren't you?' she laughed. He steered her through the open door to her sitting room. Roger, from the recreation room, watched them. They sat facing each other, she in a small upholstered chair and he on the window-seat. It appeared to be a serious conversation; Oliver, leaning slightly forward and looking into her eyes, Alice, sitting bolt upright with her hands clasped in her lap. She looked, Roger thought, slightly ill at ease. Almost cornered. He wished he could lip-read.

'It isn't my intention to pressure you, Alice,' Oliver said. 'As you know, I never have and I've always accepted our relationship exactly as you wanted it to be. But my circumstances are about to change.' He told her that he had just received a promotion that involved a posting to Greenock. This was to take effect in early January. Alice remembered him telling her about the house he and his wife had bought when he had been given a permanent, peacetime posting there.

'How splendid, Oliver,' she said. 'You'll be going home! Diana must be—'

'Diana isn't there, Alice. Hasn't been for months. As you know the marriage has been wobbling for a while. Now it's over. She wrote last week. She's been posted to a US airbase in Norfolk. There's a Canadian wing commander there. Someone she's known for a while. She's had a few flings, old Di, but this one is serious apparently and she says she wants to be free – presumably to marry him. So you see, we're in the same boat, Alice, you and I. You'll be divorced in a few months' time and I…' He smiled a warm, uncertain smile and waited. After a moment Alice felt compelled to ask, although she had already guessed the answer.

'You…what, Oliver?'

'Would very much like some sort of commitment from you. An indication, perhaps, that sometime soon, you and

I… That you might join me in Greenock.'

Alice had only been proposed to once before and on that occasion had not considered the possibility of it ever happening again. She had loved James in a fervent, youthful and uncomplicated way. The failure of the marriage had both shocked and scarred her. She remained bruised by it and only if she had fallen heavily in love with Oliver, or indeed, with anyone, which she had not, would the damage caused by James have been overridden by the blinding optimism of a new relationship. She shook her head and told him gently that she was sorry but it was too soon after the breakdown of her marriage for her to consider what he was suggesting. She had half expected him to protest and was slightly surprised by how easily he accepted her refusal. It suddenly occurred to her that she might not have been the only woman with whom Oliver had shared his off-duty hours since his driver had knocked her off her bicycle almost nine months previously. The war had separated thousands of couples and put hundreds of marriages into jeopardy, creating countless lonely people amongst whom there lurked a percentage of unscrupulous and predatory ones. Not that Oliver fell into either of these categories but it was nevertheless feasible that he had assembled a list of possible partners and Alice wondered, if this was so, where she would feature on that list. Would she be at the top of it? Halfway down it? Or at the bottom? She found herself smiling.

'So you find it amusing?' Oliver asked tightly. 'Encouraging people to declare their feelings for you and then rejecting them?'

Alice explained, as inoffensively as possible, what it was that had made her smile, realising almost at once that Oliver was unlikely to share the joke. She felt suddenly relieved that Oliver's posting to Greenock was to take effect almost immediately and glad when a diversion, which was taking place in the recreation room, ended their conversation.

'Mrs Todd! Come here, quick,' Annie laughed, taking Alice by the hand and towing her into the crowded recreation room.

Hester and Reuben were at the centre of a throng of beaming faces. She was displaying her left hand. On its third finger was a modest ruby, set in gold and circled by small diamonds.

'It was 'is grandma's!' Hester announced, transfixed with joy. 'A legacy! 'E sent for it! All the way from North Dakota, it's come! We're getting married, Reuben an' me!'

After this news had been properly celebrated it took Oliver Maynard very little time to wind up the festivities. Within ten minutes the kitchen was cleared and his men were saying their goodnights to the land girls, trooping down the path and climbing aboard the Bren-gun carrier. Roger, having thanked Alice for her hospitality, had reached his tractor but decided to wait until the carrier, being the larger vehicle, was clear of the confined space outside the farmhouse gate before making his own departure. He stood watching as the last of the soldiers left the porch, saluting or shaking Alice's hand as they went. Oliver Maynard brought up the rear. He took Alice's hand. She saw him glance across to where Roger Bayliss was hesitating beside the tractor. With his eyes still on Roger, Oliver raised Alice's hand to his lips and very deliberately kissed it. This gesture was not lost on Alice or on Roger, who turned away, climbed onto the tractor, switched on the ignition and sat staring ahead while he waited for Oliver to reach the Bren-gun carrier. As its engine revved and the massive tracks turned, hauling it, together with its trailer and its load of men, away along the narrow lane, Roger began to ease the tractor forward, its huge tyres biting into the ice. Alice, watching from the porch, raised her hand to wave, half expecting Roger to look back. He did not. He felt embarrassed that he had allowed himself to be outmanoeuvred by Maynard and annoyed with himself for being irritated, even disconcerted, by the fact that the warden found the man attractive.

'Well, 'e can't sleep here!' Rose had announced firmly, fixing Reuben with her beady Devonian eyes.

'You reckon he should walk back to Salisbury Plain, do you? You evil old—' Gwennan stopped in mid-sentence as Alice entered the kitchen.

'It's Reuben, Mrs Todd.' Hester fixed Alice with her wide eyes. 'We thought p'raps he could kip in the recreation room but Mrs Crocker—'

'Mrs Crocker said no!' Rose confirmed emphatically,

daring Alice to flout the number-one rule of the hostel. 'And I'm sure Mrs Todd will agree!' Alice did agree but, after some discussion and much to Dave's annoyance, it was decided that Reuben should sleep on the kitchen floor of Rose's cottage. Blankets and pillows were piled into his arms and after kissing his fiancée goodnight he followed Rose across the snowy yard. Dave, bringing up the rear, was heard muttering, with more feeling than originality, about GIs being 'oversexed, overpaid and over here'.

'Don't say I didn't warn you, boy!' his mother hissed back at him. 'Told you she was spoke for!'

They told their parents at breakfast. Georgina's news did not surprise them. The 'de Havilland godfather' had in fact, and unknown to Georgina, warned them of it. Lionel's case was different and both his mother and his father accused him, a charge he hotly denied, of being too easily influenced by his sister. Eventually he agreed to postpone his enlistment at least until his father, who had come to depend heavily on his strength and expertise on the farm, could find some way of replacing him. Georgina had joined her parents in persuading Lionel to make this compromise and he had reluctantly agreed to it.

Although both parents were disappointed that Georgina had rejected a philosophy in which they passionately believed, they were wise enough to accept her decision, possibly because they knew their daughter too well to expect, at this stage, to influence her. Their focus now must be on Lionel. With an allied invasion of occupied France looming, they were well aware that were he to enlist in whatever service, he would be in greater danger than his sister would soon be facing. Although this aspect of the problem should not have been the primary one, they were honest enough to accept that it was and that the longer they could delay Lionel's enlistment the more likely they were to reach the end of the war with their family, if not their principles, intact.

The morning passed awkwardly. By noon the wind had backed to the south-west and the temperature began to rise. Icicles dripped and then fell, the outline of yesterday's snowman was already softening and the carrot that formed his nose had slipped sideways. Christmas in the Webster house seemed to be over and Georgina, feeling responsible for this, decided to return to Lower Post Stone. After an early lunch she climbed onto the pillion seat of her brother's motorbike, waved as happily as she could to her parents and was borne away.

They had covered half their journey when Lionel turned off the main road and headed west, towards the moor. Georgina dug him in the ribs and, shouting through the slipstream and the wind, demanded to know where he thought he was going.

'Small detour,' he yelled back.

As they climbed onto higher ground the snow was still

thick and Lionel was forced to reduce speed. Georgina had already guessed where he was heading. She didn't know the exact location of the woodsmen's cottage but she was familiar enough with the land around the Post Stone farms to be sure that her brother's detour was going to involve Christopher Bayliss and she protested vigorously.

'This is stupid, Li! He doesn't want to see me and I don't want to encourage him to think—'

'Think what?' Lionel shouted. 'That you're too wrapped up in yourself to pay a friend a Christmas visit?'

The steepening lane had become little more than a track and their progress was reduced to a slithering crawl that demanded all of Lionel's skill and attention. 'Now, shut up, Georgie and hold tight!'

At Lower Post Stone, Marion, Winnie and Gwennan had dozed their way through their hangovers. Reuben, promised a lift from the nearby camp back to his unit, had said his farewells to Hester. They planned to visit her parents at the next available opportunity in order to formalise their engagement and if possible arrange for the marriage to be celebrated by her father at his church. Both Reuben and Hester understood the unlikelihood of achieving this and, if her parents obstructed the wedding, were prepared to be married at the barracks and by the regimental chaplain.

Ferdie had slithered down from Higher Post Stone on a toboggan that dated from Christopher Bayliss's childhood. Watched by Alice, he and Mabel had shown Edward-John how to negotiate the lower slopes of one of the pastures that rose from behind the farmhouse where, having become quickly proficient, he was soon flying downhill with Mabel's 'little brother' safely wedged between his knees and squealing with delight.

'You take care, Edward-John!' Mabel called anxiously. 'He's on'y a baby and any'ow, Annie wants a go now, don't you Annie!'

Rose's Dave produced from somewhere a sledge that, twenty years previously, his father had built for him. Sections of it were rotten but after some hammering it was serviceable and he persuaded Hester, whose engagement ring was glittering very satisfactorily in the sunlight, to trudge up the hill with him and ride precariously down again.

Fred arrived with a load of firewood and a churn of milk. Roger Bayliss, who had declined an invitation to drinks at the vicarage on the grounds that he needed to check on his land girls, rode down to Lower Post Stone on his mare. He doffed his hard hat to Alice, who, beginning to feel the cold, invited him into the farmhouse.

They sat on either side of the recreation room fireplace relishing the heat of the flames that were roaring extravagantly up the chimney. He had brought with him a cocktail shaker that contained what he described as a stirrup cup. She fetched glasses and they toasted the New Year.

'It's an old family recipe,' he told her, watching her sip.

'What d'you make of it?' She tasted it carefully.

'My goodness!' she said, blinking at the strength of the liquor. 'Well… It's too appley for brandy… Calvados?' She looked at him and had never seen him smile so unreservedly. 'But that's not all…' she went on, concentrating on her analysis. 'There's something nutty… And a sweetness there, too… Armagnac?' Yes! Armagnac!' Roger Bayliss was delighted with her.

'Well done, Mrs Todd!' he said. 'Very well done!' They laughed and sipped.

'We've known each other for almost a year. Won't you use my Christian name?' Alice asked. Then, having agreed that she, in turn, though possibly not in front of the girls, would call him Roger, he refilled her glass and they talked about the success of the previous day.

'Very good of Major Maynard,' Roger said. 'Christmas wouldn't have been nearly so much fun for your girls – or indeed, for you – without his company and that of his men.'

Alice agreed, adding, almost without thinking that, yes, she would miss Oliver. There was a slight pause before Roger spoke.

'Off somewhere, is he?' He had managed to keep his tone as casual as possible but he was watching Alice carefully as he waited for her reply.

With the onset of the cold weather, Christopher's fire had been consuming fuel faster than he was adding to his store of dry wood and the pile of split logs he had stacked undercover was dwindling alarmingly. On the morning of Boxing Day he was wielding his axe, bringing it down hard, making the logs crack satisfactorily apart. He had already wheeled three heaped barrow-loads into the lean-to. The exercise had made him sweat and he had soon discarded his scarf, his jacket and his pullover. He felt fit. The concentration necessary to achieve the maximum result from each stroke of the axe pleased him, focusing his attention, his muscles and his brain perfectly synchronised.

It had been two months now since he had retreated, alone and broken, to the forest. Since then, the life he had chosen had rested his mind and exercised his body. Both had responded. Although unaware of it, the months in the forest had physically and emotionally changed him. His bearing was altered. He stood erect now, not stooped and tense, as though braced against catastrophe as he had been when, 'scrambled' into mission after mission, his plane had flung him skywards and into the path of the bullets and the shrapnel that were intended to end his life or leave him maimed. His face was no longer the gaunt mask it had become before – and had remained during his breakdown. His eyes were clear, his uncut hair shoulder length and glossy. As a result of the good food, consistent exercise and lack of stress he had gained weight. Still perspiring, he dragged his flannelette shirt off over his head and had just brought the axe down hard on a resistant log when he caught the sound of the motorbike and turned, axe in hand, to face it.

At first Christopher saw only Lionel, who was a stranger to him. When he recognised the well-wrapped figure perched behind him, he laughed. It was a delighted and delightful sound of jubilation which echoed through the bare trees surrounding them. Lionel watched his sister and Christopher Bayliss stand smiling at one another. After a moment he felt it necessary to introduce himself.

'Brought you a late Christmas present!' he added after Christopher had shaken him by the hand. Neither Georgina nor Christopher appeared to hear him. She watched as Christopher pulled his shirt back on, his smile reappearing, charmingly, through the open neck. 'I knew you'd come,' he said and when she started to speak he silenced her. 'No, no. No need for any explanations! You must be frozen! Come inside.'

He made tea for them and cut large wedges from Eileen's cake. Georgina told him she could not believe how well he looked.

'I've never seen you like this! You are…' She hesitated. 'Transformed, Chris! I hadn't realised…' Again she paused, trying to choose her words carefully.

'How messed up I was before? It's the life up here, Georgie,' he went on. 'Basic and simple – with some useful back-up from Pa's housekeeper, of course! Hence this noble cake!'

It was, she considered afterwards, almost like meeting a stranger. The clinging, self-deprecating wreck that had both scared and depressed her was gone. Now, just as she had been when they had first met and he had been concealing his imminent breakdown under a carapace of swaggering arrogance, she found herself attracted to him. But with this realisation came a sense of guilt. Her initial reaction to him had been superficial. She had, to begin with, lacked perception and then, when the wretchedness of the breakdown had stripped him of the qualities that, despite herself, she had found attractive, she had almost despised him. Now, having misunderstood him, she felt, as they sat in his firelight and he enthused about what he had already achieved in the neglected woodland, unworthy of him.

After half an hour or so Lionel got to his feet. 'Better make tracks, sis,' he said. 'It'll be dark soon and after I drop you off—'

'You're taking Drusilla to a party. I hadn't forgotten.' She stood, winding her scarf round her neck, smiling at Christopher.

'You're still going, then?' he asked her as they moved out into the half-light where the thaw was steadily reducing the patches of snow. 'To do this flying thing?'

'Yes. I'm still going. But I could come and see you… When I get some leave… If you'd like me to?' Christopher took her by her shoulders, kissed her and told her there was nothing in this world that he would like better.

Then Lionel was revving the bike, she was on the pillion and they were negotiating the slushy track. Christopher's mouth had felt warm. This kiss was quite different from the cold neediness of their first, when on a sharp April night, after an awkward dinner together, she had volunteered to drive them home because his burnt hands were hurting him.

'Coming in for a warm-up?' she asked Lionel when they arrived at the farmhouse.

'I'd better crack on,' he said, the noise of his bike echoing round the yard.

'Don't want to be late for your bit of cradle-snatching!'

'Cradle-snatching? Dru's almost eighteen, Georgie!'

'And you've been going out with my friend Annie for the past six months!'

'Annie's lovely,' he said, 'absolutely lovely and great fun and everything...but...'

'But what?'

'Oh, you know, Georgie... She's...well, she's...'

'Not posh enough for you? Is that the problem? Are you a bit of a snob, little brother?' He pulled down his goggles and shut her out. She watched him turn the heavy machine and ride off, the beam from his headlamp wavering down the lane.

Annie must have heard the bike. Georgina would lie. She would tell Annie that Lionel had to get back to their parents' guests. Avoiding the girls she climbed the steep stairs to her room and stood for a moment, looking round it. At the desk where she had studied for her Ministry of Agriculture exams. At the narrow bed in which she had lain, arguing with her conscience about pacifism, and about Christopher. And up at the small, ill-fitting window, the blackout curtain pulled across it.

From the recreation room Georgina could hear someone at the untuned piano, picking their way through the refrain of 'Don't Sit Under the Apple Tree'. She recognised Annie's voice, hesitantly singing the words as her fingers fumbled over the keys. As she mastered each phrase of the song, Annie's pace quickened and some of the girls broke off their conversations and began singing with her, stopping, starting and laughing as she stumbled through the familiar tune. Georgina identified Gwennan's heavy Welsh contralto and snatches of Winnie's thin soprano. The voices and the laughter rose and fell, reaching Georgina through the gaps in the floorboards of the draughty little room above the porch.

After supper she would slide her expensive monogrammed suitcases from under her bed. In three days' time she would no longer be a land girl, a member of what was still disparagingly referred to as 'the Cinderella service', and she would leave Lower Post Stone Farm for what would probably be the last time.